GOOD
GUYS

BOOKS BY STEVEN BRUST

THE DRAGAERAN NOVELS

Brokedown Palace

THE KHAAVREN ROMANCES

The Phoenix Guards
Five Hundred Years After
The Viscount of Adrilankha, which comprises
    The Paths of the Dead, The Lord of Castle Black,
    and *Sethra Lavode*

THE VLAD TALTOS NOVELS

Jhereg	*Issola*
Yendi	*Dzur*
Teckla	*Jhegaala*
Taltos	*Iorich*
Phoenix	*Tiassa*
Athyra	*Hawk*
Orca	*Vallista*
Dragon	

OTHER NOVELS

To Reign in Hell
The Sun, the Moon, and the Stars
Agyar
Cowboy Feng's Space Bar and Grille
The Gypsy (with Megan Lindholm)
Freedom & Necessity (with Emma Bull)
The Incrementalists (with Skyler White)
The Skill of Our Hands (with Skyler White)
Good Guys

STEVEN BRUST

GOOD GUYS

TOR

A TOM DOHERTY
ASSOCIATES BOOK
NEW YORK

GOOD GUYS

Copyright © 2018 by Steven Brust

A Tor Book
Published by Tom Doherty Associates
175 Fifth Avenue
New York, NY 10010

www.tor-forge.com

Tor® is a registered trademark of Macmillan Publishing Group, LLC.

The Library of Congress Cataloging-in-Publication Data

Names: Brust, Steven, 1955– author.
Title: Good guys / Steven Brust.
Description: First edition. | New York : Tom Doherty Associates, 2018. |
    "A Tom Doherty Associates Book."
Identifiers: LCCN 2017039425 (print) | LCCN 2017045081 (ebook) |
    ISBN 9780765396389 (ebook) | ISBN 9780765396372 (hardcover : alk. paper)
Subjects: LCSH: Paranormal fiction. | GSAFD: Fantasy fiction.
Classification: LCC PS3552.R84 (ebook) | LCC PS3552.R84 G66 2018
    (print) | DDC 813/.54—dc23
LC record available at https://lccn.loc.gov/2017039425

Our books may be purchased in bulk for promotional, educational, or business use. Please contact your local bookseller or the Macmillan Corporate and Premium Sales Department at 1-800-221-7945, extension 5442, or by email at MacmillanSpecialMarkets@macmillan.com.

First Edition: March 2018

Printed in the United States of America

0 9 8 7 6 5 4 3 2 1

FOR SKYLER

AUTHOR'S NOTE

I never know where an idea is going to come from—what combination of reading, life, research, and random events is going to make me go, "Oh, hey, I know what'd be fun." But sometimes I can identify the final piece of it. The idea for this book came from a conversation with my friend and poker teacher Chris "Pokerfox" Wallace. We were discussing a writing project of his, and he mentioned some things that he was doing that made me go, "Oh, wow, I gotta try that." So I stole it.

How much of what I grabbed and ran through my own process would be recognizable from the idea he gave me? I don't know. But if his work makes its way into the world, and you read it, and something strikes you as familiar, I want you to know that he didn't get it from me, I got it from him. Thanks, Fox.

Steven Brust
May 2015
Minneapolis

GOOD GUYS

THE LIST

1

The first one on the list was Georgio Byrne Lawton-Smythe. I found him at the Maumee Grill on Mulberry and Fifth, just south of the river. There was no good way to talk to him, under the circumstances, but that didn't bother me. Nothing he said would have made any difference to me, and nothing I said would have made any difference to him. Or to put it another way, I didn't hate him enough to bother. I just walked up to him and put three 12-gauge solid slugs into his chest, like, blam cha-chink blam cha-chink blam. Then I dropped the shotgun, walked out the door, and turned left. I threw my gloves into the river and hiked all the way to East Broadway before I caught a cab to bring me back to Toledo and my hotel.

||||||||||||||||

Just after 2:00 East Coast time on Thursday morning, Donovan Jackson Longfellow initiated a Skype call to Marci No-Middle-Name Sullivan. She came on quickly enough that he could be pretty sure she'd been awake and at her computer, so he didn't bother asking if he'd interrupted anything.

"We caught one," he said without preamble.

"Oh, my."

"Yep. Ready to go into action?"

She might have nodded, but then remembered how hard it was to make out gestures on Skype, so she said. "Yes, sir."

"Don't call me sir. My name is Donovan, or Don, or Donny."

"All right. How does this work?"

"You ask me what's up, and I tell you what we know."

"Um. Okay. What's up?"

"West Nowhere Ohio, a place called Perrysburg. Guy torn in half with a shotgun."

"A shotgun? That doesn't seem like, you know, our kind of thing. I speak under correction, of course."

"Yeah, you'll stop doing that soon. Here's what we know: It happened in a restaurant in the middle of dinner hour, there were plenty of people there, and no one saw anything." Before she could ask, he elaborated. "I don't mean couldn't ID the shooter; I mean I saw nothing. One second everything is fine; next second there's a dead guy messy on the floor with a shotgun next to him and blood spreading out and all the nice people freaking out and throwing up. The PO-lice are stumped, and Upstairs is talking nightmare scenario. Of course, they do that all the time, so I figure mildly troubling dream scenario until proven otherwise. But we still need to check it out."

"How are they explaining it? I mean, the police."

"They figure everyone was shocked by the horror of it all, or some shit. Customers and staff are under scrutiny. They won't get shit that way."

"So the police believe it was someone in the restaurant?"

"What else *could* they believe? But the important thing is that we don't believe it, so we need to investigate."

"Do we know who the victim is?"

"Name hasn't been released. Upstairs has ways of getting past that, but they're still working on it."

"Okay," she said. "Just you and me?"

"I'm also calling in the hippie chick, because it's better to have her and not need her than, you know."

"Hippie chick?"

"Susan."

"Oh! I know her. She's the one who pulled me out of the kiddie pool."

"Right."

"So, now what?"

"Now you ask how you're supposed to get there."

"All right. How do I get there?"

"Um, yeah, good question. Let me think." Donovan weighed the pros and cons of delaying half a day, went through an imagined conversation with Oversight, and said, "You've been checked out on your slipwalk, right?"

Marci might have nodded again, but then said, "Yes."

"We'll go that way, then. The scene is already two days old. Can't expect you to sense it if we wait another twelve hours for travel."

"Two days?"

"A bit more."

"I probably won't get anything as it is. Why so long?"

"Access. The crime scene is still closed, but they've stopped guarding it."

"Oh. I don't know how these things work. Couldn't the Foundation have pulled strings and gotten us in earlier?"

"They probably don't think it's important enough to pull the big guns out. It's critical and could mean the end of the world,

but we can't spare any resources. That's sort of how things work."
He shrugged, though she wouldn't see it. "I don't know. That's above my pay grade."

Marci muttered something non-committal.

"Look," said Donovan. "Don't sweat it, all right? We go in, check it out. You get something or you don't, I report to Upstairs. If you get something, we try to figure out what it means. If not, I go back to Internet hearts, Hippie Chick goes back to organic gardening, and you go back to whatever it is you do."

"All right. I just hate it when—all right."

"Also, what are you wearing?"

"What? Seriously?"

"Yeah."

"Is there a dress code?"

"Kind of. Business casual is all right, or jeans and a T-shirt."

"What *isn't* all right?"

"Don't look like you're going clubbing."

"Is this really a thing?"

"Look. It matters. There are practical reasons."

"What practical reasons?"

"You'll figure it out."

"I—all right. I'll trust you on that. For now."

"Thanks."

"Anything else?"

"No, that's it."

"Are you calling Susan or am I?"

"I am."

"Does she really do organic gardening?"

"Wouldn't surprise me. The place is called the Maumee Grill." He started to give her the whole command line for the slipwalk, but decided it was disrespectful. If she ended up in Greenland or something he'd regret it, but she was now on his team, so he'd assume competence until proven otherwise. "I'll meet you outside the yellow tape. See you in an hour?"

"An hour," she said, and he disconnected.

He made the next call, which took a little longer to connect. Susan Dionisia Kouris eventually appeared. Even though it was before midnight in her time zone, she looked more than half-asleep. She was wearing a blue terry-cloth bathrobe.

"Sorry to wake you up," he said.

"Ugh," she explained.

"Need some time?"

"No, it's all right. I'm at the tail end of a chest cold. I'm trying to sleep it off. We have something?"

He nodded. "Yeah. A body. Up for it?"

"Always. I'll take a decongestant."

He gave her what details he had and hung up.

Donovan stood up and stretched, then put his coat on—the ugly-but-warm fleece-lined one. He also put on a stocking cap, because sometimes when it's cold you just have to sacrifice looks for survival, or comfort at any rate.

He checked his pockets to make sure he had his wallet, knot-not, latex gloves, and blackjack. He was unlikely to need the blackjack, especially with Hippie Chick there, but he felt naked without it. He left the apartment, took the elevator to the basement, and let himself into the laundry room.

Building management had thoughtfully provided the tenants with a washing machine and two dryers, one of which sported a sign that said: "Out of order." He switched that one from "high heat" to "air dry," then set the timer to 8 minutes, then moved it to 31 minutes, then to 19 minutes, then to 39 minutes. He switched it from "air dry" to "high heat" and stepped to the side. The dryer swung back, taking a section of wall with it. Donovan went into the stairwell it had revealed, lit by a single fluorescent bulb, and pulled the wall shut behind him. He said in a clear voice, "Outside the Maumee Grill, Perrysburg, Ohio, USA." Then he went down the stairs. After about ten steps, the hallway dissolved.

Aw shit, he thought just too late. *Did I leave the milk out?*

It was full dark in western Ohio. Once the ground stopped turning, he looked around to make sure he was alone. The temperature wasn't bad, but there was a wind that stung his face. He took a long sniff of the air: stale fryer oil and river. He walked around the building, staying outside of the crime scene tape; after a good look, he slipped under it. *I have now broken the law*, he thought. *Gosh gee.*

The main door was closed by more than bureaucratic theory— there was a particularly heavy padlock there: an Abloy PL 362. He recognized it because it was the same one he used for the closet where he stored his gear. Using it here was pure idiocy— yeah, it was hard to get past; the knotnot might even be inadequate—but there were windows all around the place, and, in particular, four windows into the kitchen and a door in back that wouldn't stand up to a pry bar, or even a decent screwdriver.

He shrugged and went around back and put the latex gloves on. He didn't have a pry bar or a screwdriver, but he did have a gift from the good folks in the Burrow: a device that looked like a cheap ballpoint pen, because that's what it used to be, and that he called a knotnot. He pointed it at the back door and said the magic words: "Open, you piece of shit."

The door gave out a click. He turned the knob and went inside.

Forty-five minutes later he was back outside, in time to see Susan appear as a two-dimensional image that, even if you knew what was going on, made you think, *Wait, has she been there the whole time?* The image filled out so there was no question; Susan looked around and found him.

"Hey, Hippie."

"Hey, Laughing Boy. You went in, didn't you?"

"Just for a look-see."

"Because protocol is for other people, and there was no chance of you being interrupted and, like, arrested or shot or something?"

"Do you see anyone around? Any PO-lice cars?"

"Not the point and you know it."

"How's the cold?"

"I'll live," she said, and sniffed. In person, her eyes were certainly bloodshot, but he wasn't her nurse. If she'd been too sick to take the job, she could have said so.

She glanced around, then looked a question at him.

"Soon," he said. "If she doesn't screw it up."

Susan nodded, and they stood there in silence, waiting.

A minute or two later, Marci appeared, stumbling a bit. Everyone stumbled at the end of a slipwalk, except Hippie Chick, because she was a freak. Marci smiled a little hesitantly to him and Susan. "That was weird. And kind of fun."

"Yeah," said Donovan. "Bad news is, you'll get used to it."

"Except the climate changes," said Susan. "That always catches you by surprise, even when you're expecting it. And you can get a cold from the temperature shifts if you do it too much."

"Is that what happened to you?"

"This? No, this is just Oregon winter."

Marci nodded and turned to Donovan. "Have you learned anything new?" she asked.

"I couldn't learn anything new without going inside, which protocol forbids without the full team."

"Oh. Right. Sorry."

"As it happens, I don't give a shit for protocol. So here's what I got: Blood spatter tells us that the victim didn't move, and the

PO-lice report Upstairs passed on says that he was shot three times. If you work out the timing on three shots from a pump-action shotgun, it means something was holding him still. Dropping the weapon at the scene—and right there next to the victim's table—would usually indicate a professional killer, or someone who planned the whole thing out in detail and was cool enough to follow through with it."

"Usually?" said Susan.

Donovan nodded. "Thing is, shotgun slugs can't be identified. Either he doesn't know that, which means he's new at this, or he had another reason to drop it. No witnesses report cars leaving the lot afterward. There was a duffel bag just outside the door, and they found traces of gun oil in it."

He paused for a breath and to see if there were questions yet, then continued.

"So he walked from—somewhere—holding a shotgun in a duffel bag. He dropped the bag, came in, did his thing, dropped the gun, walked out again all with no one seeing anything. Or hearing anything."

"No one heard anything?" said Marci. "No one heard the shotgun fire?"

"Correct."

"So it wasn't just invisibility."

"Right."

"Maybe a combination of—no, I shouldn't speculate. Let's go in. From the sound of it, it was a major working, so there could still be traces. And we're far enough from a grid line that it might not have covered it over."

Donovan nodded as if he understood that—well, he sort of did, in theory—and indicated the way around the back. Susan led, because protocol; Donovan at the back. This was in case of danger that didn't exist, but it was silly to argue about. Marci walked almost in a straight line, like she wanted to put one foot directly in front of the other, giving her a strangely dainty stride that reminded Donovan of cartoon Japanese women. Susan walked like someone you didn't want to tangle with, but a lot of that was that she didn't swing her arms at all, which gave her a sort of threatening aspect. And the rest was because Donovan knew her.

They reached the back door. "Gloves," he said, "if you plan on touching anything. I have extras."

"I shouldn't need to touch anything," said Marci.

Susan pulled out her own gloves and put them on without a word.

"Okay," said Marci once they were inside. "I'm going to see what I can find. Can you two wait here?"

Donovan and Susan remained by the door to the dining room. "Watch the crime scene markers," he said.

"I know."

Marci walked up to the blood spot, stopping just short of it—it was big. There'd been a lot of blood. Donovan and Susan waited while Marci investigated her way.

"Well," she said a moment later. "This is quite something."

"What—"

"I hope you didn't have any plans," she said in a suddenly all-business voice. "This is going to take a while."

"If I had a life," said Donovan, "I wouldn't be here."

Hippie Chick nodded beside him.

‖‖‖‖‖‖‖‖‖‖

Around 6:00 AM, Donovan stepped out of the laundry room, took the elevator back upstairs to his apartment, put his coat away, returned the blackjack and the knotnot to the closet (*no—that shelf, you idiot, so you'll remember it's been used*), and sat down at his computer. He brought up Skype, and selected a name. The face that appeared was a pasty, sickly white as of someone who never went outside—you could even tell through the distortion. The man was clean-shaven and bald save for a fringe of light brown hair, and was wearing a white shirt and thin, dark tie. His collar looked very tight.

The man on the screen said, "Good afternoon, Mr. Longfellow."

"It's morning here, Mr. Becker. Very early morning, after a very late night."

"Report, please."

"He used a time-stop. And he used it over a wide area—he covered the whole building so he wouldn't be seen even in the parking lot."

"That's a lot of power, Mr. Longfellow. I trust you're certain it was a time stoppage, and not high speed?"

"Marci is sure, so I'm sure. There was also a gradual release, so it covered up the sound of the shots."

"Explain that, please?"

"Marci says if the time-stop releases gradually, the sound will be whole octaves lower than usual, and drawn-out, and the human ear won't pick it up."

"I'm not certain I understand, Mr. Longfellow."

"Nor am I, Mr. Becker."

"Very well. Did this take place close to a grid line?"

"None within half a mile."

"That is extremely impressive."

"Yeah."

"What else?"

"Shotgun, three to the chest, just like the PO-lice say. From under a foot away."

"How did the shooter cut through the air?"

"Uh, what?"

"If time has stopped, surely that means the air molecules are also stopped? So how did the shooter get past them?"

"Oh. According to Marci, a time-stop field takes effect an inch or so from the caster, otherwise he'd have stopped himself. I hadn't thought about the air movement thing."

"An inch from the caster, Mr. Longfellow? But the barrel of the gun is farther away than that."

"Yeah, I asked about that. If the caster is in contact with the gun, the gun is part of the field; otherwise it wouldn't fire."

"I see. Ms. Sullivan. It sounds like she's working out."

"It was her first case. But yeah, I think so. She knows her stuff."

Becker was silent for a moment, then said, "Take me through the events."

"All right. I'm going with 'he' for now, because a man is more likely to use a shotgun. Marci didn't get any personality indicators—which says something by itself. Anyway, yeah. He arrives, walking, at about six fifty PM local time. No sign of magical travel of any sort, although after two days that doesn't prove anything. He casts a time-stop from about twenty feet from the door. He goes in. Dining room has seating for fifty-six, and it's about half-full. Or half-empty, in your case, Mr. Becker."

Becker didn't appear to hear that; Donovan went on.

"He walks up to the table and shoots three times. Now here's the thing: Marci figures that as soon as the slug clears the barrel, it hits the time-stop. Like, if you'd been able to watch, you'd have seen the slug freeze in midair, and then the next, and then the next. Which is why it looked like the guy didn't move when he was hit—in effect, when the time-stop released, all three slugs hit him at the same instant."

"And yet, you said the time-stop was released gradually."

"Gradually, Mr. Becker, meaning over the course of about a second subjective time."

"I see. And speaking of, is there any way of knowing the elapsed subjective time for the shooter?"

"Marci says that time-stop, at best, doesn't last very long, and takes a lot of concentration to maintain. I can't imagine he spent more time than he had to. And there are no reports of anyone in the place having a watch that's suddenly off. All in all, I'd guess about a minute. Not more than two. I should add, this is from historical reports; she says that no one has been able to perform that spell in over two hundred years. It's a fluke talent, like direct flying or becoming discorporeal."

"Thank you. I believe I'm caught up."

"Have you managed to learn anything about the victim?"

"Yes, some things have come in."

"I'm listening."

Becker may have nodded—it was hard to be sure. "Our victim wasn't a very nice man, Mr. Longfellow."

"Very not nice?"

"Yes."

"So we might be dealing with a personal grudge, or a vigilante?"

"Either one is possible. We know that the deceased, a Mr. Lawton-Smythe, emigrated from Bristol, England, ten years ago and took a tenure-track position at the University of Toledo. Married to a professor of modern languages, two children, aged fourteen and eleven."

"What did he teach?"

"English literature and philosophy, with a specialty in Heidegger."

"Sounds pretty evil."

"You've never heard of Heidegger, have you, Mr. Longfellow?"

"Not as such. Does it matter?"

"Probably not. More significantly, Lawton-Smythe had ties to the Roma Vindices Mystici."

Donovan sat back. "Why would they want someone in western Ohio?"

"Why would we want someone in New Jersey?"

Donovan took the point: They didn't particularly want someone in New Jersey—that's just where he lived.

"What sort of ties?"

"He was a sorcerer. Not especially strong, but still. A sorcerer, and one of theirs."

"Do we have him for anything?"

"In England he was responsible—indirectly, of course—for random beatings of Pakistanis, and some football hooliganism."

"Football hooliganism. Is that a thing?"

"It's the game you would call soccer, and yes."

"Did he have a reason? I mean, other than being a prick?"

"If by 'being a prick,' Mr. Longfellow, you mean being an extreme racist, none we are aware of."

"What's he done since he came here?"

"Nothing we've found so far, but we're still looking."

"You said he wasn't very strong."

"Just mental and emotional effects—suggestions, mood altering. But good at it. In England, you might say he did a great deal of damage on a small scale, if that makes sense."

"What did he do for the Mystici?"

"We don't know exactly. If I had to guess"—Becker said this as Donovan might say, *If I had to stick my hand into sewage*—"I would say that they brought him in when they needed subtle manipulation done."

"All right. So, how do I find the shooter?"

"You're asking me, Mr. Longfellow? That's your specialty."

"All we know is that he's willing to throw away a shotgun. I need something to go on."

"Such as?"

"A sorcerer who can do a time-stop over that much of an area must have left traces somewhere. Where did he get his training? Or, to put it another way, is he one of ours, one of theirs, a renegade, or a weirdo? Odds are good he's one of theirs—Marci is sure we don't have anyone with that talent. If that's true, it's one of theirs attacking others of theirs. That means talking to them and convincing them to cough up information, and that's your department, Mr. Becker. Although one other possibility comes to mind."

"Go on."

"A powerful spell, cast half a mile from the nearest grid line, using a spell no one has been able to do in generations. What does that suggest to you?"

"Ah. Yes. It is possible. Good idea, Mr. Longfellow. I'll have our people look into it, though we're unlikely to have a positive quickly, and of course we'll never have a definitive negative. What will you be doing in the meantime?"

"I'll be sleeping, Mr. Becker. After that, my niece is having her sixth birthday, and I haven't gotten her anything."

"Please, Mr. Longfellow."

He shrugged, even though Becker wouldn't see it. "We got what we could get. Now we wait for you to find something, or for something else to happen."

"Something else, Mr. Longfellow? Such as what?"

"Another killing, Mr. Becker."

"You think there will be more?"

"I have no idea. It's a trade-off, I guess. More killings will make our shooter easier to find."

"You are very cold-blooded sometimes, Mr. Longfellow."

"You would know, Mr. Becker."

It seemed on the screen as if Becker may have smiled a little. Donovan closed Skype, then stared at his computer's wallpaper—a British Columbia lake reflecting mountains that looked like it should be on a beer can—for a good five minutes. Then he got up, found the milk, sniffed it, and put it in the refrigerator.

||||||||||||||||||

Manuel Becker stretched his legs, then stood up. He could have phoned, Skyped, emailed, or sent a memo, but he always preferred to ask favors in person. He took the elevator up to the Burrow. Many Foundation members, over the years, had remarked with amusement that the Burrow was actually on the second from the top floor; Becker was not one of them. Many had also, on the way to the Burrow, stopped to admire the view of Paseo del Prado through the window opposite the elevator. Becker wasn't one of those, either. He just stepped out of the elevator and went down the hall to the room labeled, in Spanish, German, English, Russian, French, Mandarin, Farsi, and Hindustani, "Artifacts and Enchantments."

The department secretary, a young man named Anthony, did a credible job of appearing to snap to attention without moving. "Mr. Becker," he said in American-accented English. "How can I help you?"

Becker had years ago given up on trying to convince him to speak Spanish; it was one of few things he had ever given up on. He nodded. "Hello, Anthony. Is Ms. Ramirez available?"

"I'll check, sir."

Anthony picked up the desk phone, punched a button, and waited. After a moment he said in Spanish, "Julia? Mr. Becker from the Ranch—I mean, from I and E—would like to see you, if you have time. . . . All right."

Anthony hung up, and said in English, "Just go on back, sir."

Becker nodded and did. Julia Ramirez stood up from her desk as he approached. She was wearing a red dress that matched some of the appalling fake gemstones on her glasses. "Mr. Becker," she said in a thick but pleasant Catalonian accent. "Please, have a seat."

Her L-shaped desk held a computer with a pair of monitors, and a picture of her husband and their two boys, both in the eight-to-ten range; the picture was new since the last time Becker had been to see her. He did not remark on it. He sat down opposite her and said, "Thank you for making the time, Ms. Ramirez."

"Of course. How can I help Investigations?"

"We have an unusual case, Ms. Ramirez. A sorcerer has used a time-stop to commit murder."

Ramirez nodded. "Go on."

"It was cast in a place far from a grid line. This makes us wonder if an artifact or a device of some sort could have been used."

Her brows—pencil thin and artificially darkened—came together. "We have no such device, nor the capability of making one."

"Yes. My understanding is that none of our people are able to cast it."

"That is correct. If the Mystici do, they are keeping the secret well guarded."

"I understand. But something from antiquity?"

"Well, of course, it's possible. But I've never heard of anything with that enchantment on it."

Becker nodded. "Could I trouble you and your team to do

some research? If there is, or was, such an item, and it has been found, it could help us identify the individual responsible."

She flashed a quick, uncomfortable-looking smile. "Of course, Mr. Becker. We'll start at once."

"Thank you, Ms. Ramirez." He stood up. "I look forward to hearing from you."

He gave her what hoped was a friendly smile, and left, only vaguely aware of how the entire room seemed to emit a sigh of relief as the door closed behind him.

2

GOOD-BYE, MR. BLUM

Next on the list was Richard Nathaniel "Nate" Blum. He had an office in the MetLife Building. He used a town car to get to and from his condo around the corner from a restaurant called At Nine, where he liked to eat. I could have done it there, but outside the building was too convenient, and crowded, to pass up.

He worked a little late that night, but there were still a lot of people leaving the building when, just twenty feet from his ride, he gasped, clutched his chest, and fell to his knees. I was the first one to him. I squatted down facing him and said, "Heart attack. That must really suck. Tell me, does it make you wish you'd lived a better life?" He looked at me, his mouth open, but of course he had no idea who I was.

A crowd gathered quickly and someone knew CPR, so I got out of the way while various people did chest compressions until the EMTs arrived. Charlie had said that would likely happen and not to worry about it, so I tried not to. I examined my feelings to see if there were any, and, except for a certain satisfaction, there were none. I was fine with that.

It took a while to figure out which train would take me back to Brooklyn, but I did, rode it, then took a cab to my hotel. I settled into my room and started looking at flights out of Newark because everyone says LaGuardia sucks.

‖‖‖‖‖‖‖‖‖‖‖

When Donovan stepped out of the shower, the beeping from his computer informed him he'd missed an important call. He studied the screen. Becker. Donovan finished drying himself and got dressed before returning the call; Becker wouldn't have cared either way, but Donovan did.

Becker appeared instantly. Donovan tried to remember a time when Becker hadn't, but couldn't think of one. Did the man never use the bathroom?

"You called me, Mr. Becker?"

"There may have been another killing, Mr. Longfellow."

"May have been?"

"This one isn't as clear-cut as the Lawton-Smythe matter. It appears to have been a heart attack. Late twenties, good condition, no history. Of course, that happens."

"But?"

"But he is connected to the Mystici."

"With all due respect, Mr. Becker, tens of thousands of people are connected to the Mystici."

It seemed as if Becker may have bowed his head—as close as Donovan had ever seen him come to a gesture of regret. "I beg your pardon, Mr. Longfellow. I should have said, close ties to the Mystici. From the amount of communication between him and London, we assume he was an actual agent, as opposed to an occasional asset like Lawton-Smythe. We do not know what he did for them, however."

"I see."

"Again, perhaps it is only the heart attack it appears to be. But we feel it is at least worth bringing your sensitive to the scene and looking it over."

"When did it happen?"

"It's still fresh, only a couple of hours ago. If sorcery was used, there should still be traces."

"What can you tell us about the heart attack guy?"

"Nate Blum. Iraq War veteran, Marine. Honorable discharge in 2013. Divorced, three children aged three, four, and six. He lives with the oldest, a boy; his ex has custody of the other two. No job, but he keeps—kept—a nice apartment in Greenwich."

"Is that what the PO-lice would call 'no visible means of support'?"

"That is exactly right, Mr. Longfellow."

"But he worked at the MetLife Building?"

"He had an office there that he went to every day; we aren't aware of anything he actually did except communicate with London a great deal."

"Maybe I'm just crazy, but shouldn't we find out?"

"We're working on it."

Donovan exhaled slowly. "All right," he said. "What else?"

"There are indications that he's been responsible for the disappearance of reporters looking into government corruption."

"Indications?"

"Same time and place more than once. It could be a string of coincidences, but it seems unlikely."

"A sorcerer?"

"No."

"Very well, Mr. Becker."

"I'll email details of the location."

"All right. I'll get the team on it. What time is it there, Mr. Becker?"

"One-oh-six AM."

"And you've been hanging around the office waiting for me to call? Maybe you should go home."

Becker signed off without further comment, and Donovan started placing calls.

|||||||||||||||||||

Two hours later, just after 10:00 PM, Donovan stood outside the MetLife Building in Manhattan with Marci and the hippie chick. This time he'd used mundane travel—PATH across the river to the MTA. The others had had farther to travel, so he'd authorized slipwalks for them. It was late, but there was a lot of traffic, and people kept moving to and from the station directly below them. He was aware of the attention he was attracting—standing on a public street with two white women was going to get him noticed—but so far the attention was subtle, and not overtly hostile. And, as always when out in public and not in his own neighborhood, he had the Face on.

"Oh," said Marci.

"Hmmm?"

"The dress code. I get it."

Donovan nodded and turned his mind to the case.

"Somewhere around here," he said.

Susan said, "You're sure this is our business?"

"Nope. That's the first thing to check."

"Why do you suspect?"

Donovan explained Becker's thinking; Susan and Marci nodded.

"How long this time?" asked Marci.

Donovan pulled out his cell and checked the time. "A bit under four hours."

She nodded and, with her arms at her sides and her palms out, she closed her eyes and turned in a slow circle. She got a couple of glances from passersby, maybe waiting to see if she was about to do a street performance, but this was New York, so they just moved on. After a moment, Marci opened her eyes and said, "Nothing. How sure of the location are you? I mean, the precise location."

"Not very. He came out that door, was heading in that direction, toward Forty-First. Somewhere in between he collapsed. But with the amount of power you detected last time, if there was anything you'd pick it up, right?"

"If it was another time-stop, yes. Let me do a couple more checks; then we'll call it a day."

"All right."

She moved around and repeated her exercise, while the others waited. It was strange watching Marci work. Her face was usually so animated, every nuance of emotion expressed in the twitch of a lip or the furrow of brows. But when she was sensing an area, she was like a fine marble sculpture before the artist had finished the face. There was nothing, except that, if she found what she was looking for—

The third place she checked, just past what Donovan thought of as the cement garden, her body went rigid, only her hands moving, slowly curling into fists and then uncurling again.

"Fuc*k*," said Donovan, hitting the *k* particularly hard.

Susan nodded.

After about twenty minutes, Marci's face returned to normal. She blinked, shook her head, and walked up to the others. "Yeah," she said as if they hadn't just seen.

"What can you tell us?"

"It wasn't big like the time-stop. It was something subtle. Heart attack fits. The sorcerer just stopped the guy's heart."

"Is that hard to do?"

"Not terribly."

"Okay," said Donovan. "Now I'm really curious."

Donovan looked at the MetLife Building, looming over them. "I wonder what kind of security they have."

"What are you thinking?" said Susan.

"I want to know who this guy was. According to Upstairs, he came to work every day and no one knows what he did. Becker said, 'We're working on it,' in the tone that means 'in six months or so someone might deign to pull the assignment out of an in-box somewhere.' Marci, do you have something that could get past security, in case they're checking?"

Marci looked doubtful. "I can do emotional stuff, and trust falls in there. But I can't do illusions. I suck at light manipulation."

"So?"

"So . . . maybe. Not exactly my area."

"Welcome to fieldwork. Give it a shot?"

"All right."

They walked in the door, Susan and Donovan pretending to be in deep conversation, Marci a step ahead of them. He saw her shoulder's tense, and her fingers twitched a little. The security guard looked up, smiled, and, "Hey, Sherri." He gave Donovan and Susan a smile and waved them through. When they were inside an elevator, Donovan said, "Sherri?"

"I have no idea," said Marci.

"Well, good work," although, in fact, he almost regretted it; he'd had thoughts of going to a costume shop and dressing them all like a cleaning crew like they do on TV. He'd always wondered if that would actually work.

The office was on the forty-first floor. They stepped out of the elevator into a wide hallway. *Showing off*, thought Donovan. *See how unconcerned we are with the cost of space? You can drive a truck down our hallways. Whatever.* The hall was illuminated by fluorescent light fixtures every five feet, with smaller ones to the side.

They found the office. Donovan put his gloves on; Hippie Chick did the same. He took out the knotnot and said the words. Marci giggled, which made an odd sound in the empty hallway. Donovan opened the door, and looked inside. Then something slammed into him and he was on the floor.

"What the—"

Susan jumped over him, into the room, rolling.

It was over before Donovan had time to know it was going on: Susan was straddling a man who was facedown on the carpet; she had his arm up behind his shoulder and was gripping his hair with her other hand. Then Donovan noticed, a foot or so from the guy, a gun: a semi-auto complete with silencer, just sitting there. Donovan glanced over at Marci, who was pale, but seemed steady. Then he smelled cordite. He looked back and saw the bullet hole in the wall behind him, and he didn't feel at all steady himself.

"We need to get out of here," he said.

Susan nodded. "What do we do with this guy?"

"Let me see him."

Susan pulled the man's head up by the hair. The man had scar tissue around his eyes, and his nose had been broken at least once. His clothing was dark and loose fitting, not overly expensive. His hair was a little shaggy—he hadn't had it cut in several weeks—but his face was well shaved. He seemed more dazed than either frightened or angry, but that wouldn't last. Donovan said, "We need to question him. We're going to feel pretty stupid if he's the guy we're looking for and all we do is turn him over to the PO-lice. Is your place good for that, Hippie?"

"No," she said without hesitation.

"Then I hope yours is, Marci—because we're sure as hell not hauling this asshole back to my place on a train, and I think a taxi might present problems even if we can find one to take us to Jersey."

"I think I might be able to manage a sort of slipwalk, now that I've done it," said Marci. "I mean, not a full slipwalk with all the bells and whistles, but I think I can duplicate enough of the effect to get us there. Or, I know. This is better." She walked forward, knelt, and touched the man's forehead.

The guy's eyes suddenly looked even more dazed.

"You two will have to support him," she said. Then she looked back and forth between Susan and Donovan, as if she'd been doing this all her life. "Come on," she said. "Let's get our poor, drunk friend back home."

"I'll get the cab," said Susan. "I can talk a cabbie into anything."

"A New York cabbie?" said Donovan.

"It's my super-power," she said.

Donovan and Susan helped the man stand; he really did act like he was drunk. Donovan said, "Can you hold him for a second?" Susan nodded. Donovan took a quick walk around the room: There was one small bookshelf, a table covered with newspapers and magazines, a desk with half a dozen more books and a few papers on it. Hanging near the one window was what looked like a cross between an American Indian dream catcher and a mobile made of stained glass.

"All right," he said. He took their prisoner's other arm. "Marci, get the lights. Use your elbow, not your fingers. And shut the door, but don't touch the handle."

"What about the gun?" said Susan.

"Not my gun, not my fingerprints."

"All right."

They set off back toward the elevators.

|||||||||||||||

"So," said Becker. "You interrogated him yourself?"

"Yes."

"Because?"

"Because you're in Spain and I didn't want to keep him trussed up in my apartment until you could get here. And because I don't like your interrogation techniques, Mr. Becker."

"I see. We will discuss that another time, Mr. Longfellow. For now, what did you learn?"

"None of the facts are useful; some of the conclusions are."

"Please, Mr. Longfellow. I know how clever you are. It is why you were brought into the organization. What did you learn?"

"He was hired anonymously; all he has is an email address. I'll text it to you if you want, but good luck tracing it. He was paid in cash, unmarked bills left at a drop; he has no idea who hired him or how that person picked or found him. But what's interesting is what he was hired to do. He was given a key to the office and told to enter it at six o'clock that evening, remain for fifteen hours, and kill anyone who came in during that time."

Becker was silent for nearly a minute. "Yes," he said at last. "I see what you mean about drawing conclusions. Who is he?"

"Ex-army, ex-boxer, ex-merc. Did a stretch for armed robbery, was arrested for manslaughter once, but no conviction."

"How much was he paid?"

"Five hundred bucks, with the promise of a thousand later for each one of us he killed."

"Not very much as such things go."

"No. Mr. Becker, why is it that we don't have someone who can use magic to trace an email address?"

"I'm told Research and Development is working on it, but it isn't easy for reasons I'm afraid I do not understand, and that I doubt you would, either."

"It'd sure be useful."

"No doubt it would. How did you get the information from the attacker?"

"I asked nicely."

"Please, Mr. Longfellow."

"I'm mostly telling the truth, Mr. Becker. There were a few subtle threats, maybe, but for the most part, we just talked. We cooked him some roast chicken, gave him some beer, and had a conversation. No torture, not even a hint of a spell from Marci. We convinced him that if he cooperated we'd let him go, and that he had no reason to protect those who hired him."

"And you think he told the truth?"

"We know he did. Marci can tell; that sort of falls within her skill set."

"What did you do with him?"

"Let him go."

"Do you think that was wise?"

"I don't see the harm."

"He knows where you live. He can report it, and our enemies can find you."

"Yeah? That'll be interesting."

"We do things differently, Mr. Longfellow."

"Yes, we do, Mr. Becker."

"In any case, we've established that they're on to us. Or they are now, if they weren't before."

"Yeah. We also know that their resources are limited if they have to go outside their group to take a shot at us, and not all that effective a shot at that. Five hundred? A thousand per? That's not big-budget stuff."

"Agreed."

"And?"

"Yes," said Becker. "I was able to confirm the nature of his connection to the Roma Vindices Mystici."

"So was I," said Donovan.

"Were you indeed? How so?"

"That's what he did in that office for eight hours a day: He was recruiting for them. His area ran as far west as the Ohio border, as far south as the Maryland border, north to Canada. And he also kept track of who was looking into government corruption. Your assumption about him being involved in making reporters disappear is almost certainly true. From what I know of the Mystici, he would have been doing that on his own as a private contractor for someone, not for the Mystici, but I speak under correction, of course."

"Good work, Mr. Longfellow."

"What is it with these people? Are they just, you know, doing bad stuff because they're bad, and like to twirl their mustaches and say, 'Bwa ha ha'?"

"They protect each other, just as we do."

"But the things they do—"

"You know their history, Mr. Longfellow."

"Some of it. The Foundation isn't especially forthcoming with those of us who are merely employees, Mr. Becker. And none of my cases so far have brought me up against them."

"You aren't *against* them now, Mr. Longfellow. The members of their order are sworn to defend each other. They have no goals, or master plan."

"But they're such *assholes*."

Becker might have smiled. "Some of them," he said. "But then, similar words have been applied to me at times."

"That's hard to believe, Mr. Becker. So, our shooter. He either doesn't like the Mystici, or doesn't like some assholes in it."

"Yes."

"Other than being frat brothers, do the two victims have any connection?"

"We're still checking. I'll let you know if we find anything. I assume you will also look into the matter."

"Yeah. So here's the question: Why do we care?"

"You care because you're being paid to, Mr. Longfellow."

"What, a hundred and thirty dollars a month? That's not a lot of caring, Mr. Becker."

"And a place to live. And that's just the retainer. For active service, you're paid by the hour."

"Right. Eight dollars and fifty cents."

"That is the best we can do, I'm afraid. You know we're not wealthy."

"But why do *you* care? Your people, the ones who pay me? What's the Foundation's stake in this?"

"Mr. Longfellow, anyone able to stop time and willing to murder presents a danger, don't you agree?"

"Mr. Becker, we both know you sent my team to look into Lawton-Smythe's death before we knew about the time-stop. So, what is it?"

"Your job is to prevent knowledge of magic from leaking out into the awareness of the general public. You truly cannot see how exactly this sort of thing could lead to that?"

"Not really. Especially the coronary. It isn't like the Arizona business, with pyrotechnics that everyone could see and had no good explanation. Or that mess with the flying ship in Biloxi.

And it seems like the people being killed are bad guys. Isn't that one of the things carved into the plaque? 'People shouldn't use magic to do bad things to each other,' or whatever it is in Latin. So, what is it really?"

"If that is all, Mr. Longfellow, I should follow up on your intelligence and see if it leads anywhere. I'll be in touch."

Donovan stared at the camera long enough to make his point, then said, "I'm including the interrogation on my time sheet, Mr. Becker."

"Very well, Mr. Longfellow."

"Marci and Susan were there for the whole thing, so I'm going to tell them to include it on theirs, too."

"Very well, Mr. Longfellow."

"I'll talk to you soon."

Donovan closed Skype, and turned around. Marci and Hippie Chick were sitting on his sofa, in earshot of the computer, though not in range of the camera. Marci was drinking tea. Susan had white wine. Donovan was drinking horseradish-infused vodka on the rocks because he felt like it, that's why. Three of Donovan's knotnots were sitting on the table, next to Marci—she'd recharged them while he was talking to Becker, which would have been distracting if it had involved anything more dramatic than her face going blank and the room warming up a little. He picked up the devices with a nod of thanks and put them in his closet, then came back, sat down, had a sip of vodka. It burned pleasantly.

"All right," he said. "You heard all that. Anything come to mind?"

They both shook their heads.

"Me neither," said Donovan.

"You have a nice place," said Marci, looking around. "It's cozy."

"You mean tiny."

"I guess."

"It's what they gave me."

"How'd they recruit you?" she asked. Then she looked suddenly hesitant and said, "Or are we not supposed to talk about that?"

"I don't mind. Do you mean how, or why?"

"I was asking how, but now I'm curious about why."

"Why is because I had the right skill set. I was going to be a private investigator. I had an uncle who was an ex-fed, if you can believe it, and he trained me."

"What happened to that plan?"

Donovan considered, then shrugged. "He lived in Los Angeles, and I was staying with him there while he taught me. He died, and after the funeral I was going to take a flight home. The TSA guy decided I needed to be frisked, and he touched my junk."

"Uh-oh."

"Yeah. I broke his wrist. And a couple of ribs and his jaw. So all of a sudden I can't fly, and I can't get a PI license."

"Really!" said Susan. "I never knew that. No offense, Don, but you don't look like a bruiser."

"I'm not. He was a little guy with a lot of attitude." Donovan didn't mention his own broken ribs, from where the other TSA guys had held him down and kicked him. It didn't seem germane.

Marci nodded. "Well, so that answers the why. Now, how?"

"I should have let you interrogate our friend."

She smiled nervously. "Sorry if I'm being—"

"Naw. It's all right. The how is easy enough: They brought me back from the dead."

"Literally?"

"Almost. I was shot by a PO-liceman. For jaywalking."

"Really?"

"That's not what he said. And there were words exchanged first, and I probably shouldn't have tried to run. But yeah. They brought me back from nine shots, at least four of which were fatal. I guess I wasn't technically dead at the time, or they couldn't have managed it, but technically dead doesn't have a really good definition when it comes to medicine, and less when it comes to magic."

"I know," said Marci.

"Anyway, yeah, back without any what they call 'deficits.' Gave me a new identity, new face, set me up. I could get a PI license now, but I figure I owe them."

"So," said Susan, "you knew about the magic from the start."

"You didn't?"

She shook her head. "They handled it well. I'd see something bizarre, and they'd shrug it off and refuse to explain. It went on for months like that, all during my training. By the time they told me what was really going on, I was in a head space to accept it."

"They're clever," said Marci.

"That they are," said Donovan. He looked at Susan. It was interesting that they'd never talked about this before. He said, "Do you know why they recruited you?"

"Yeah. Because I got too big to be an acrobat." She turned to Marci. "How about you?"

"Me?" said Marci. "When I was fifteen, I levitated a paperweight and threw it at a guy who—who I didn't like."

"That was it? You just levitated something out of nowhere?"

"That was the first time I did something I couldn't explain away. The next day William sent me a text message."

"William?" said Donovan. "I don't know him."

"Head of recruiting."

"Must have been after my time."

"I guess. He specializes in magic training and fart jokes. The message said: 'You can do more than levitate things, and I can help.'"

"Huh," said Donovan. "That'll get your attention."

Marci nodded. "I used to sneak out to practice with him two or three times a week, whenever I could. Once I was on my own, working for them just seemed obvious." Then her brows came together and she tilted her head. "Hey, tell me something?"

"Sure."

"Were you just, ah, blowing smoke up Mr. Becker's ass?"

Donovan frowned. "Huh? No, that turns out to be a bad idea. What do you mean?"

"All that stuff about what Blum did."

"Oh. Yeah, that's real."

"How could you know that?"

"I told you, my uncle was an ex-fed and he trained me."

"But—"

"Did you see a computer on his desk?"

"Um. I don't remember. I was kind of excited."

"There wasn't one. But there was a CAT Five cable sitting on it, so what do you conclude?"

"That he uses a laptop and brings it home with him."

"See? It isn't that hard."

"But how does that—"

"It was just an example." He drank some more vodka and leaned back in his chair. "Of course, we can go a little further: that he's using CAT Five instead of the building's wireless means he's concerned with security, and that he doesn't know a lot about how computer security works. But that doesn't get us very far, either."

"So then how did you know all that stuff?"

Donovan drummed the fingertips of his left hand on the arm of the chair, and looked at Susan, who was a wearing one of her little smiles. "All right," he said. "Next to the cable—I mean, right next where his laptop would be—was a map of the northeastern United States, with nodes marked on it. One of the things nodes are used for is recruitment—a sensitive might be drawn there, so the Mystici, and us, keep a watch on the major ones to see who shows up. Pretty much anything else, like most uses of magic, he'd have the lines, the points, *and* the nodes. Also, right on his desk, in easy reach, he had a listing of psychiatric hospitals and wards in New York, New Jersey, Massachusetts—all the states in his area. Sometimes sensitives are first diagnosed as schizophrenics, so keeping track of those is something else a recruiter would do. The thing hanging from the ceiling is one of the standard ways to construct—hell, I don't know what they call it; ask the kiddie pool. But it can detect when magic, especially uncontrolled magic, is used within a certain distance. That's probably how your friend William found you. Put it all together, he was doing recruiting."

Marci nodded. "And the stuff about the reporters?"

"The magazines on the table. *The Washington Post, Rolling Stone, The Guardian, The Boston Globe, Harper's, The New Yorker:* newspapers and magazines that are known for revealing political scandals. Upstairs told me that Blum might have been involved in that, so I was looking for it."

"But you were only in there for a few seconds."

"As I said, I've been trained."

"What was in the bookcases?"

Donovan nodded. "Ah. Now, that is actually interesting. They were all novels. Mysteries, thrillers. A complete set of Anthony Price. And Patrick O'Brian."

"How is that interesting?"

"A bookshelf full of fiction? At the office? Why not keep them at home?"

"Oh. Well, why?"

"I don't know yet. I'm going to guess that we'll never find out, and, if we do, it won't matter. But it's a thing I noticed, so I'm going to keep track of it."

"Wow," said Marci. "You're good at this."

"Yeah, and you're good at what you do. And Susan's good at what she does. And so are most of the rest of the Foundation. They're all good at what they do."

"Nice to know we're the good guys," said Marci.

"If we are," said Donovan.

Susan's head snapped around. "What do you mean?"

"I mean, I'm not sure they—we—are the good guys anymore."

"Why?" said Susan.

"Why do I wonder? Because we're after someone who's killing members of the Roma Vindices Mystici, and from everything I know all the people he's killing are assholes."

"I think they—I mean we—are still the good guys," said Susan.

"Yeah, because you're a hippie chick who trusts everyone."

"No, because if we were bad guys we'd be getting paid more than minimum wage."

"Huh," said Donovan.

"You know," said Marci. "That's actually kind of a good argument."

Donovan thought about it. "Make sure you include the interrogation on your time sheets," he said.

MYSTERIOUS CHARLIE

3

I called him Mysterious Charlie for a reason. Face-to-face meetings with him were rare, and strange, and not really face-to-face. Once we met in the confessional of a church, me taking the role of the priest. Another time, booths in a diner at three in the morning, facing away from each other. My first meeting with him came when he was driving the cab I got at Denver International after I came back from New York, back when my first attempt had failed so spectacularly. He'd struck up a conversation by asking if I believed in the Devil. I wondered if I'd stumbled into a slasher film with a crazy cabbie; after what I'd just been through, that didn't seem impossible. But I ventured to say no, I didn't believe in the Devil, and he said, "How about metaphorically, Mr. Nagorski?"

"How did you—?" I broke off, now thinking it was a thriller instead of a slasher movie, which I supposed was a little better.

"Relax, Mr. Nagorski. We'll talk, and I'll make you a proposal, and you'll either say yes or no, and if you say no I'll drop you off at your home and you'll never hear from me again."

"What if I say maybe?" I said, because my head was spinning a little and I was having trouble processing.

"'Maybe' counts as 'no,' I'm afraid."

"Oh," I said, and tried to get my brain to form thoughts. "Who are you?"

"Call me Charles. Or Charlie."

"How did you know my name?"

His rearview mirror was tilted up so I could only get a bit of his profile—he had a sharp nose and a sharper chin, a long neck, and short, dark hair; that's about all I can tell you. He said, "I will answer your question, Mr. Nagorski. I will answer as many questions as necessary for you to make an informed decision, and eventually, if we work together, I will answer others. But humor me and answer mine first. Do you believe in the Devil metaphorically?"

"You mean, do I believe in evil?"

"Yes."

That was an easy question to answer, especially just then. "I believe in selfishness and greed and people who don't give a shit who gets hurt," I said. "So I suppose I do."

"How about magic?"

"Metaphorically?"

"Literally. The supernatural, subject to conscious control."

"No."

"Really? Then there are a few things you must have trouble explaining. Not only how I know your name, but how, in the line of cabs and the line of passengers, I happened to be the one to pick you up. And more than that, you have to ask yourself how it is that Paul Joseph Whittier Junior is still alive."

Suddenly, the cab seemed very warm, and I wanted to open the door and jump out, or maybe just throw up. I guess he knew that, because he said, "Don't be frightened, Mr. Nagorski. At least, not of me. I will let you out if you wish, or take you home. But if you want, I can help you kill Paul Whittier. And I would like to do so. I have my own reasons, naturally. May I call you Nick?"

"Um. Sure."

"Thank you, Nick. As I say, I can help you. But it won't be easy, and the first thing you have to do is believe in magic."

"I'm not sure I can do that."

"You have to believe in something, Nick. You believed in marriage, and that didn't work out. You believed in hard work and loyalty, and that didn't work out, either. You believed in the law, and that life was fair, and—"

"I get the point. You know all sorts of things about me."

"I'm trying to explain, Nick. What do you believe in?"

"I believe in God. I mean, sort of. Maybe."

"What is God except magic, Nick?"

I was starting to recover—or maybe I was just emotionally distancing myself from the weirdness. I'd had a lot of practice at emotionally distancing myself lately. I said, "There's something wrong with that logic, Charlie, but I'm not sure what it is."

That was the first time I heard him chuckle. He didn't do it often; he was a serious kind of guy. He said, "Whittier is protected by magic, Nick. That's why you failed. You'll need magic of your own to kill him. It's that simple."

"Yeah. Uh, look, Charlie—"

He said, "What would it take to convince you?"

I thought about it. "I suppose empirical proof, like the business with the cab, but more tangible, and a way to convince myself I wasn't hallucinating, and that it couldn't be faked."

"That sounds impossible, Nick."

"Sorry."

"Sounds impossible, not *is* impossible."

"All right."

"So, should I take you home, or should I convince you?"

"Convince me," I said.

He crossed two lanes of traffic and took three rights, taking us back the way we'd come. "Let's get started," he said.

Later, he explained that getting me in the cab hadn't been magic at all—he'd just spotted me, counted, and bribed a few other cabbies to let him in front. But by then it didn't matter, because I'd been convinced.

||||||||||||||||

The words that greeted Marci when she walked through the door were, "Where have you been? You were gone all night." There was also a delicious smell, but the sour tone of the question demanded her attention first.

Lawrence sat at the kitchen table, cheek on hand, holding a ginger ale that, no doubt, he'd been staring at until the door opened. Marci went over, sat down, and looked at him. No, it wasn't magic. She never used magic on him. She could have, but she didn't. She just looked at him and waited. He stared back, then dropped his eyes. "Sorry," he said.

She leaned over, kissed his forehead, and put her hand on his. "Bad day?"

"Why," he said, "did I get a job where I have to interact with the public? And especially the kind of public that owns SUVs and lives the way they drive?"

"I don't know," she said. "Maybe something about nothing else being available? Or else the gods are trying to teach you patience."

"Yeah, that must be it. A growth opportunity." He managed a smile and kissed her cheek. "How about your day?"

"It was all right." *Except for getting shot at. And taking part in the interrogation of someone who tried to kill me. Achievement unlocked?*

"You look beat."

"Yeah, a bit. It was tiring."

"Are you ever going to tell me what you do?"

"No, love."

"Is it okay if I keep asking?"

"Yes, love."

"Okay, then. Hungry?"

"Yes, love. Did you cook?"

"Rice and beans with Chorizo."

"I swoon; I die. Feed me, then put me to bed."

He did, and they made love, and that was better. Then they slept, spooning, his arm around her, which may have been better still.

Marci slept until the middle of the afternoon, and Lawrence was at work when she woke up. She spent the a few hours indulging herself by reading papers by Stanislav Smirnov on Percolation theory, then made herself stop. She did a load of laundry, went through the fridge and the cupboards and started a shopping list, then, braced by both fun and tedium, tackled the bills.

An hour later she rubbed her eyes and glared at the computer, wanting it to notify her of a Skype call that would take her to anything, even another corpse, even someone else shooting at her. It was obstinately silent.

I am a sorcerer. I can sense grid lines. I can stand at a node and feel the power flow through me. I can dive into the remnants of a spell and tell what has been cast, how long ago, and sometimes even sense things about the caster. I can make strangers trust me by willing that they do so. I can conjure a shield that will stop bullets. I know how to create an artifact by sending my spell into an object to be cast later by anyone who knows how to release it. I embody a tradition stretching back to the 1930s, and before that to the Middle Ages, and before that to the nameless pioneers of the Art who, through trial and error, learned truths and created superstitions. That is who I am. That is what I am. And I'm stumped trying to figure out how to pay the fucking rent and the minimum payment on the Visa and two cell phones and not have our Internet turned off and still leave Lawrence enough money for bus fare to work.

The amazing thing isn't that sorcerers become criminals; it's how few of us do so.

But her teachers had been insistent that willpower was the key to making the world do what you wished, so she used hers and returned to the bills.

||||||||||||||||

I had a face-to-face with Mysterious Charlie before leaving New York. Or, well, back-to-back, I guess you'd call it. This time, we met at Washington Square Park, about one in the morning, at an empty chess table. More precisely, I was at the chess table, with my back to the wall, and he was on the other side. It was like a bad spy movie. I wondered if he was an actor or a politician, someone I'd recognize. I suspected he was just trying to be mysterious, but I knew for sure he wasn't anyone to mess with. He knew things, and he knew people who could do things. Even more, he was helping me get what I wanted. What with one thing or another, if he wanted our meetings to go like a parody of a Michael Caine movie I wasn't going to object.

"You're doing well, Nick." He kept his voice low and rough, which added to the sense of someone playing at spy. But I've never met a real spy, so for all I know that's how they are.

"Thanks, Charlie. There's still a long way to go. You have something for me?"

"Yes. When I leave, there will be a paper bag containing what you need."

"Thanks."

"If you remember, I told you that if things went well, I'd be willing to start answering your questions. So, what do you want to know?"

"What's your game? I mean, what is it you're after? Why are you helping me?"

"A good question, but I'm not ready to answer it. Ask me another."

"All right. Since it's on my mind: Why won't you let me see your face?"

"For the same reason I won't answer your last question. Because there is danger of you being captured, and forced to reveal everything you know. I want you unable to identify me."

"I don't like how 'forced' sounds in that sentence."

"I never denied there was danger."

"True. All right. Next question. What is—"

"No, just one question, for now."

"Huh," I said. "If I'd known that, I'd have asked something different."

||||||||||||||||

Donovan sat in the office chair at the kitchen table, laptop in front of him, but he didn't touch it. The medical billing work was building up next to him, but he ignored it. The screen for Internet hearts was up, but he didn't log in.

Okay, then. Let's assume Hippie Chick is right and we are the good guys. How do we find this fuck?

He plugged in the speakers, found some Beastie Boys, cranked it, and wallowed in synthesized drums and nostalgia and memories of a girl named Diane whose hair smelled like vanilla. That didn't provide any answers either, but it made Donovan smile.

After an hour or so, he turned off the music; he was only vaguely aware that his foot kept tapping.

Well, shit. The obvious question is, other than the Mystici, what connects these two? It isn't geography, or profession. He took out his cell, and selected a name. After five rings, a deep voice came on. "Donny. What's up?"

"Jeffrey my hero. Got a question. How long do phone companies keep records of calls?"

"Six weeks to ten years, depending on the company. Why?"

"I'm going to text you two names, with cities and approximate ages. See if you can find a connection between them."

"Do I get paid for this?"

"Jeffrey! How can you even ask?"

"Because we've been here before."

"Yeah. How much will you want?"

"Five thousand."

"Five thousand. They'll have a cow. Okay, tell you what. If you find a connection, I'll pass the bill up, and raise a big stink if they don't want to pay it."

"What if there isn't any connection?"

"Then I owe you a drink."

"Sheeeeeeit."

"Welcome to my world."

"Can we at least make it dinner?"

"Cheap dinner."

"Not fast food."

"Agreed. One step up."

"All right. I'll look into it. But only because it's you."

"You're a hell of a guy."

"Are you ever going to tell me who I'm working for?"

"Seriously, Jeffrey? You really want to know?"

"Of course not, I just like asking."

"Look forward to hearing from you."

"I'll be in touch."

Donovan disconnected, then stared at his phone, wondering if at some point someone would be looking at the records of the call he'd just made, maybe to track him, maybe to use as evidence of some crime as yet uncommitted. *What the hell. The NSA has it already. Why worry about it?*

||||||||||||||||

I caught a red-eye to San Diego, and checked into the Hilton San Diego Airport. This time I used a fake ID that Mysterious Charlie had gotten for me, because this one was going to be different. Well, they're all different, but this one—

First, I carried out my plan of getting a whole lot of sleep. When I finally woke up, I stumbled downstairs for breakfast—no coffee, thanks—then slept some more. Travel takes a lot out of you.

When I woke up again it was after noon local time, and I was groggy. I went down to the Odysea and read the paper and drank coffee. The news was full of bad, and for the thousandth time, I wished I cared about sports—this would have been a perfect day to read up on how my local team had done, and study the statistics of my favorite players. Too bad. Eventually I put the paper down and just watched the Pacific.

When I got back to my room, feeling much better, I took out the file. The next name on the list was Caren Wright. I needed to take my time and be sure with this one. This one would be noticed, which meant I might be noticed; and I didn't want to be noticed until my work was done.

I knew a fair bit about Caren Wright. Aged fifty-three, divorced twice, no children. She came from money and still had it. She had a mansion in La Jolla, and a winter home in Aspen, a condo in Sacramento, and a "cottage" in Nantucket. A few years ago, she'd gotten herself elected to the State Senate, where she had helped pass a bill making it illegal for persons under eighteen to use tanning beds. Important stuff, that. Oh, and she did some work to prevent the proposed football stadium in Los Angeles from being thoroughly reviewed. I don't know how much she made from that one—my sources of information aren't perfect.

But I can usually find out what I need to know, like what bills she voted for, or what kind of cars she owned, or the security codes for the two gates to her backyard, or when she would relax in her heated pool.

4

State Senator Caren Wright was swimming laps naked. I wished she were wearing a suit. Yeah, I know, that's stupid: If I'm going to take someone's life, feeling shitty about invading her privacy is kind of mindless. But the fact is, I did.

I made it happen as fast as I could. I remained behind the shrubs and pulled the smooth, polished, glimmering red and gold stone from my pocket. I wasn't in direct sunlight, but it seemed to sparkle nevertheless—was that magic, or just a property of the stone? I don't know. I'd never seen one like it. I held it in my palm, and extended my hand, fingers pointing toward the pool. I didn't shout; I didn't whisper. I just said, "Kahta dondurauma" or something like it, making sure I trilled the "r" as Charlie had taught me.

The stone did nothing, but I heard a gasp, and then a scream. I moved out from the shrub and watched. When the spell was done, she was still alive, still thrashing about. Somehow it seemed as if she saw me, but the pleading look in her eyes has to have been my imagination. Fuck my imagination. I did it, and I did not—do not—regret it.

Eventually she stopped moving, and I left the way I'd come.

|||||||||||||||||

They sat in a rented Toyota, Donovan at the wheel, Marci next to him, Hippie Chick in back. The scent of the ocean was unmistakable, maybe two hundred yards northwest of them, just past a close-packed pair of what Donovan supposed could be called houses, although "mansions" might be more accurate.

"Jesus H," said Donovan. "What would you guess is the square footage on that thing?"

"Nine thousand feet?" said Susan. "Ten? Eleven?"

"God. Who needs that much space?"

"Well, Caren Wright doesn't," she said. "Not anymore."

"That's cold," said Marci.

"Yeah," said Donovan. "All right. Anyone have any ideas? We don't have a lot of time—the PO-lice around here don't like cars that are just stopped for no reason, especially at night."

"We haven't looked at the scene yet," said Marci. "We have no idea how to get there, much less what to do."

"That's what I meant. Any ideas for getting into that place. There must be alarms. For all I know, there's even a rent-a-cop. It's not a public place. We need to figure out how we're going to get in there without inviting the PO-lice to the party."

"That's why you told us to wear black," said Marci.

"Well, that, and I was afraid Susan would show up in tie-dye."

Hippie Chick ignored that. "The pool is supposed to be outside, right? So we don't have to actually break into the house."

"There's that," said Donovan. "But I wish I knew what we're likely to find getting to the pool."

"Would you like an aerial view?" said Marci. "I can get you

some pictures of the pool and the approach. It might help figure out where the alarms are, and if there's a live guard."

"That'd be good," said Donovan.

Marci took out her cell phone and stared at it.

After a couple of minutes, Donovan turned the key in the ignition and rolled the window down. At about the same time, there came several "clicks" from Marci's cell as it made its camera sound.

Marci silently handed the phone over to Donovan. "Sorry about the heat," she said. "It's a bit of distance to the grid line." Donovan looked at her—she seemed a little haggard.

"I need you in top form, just in case," he said. "How long—"

"Twenty minutes, maybe thirty."

"All right."

Donovan studied the pictures silently, then passed the phone to Susan. She also studied them, then passed the phone back to Marci, who laughed.

"What?"

"I hadn't noticed before. There's a porta-potty. They have their own porta-potty. Why—"

"Construction," said Donovan. "See the sheeting around the fence? Can't let workmen into the house to pee, you know."

"Jesus," said Marci. "For real?"

"For real."

"I could get in," said Susan. "I might be able to disable the alarms."

"If you can't disable the alarms, can you avoid setting them off?"

"I don't know what the security system is, but I think so. We covered some of that in training."

"All right. We'll wait here."

Donovan switched the dome light off, and Susan got out.

She crossed the street, her pace unhurried, though with a grace that pushed the limits of what was natural.

"We should probably slink down in the seats," said Marci.

"I know," said Donovan. "Only I'm not going to do it."

"Um," said Marci. Donovan glanced over; her eyes were closed and her face had the blankness of working. Donovan kept watching until she opened her eyes again.

"That's tight. I should have asked you to do that in the first place," said Donovan.

"It isn't guaranteed. I suck at invisibility spells. This is like tinted windows. If they're determined enough, they'll see the car."

"Good enough," he said. "Let's hope no one has called about us yet, or we'll need a whole new plan. How much more time—"

"It was easy, shouldn't add much to the refractory period."

"Never call it that again."

Marci seemed puzzled. "Never mind," he said. "Anyway, it isn't just nosy neighbors," Donovan said. "We have to assume whoever tried to kill us before is watching us now, or watching the house, at any rate."

"I know."

"When Susan gets back, see if you can do that same spell like you put on the car, make it so we don't attract so much attention, all right? Keep the neighbors from getting upset, and maybe if there's some dumb fuck who wants to shoot us he'll have a harder time spotting us."

"All right. I can do that."

"Can you tell if someone is watching us now?"

"Not reliably. I can try."

"Try," said Donovan. "It'll give us something to do while we worry about Susan."

Once again, Donovan watched her face turn blank. After a moment, her face came alive again and she shook her head.

"What? We're not being watched? Or you can't tell?"

"I didn't detect any hostile attention on the car. That's all I can tell you."

"You could be more reassuring."

"I'll work on that."

They waited.

After nearly half an hour, his phone rang. He looked at the caller ID, then clicked answer. "Hey, Hippie Chick."

"Did you guys leave?"

"What? We're just where—oh yeah, Marci did a concealing spell. Just look hard."

A moment later the door opened and Susan got in. "Nice work, Mar," she said. Then, "Okay, I've killed the alarms."

"All of them?"

Susan looked at him in the mirror. "No. I thought it would be funny to leave a few on."

"Sorry."

"Shall we?"

Donovan looked over at Marci and nodded. They got out of the car and trooped through the gate and around the back as if they belonged there. There was another gate there, into the pool area itself, surrounded by a fence high enough to block the neighbors' view, though it would still be visible from the house. Susan opened the gate, and when nothing sounded, Donovan let his breath out.

"This is where it was," said Donovan. "In the pool. They found her at the bottom. She'd been dead for maybe a couple of hours."

"No chance she just drowned?" said Susan.

Donovan shrugged, but Marci was already doing her thing, slowly walking around the pool, arms at her sides, palms out.

Donovan watched her; Susan's eyes kept sweeping the area—full of palm trees and carefully manicured shrubs—as if she expected to be shot at any second. The house, three stories of it, towered over them; she kept watching it as well.

So far, so good, thought Donovan.

||||||||||||||||

It was almost like a faint ringing in the ears, or maybe a tingling in the fingertips. It was the confused warm blanket of barbiturates, the cold, sharp clarity of solving a mathematics problem. And it had a location, as clear as the direction of a strong breeze, as subtle as the pink haze of twilight. *That way—toward the ocean. Perhaps fifty feet beyond the shoreline.*

She reached out for it, touched it easily even from that distance, and let it fill her. Then she opened the eyes that could never be closed and looked-listened-smelt-touched-tasted.

Here is where it swirled, tasting green and flowing in quiet circles, spreading out to there, and there, and there, down down deeper into the slashing cutting never-stopping blossom of—what was that, chlorine? Yes, but no, and also I'm never going to swim in a chlorinated pool again. Deeper still, and there is motion and the green touch quiets it, quiets it more, the motion slows, slows, slows, and spreads—how long? Seconds, it takes seconds, and is over, and—no, this is the bad part, but let it happen, feel it, but don't experience it. Distance and control. Observe, and reflect, and ultimately know.

||||||||||||||||

Marci opened her eyes, and Donovan knew at once, but asked anyway: "You have it?"

"Oh yes. Not a very pleasant way to go. She was in the pool when it froze solid."

"What, all of it? That's—"

"I don't know if all of it. Probably not. But at least a solid layer on top."

Donovan shuddered. "Nasty."

"I'm trying not to picture it," said Susan.

"Marci, check the area for hostility again, please. If there isn't any, we can just—"

"We're being watched," she said.

"Great," said Donovan, and looked at Susan.

"Can you get a location, Mar?"

"Trying. In the meantime, I've put up a—"

A bright spark occurred twelve inches from Marci's head. She gasped.

"Shield," she finished needlessly.

There was another spark, this one also directly in front of Marci. "Don't take it personally," said Donovan. Her eyes were frightened, but she held herself still. *Good*, he heard himself thinking. *She's going to do fine.*

There was a third spark, not far from the last one. Donovan had opened his mouth to make a remark about the grouping when Susan said, "Got it. Not in the house, in the shrubs," as she sprinted off, clearing the wall like a gymnast working the pommel horse. She made no sound.

"If it turns out to be the same guy," said Donovan, "I'll have to admit that Becker was right, and I'd hate that."

"There are worse fates," said Marci.

"No, there aren't."

||||||||||||||||

Step one, don't be stupid, Susan told herself. *Stupid people get dead. You don't know there is exactly one shooter; you don't know the shooter has only mundane means; you don't know if the shooter has planned for this. Don't be stupid.*

Magic, you might almost say, is as magic does. What Susan did wasn't magic. What Susan did was the product of between four and six hours of training six days a week for eleven years, and that didn't count the acrobatics that had started when she was five. But she knew that the result of it all made it look like magic to those who hadn't been through it, and she was honest enough with herself to admit that this delighted her. That is, when there was time for delight.

Now there wasn't time for feeling much of anything; going after someone who is armed without a solid visual doesn't leave you much attention to spare for anything except eyes and ears.

Her movements were deceptively smooth—deceptive because she was doing what Sensei called the snake-walk: The traditional bobbing and weaving was hidden behind a motion so graceful that it also concealed her speed.

By the time she heard the report of the rifle, the bullet was well past her; it hadn't even been close, and then she was on him. He put up more resistance than the guy in the office had. He swung the rifle at her; she stepped inside the swing and clipped his wrist and he dropped it. His reaction was quick—he let out a flat punch with the other hand; she deflected it and hit the nerve in his biceps. That was enough time for her to realize that he'd had training. When he tried to kick her knee she swept his supporting leg out and he went down. When he started to get up she snap-kicked his jaw—not enough to break it, but enough to make him reconsider standing.

He used a bad word and started reaching inside his jacket.

"Really?" she said.

He stopped, staring at her. He spoke for the first time, his voice even. "Not really. What now?"

"Take it out carefully, two fingers, and put it on the ground, then slide it over to me."

"Give me some reason to believe I'm going to get out of this any better if I do what you say."

"I'll kill you if you don't."

"I know that."

She studied him. He was a big guy, maybe a weight lifter. His head was shaved clean, and he had a mustache joined to a wisp of carefully trimmed beard on his chin, giving him a bit of the Anton LaVey look.

"We don't torture," she said.

He nodded slowly. "All right, I'll buy it."

He took the pistol, a revolver, out as she'd said, and slid it over. She kicked it off to the side next to the rifle—a Remington Model 700 SPS Tactical bolt-action with a stock scope: a deer rifle. She said, "Now stand up slowly. If you fuck around, I'll break both your knees. And then I'll have to try to drag you, and that will piss me off enough that I'll probably break your nose, your jaw, and a couple of ribs just out of spite."

"But you don't torture."

"That isn't torture; that's just me getting annoyed." She studied him a bit more. "And you know the difference. If you do what you're told, you'll probably walk away from this."

He grunted and stood up. He really was very big—tall and wide.

"Hands laced together behind your neck, and stand still." He complied wordlessly while she frisked him, finding a cell phone, keys, a wallet, a few dollars, and an ASEK survival knife. She let him keep the wallet and the money.

"All right," she said. "You can relax."

He gave Susan an evaluating look.

"Just don't," she said. "It won't turn out well for you. Let's go this way; I want you to meet the people you were trying to kill."

He hesitated. Susan waited.

"All right," he said. Susan stepped aside, indicating that he should walk first. She took up a position four feet behind him. He was tense as he walked. *Good.*

When they reached the poolside, she said, "Stop." He did. Don and Marci faced the man. Susan walked around him and handed the knife, keys, and phone to Donovan.

"Can we keep him subdued in the rental?" said Donovan.

"I can take him to your place," said Marci.

"That thing you were talking about before? A slipwalk without the frills?"

"Yeah, kinda. I can manage it, I think. I'll meet you back at your apartment."

"You think?" said Donovan. "What if you can't?"

"I'll get hold of you and we'll figure something out." She looked at the big man, then turned back to Donovan. "I can keep him under control."

Susan saw their prisoner cast an evaluating look at Marci; evidently, Donovan saw it as well. "Better show him," he said. "It'll save trouble later."

Marci nodded and reached a hand toward their prisoner. His eyes widened and he brought his hands to his throat as if unable to breathe.

"I find your lack of faith disturbing," said Marci. Then she smiled sheepishly at Donovan. "I've always wanted to do that," and she released the man, who put his hands on his knees and took several deep breaths.

Donovan shook his head. "Stay with her, do what she says, and be nice, and she won't hurt you."

The man cleared his throat. "Where—"

"We're just going to have a chat," said Donovan.

"I don't—"

"Then don't. Let's get out of here."

"Good idea," said Susan.

||||||||||||||||||

Donovan dropped Susan off just short of where they'd appeared, near the Avis lot, and let her walk to the return point while he returned the car, and then met her at the return point, from where they slipwalked back to Donovan's apartment in New Jersey. They emerged at the bottom of the stairway behind the dryer. Marci was there as promised, looking drained and exhausted. Their prisoner with her; he seemed nervous, but not about to become violent. The tricky part was getting from the laundry room back to Donovan's apartment—but it was late and the one guy they ran into, Rob from 301, was much too drunk to be a problem.

Once they were inside his apartment, Donovan sat the man down and pulled his wallet from his coat, found his driver's license. "Matthew Castellani," he said. "Tell me about yourself, Matthew. Do you go by 'Matt'?"

Matthew or Matt grunted, shifted, looked like he was about to stand up, glanced at Hippie Chick, and reconsidered.

"Marci," said Donovan. "Can you secure him?"

Marci walked up to him. "Don't bite, now," she said, and ran a finger diagonally over Matthew or Matt's chest, then around his back, outside his arms, and finished with his legs. She stepped back and nodded.

"What the fuck?" Matt or Matthew's eyes were very wide.

"Matt, or Matthew?" Donovan asked again.

"I—Matt."

"Okay, Matt. I'm Donovan; this is Marci. You've already met Susan."

"How do you do," said Susan.

Matt struggled against the invisible bonds. "What did you do to me?"

"No, no. I'll do the asking. I'm the DJ; you're the rapper. What were you paid to kill us?"

Matt glared.

"Look," said Donovan. "There isn't a lot of point in this, is there? I mean, the whole resisting thing. We've got you cold. We can make you disappear. Or worse. But what's the point? Who are you protecting? He paid you to shoot us. Did he pay you for loyalty, too? Did he even bother telling you not to talk? Is it someone with any loyalty to you? If the PO-lice had caught you, would he have provided a lawyer? Is it someone you're more afraid of than us? Is it—"

"All right. I get your point," he said. "Are you recording this?"

"No."

Matt studied his face. "All right." He took a deep breath and let it out. "I was paid five hundred, plus—"

"A thousand per kill?" said Donovan in time with Matt.

"If you already knew—"

"Just making sure you're being honest with us. Keep doing that, and this will work out all right for you. Well, except for the part about you being dumped off in Jersey City to get back to California as best you can. Sorry about that. Do you know why someone wanted us dead?"

"No," he said.

"How were you paid?"

"Small bills, left at a dead drop. Um, a dead drop means—"

"Yeah, I know what a dead drop is. What are the specifics?"

"It was taped to the inside of a trash can at Balboa Park."

"And how did they reach you?"

"Anonymous email."

"Why did you shoot at Marci each time?"

"If I were back home, I could show you the email. There was a description of her, and it said she was the most important one to take down."

Donovan glanced at Marci; she seemed to be taking the news all right. Donovan turned back to Matt. "How did they find you?"

"I don't know."

"You didn't ask?"

"No."

"Do you have a criminal record? I'll point out that we can check on that; it's a stupid thing to lie about."

"I have a dishonorable discharge. Does that help?"

"What did you do to earn that?"

"Look it up yourself."

"So, something you're not proud of."

Matt caught Donovan's eye and held it. "That is correct."

"All right. But what I really want to know is, how did they find you? What made them think you'd be willing to take a rifle and kill three complete strangers? Can you tell me that?"

Matt looked from one of them to the other, then around the room. Donovan waited. Then Matt said, "Throw me a bone."

"What kind?"

"Who are you people?"

Donovan turned to Marci and nodded. Matt relaxed as the invisible bonds released. Donovan said, "We're the good guys. We hope. If you're asking if what has happened to you in the last hour is the product of insanity, drugs, or magic, the answer is magic."

"No shit?"

"No shit."

"The scary thing is, I almost believe you."

"Yeah. So, do I get an answer?"

"Sniper training." He gave Donovan a significant look and said, "I've also been trained in interrogation techniques."

"Torture?"

Matt held his eye. "Never done it. It doesn't work."

"Yeah," said Donovan. "There's a guy I need you to explain that to."

Matt shrugged. "Anyway, now I work as a bouncer at a titty bar because I can't get anything else. Anyone with the resources to find an ex–Special Forces Operative with a DD could have found me."

"Huh. You were a Green Beret?"

"Tell the truth, I've always thought of myself as kind of a flat cap."

"Any ink?"

Matt rolled up his eyes, then his sleeve, revealing a black knife, up, entwined with blue flowers, surrounded by fig leaves.

"Doesn't say anything about Special Forces."

Matt tilted his head. "No, it doesn't. They kind of frown on that. If you get captured, it gets hard to pretend you're an insurance salesman on vacation when you have a tattoo that says you're an S.F.O. But if you look close, you'll see a one and a nine in the leaves."

"Unit?"

"Nineteenth National Guard. Second Battalion, C Company, O.D.A."

"Where was your base?"

"Draper, Utah, then Camp Dawson."

"All right. So, if you have Special Forces training, why not go up against Susan?"

He shrugged. "She got me," he said. "How does this magic thing work?"

"Hell if I know," said Donovan. "I'm just the brains of the outfit."

"There are places," said Marci, "that a few people can tap into that allow the bending of reality. The closer we are, the more we can do easier. This apartment building is right on top of one."

She waited. When he didn't say anything, she continued. "The people who can detect and use the places are called sensitives; after training, we're called sorcerers. Or freaks."

"Nah," said Donovan. "Hippie Chick is the freak."

"Bending of reality," said Matt. "That sounds kind of . . ."

"Yeah?"

"Cool."

Marci smiled. "It is."

"What can you do with it?"

"Be easier to say what can't you do."

"Okay, what can't you do?"

"Break the law with it," said Donovan. "Or people like us will come after you and do bad things to you."

"So, you're kind of like cops?"

"No," said Donovan. The others looked at him, and he shrugged.

"You can't violate natural law," said Marci.

"Then it isn't magic, is it?"

Marci laughed suddenly. "Imagine a dozen wannabe sorcerers, ages between thirteen and twenty-five, sitting around a cafeteria table arguing that at the top of their lungs, and you'll have a pretty good idea what sorcery training is like. At least between sessions."

"How did those things you did to me not violate natural law?"

"Which things?"

"The way we traveled, and making it so I couldn't move?"

"The second is simple; I changed the makeup of part of your clothes to make it rigid and adhere to your chair. Nothing impossible about the result, just used different means to do it."

"And the travel?"

"Same thing. Think of it like a train that moves at about four hundred miles a second. That one's hard, though. You have to make sure nothing happens to the body during transit, and that the particles of your body remain coherent while passing through objects, and a host of other things. They build portals for that so even civilians can use it if they know how. It includes all sorts of technology, like voice recognition, and concealment spells, and things to check if the place you're arriving at is occupied. There are specialists who keep them operational, and charge an arm and a leg for it."

"Man. I almost believe you. How many are there?"

"In our group, or total number of sensitives?"

"People in the world who can do this."

"Something like one person in a hundred thousand can sense the grid lines."

"Seventy thousand worldwide, give or take," said Matt with no hesitation. "Not many."

"No."

"And what do the good guys do?"

Donovan, whose mind had been occupied with trying to come up with a way to find who had hired Matt, suddenly came back to the present. "Hey," he said. "How did this turn into you interrogating us?"

"I started asking questions."

Donovan smiled in spite of himself. "It's a whole thing," he said. "You know, secret foundation, all like that. We protect each other, and try to learn more about how magic works, and do what we can to prevent bad people from using it for bad things, because then it would be discovered, and we don't know what would happen to sorcerers if everyone knew about them, but I doubt it would be pleasant."

"How did you know how much I was paid?"

"You aren't the first guy who tried to kill us."

"Shit. What happened to the last one?"

"We let him go. We're generally catch-and-release types."

"Generally?"

"Generally."

"Yeah, about that. You said all this stuff is secret. How secret?"

"You mean, is it secret enough that we're going to kill you or something? No. Who would you tell, and who would believe you? The stuff we worry about is big and splashy and includes photographs."

"So, you're really going to let me go?"

"Yeah."

Matt stood up and walked toward the door, glanced back at Donovan. "You really are letting me go," he said.

"Like I said, catch and release. That's how you know we're the good guys." He decided mentioning Becker at this point would ruin a perfect moment, so he didn't.

"Well, damn," said Matt. Then he came back and sat down on the couch. He remained there for a moment, brows furrowed. "You know," he said at last. "I'd kind of like to be a good guy."

CORPORATE POLITICS

5

Donovan almost didn't take the call. He hadn't gotten enough sleep, and Matt was still there, crashed out on the couch, and the coffee wasn't done. So, when Skype notified him of an incoming call from Fenwood, Donovan very nearly ignored it. But he was awake, Susan and Marci had left, and he wasn't in the middle of anything critical; there wouldn't be a better time, and the Black Hole couldn't be ducked forever. Then he took a breath, let it out, and clicked the answer button.

The familiar long, cadaverous face appeared. "Good day, Mr. Longfellow. This is Boyd Fenwood from Budget and Oversight."

"A pleasure to meet you, Mr. Fenwood," he said.

"If you please, Mr. Longfellow. This is not a joking matter."

"Oh. It isn't? Well, damn. And all the other times we've talked, I thought you were just kidding around."

"If you please."

"Sure. Can I call you Boyd?"

"I would prefer you didn't."

"Yeah, I know. But I'm gonna keep asking. You gotta break down eventually."

"Mr. Longfellow."

"Well, all right then. I guess you'd better tell me about it. What's on your mind? How can I help Budget and Oversight? Because you know that with everything I do, keeping Budget and Oversight happy is my first concern."

"Mr. Longfellow, are you aware that every time you activate the Remote Portal Device it requires both the work of a skilled technician and certain expensive materials, costing the Foundation over two thousand, two hundred dollars to reset it? And nearly half that much for the return trip?"

"Why, no, Mr. Fenwood," said Donovan, who had been given this figure roughly ten thousand times. "I had no idea. Is that what this is about? I'd thought you were going to ask for my recent expenses, so you could make paying them your top priority, like you usually do."

Fenwood's face kept jumping around on the screen, like he was moving his head all the time and Skype was having trouble keeping up. It was oddly disconcerting after Becker's stillness.

"Mr. Longfellow, will you at least do me the courtesy of being serious?"

"I'll try."

"You have authorized the device for your team on six occasions in the last week. Are you absolutely certain that none of those trips could have been taken by mundane means?"

"Not if we wanted results. More time to the site means more time until the results of the investigation are in, and sometimes it means the thing we're trying to investigate is no longer in condition to be detected."

"I am aware of this. But you, in turn, must be aware that if we were to authorize fast travel for every investigation we would soon be out of money for, among other things, your wages."

Why wait? Haul out the heavy artillery right away, as some general somewhere must have said. "Mr. Becker was insistent on results. If you would like to check this with him, I have his number right here."

There was a pause. Becker was a trump card that could be played over and over, and the fact that Fenwood knew exactly what Donovan was doing did nothing to diminish the effectiveness. There was, however, a downside: Fenwood might cave, but he would have his revenge.

Donovan sat there for another ten minutes as the man from the Black Hole explained in detail the meticulous accounting necessary to stretch the meager funding from Grants and Acquisitions ("the Vault") to not only continue the services the Foundation provided to its members but also simply keep it operating. Was Mr. Longfellow aware of what the Euro was doing in Spain, and the mere cost of maintaining the headquarters building, and paying the salaries of the clerical staff? It was not his, Fenwood's, place to decide what services must be reduced, if not cut out entirely, but he would take his oath—yes, his oath— that it wasn't Donovan's, either, and yet by his promiscuous spending he, Donovan, was taking that decision out of the hands of both Budget and Oversight and the Executive itself, and surely even Mr. Longfellow could see that the Executive would not be pleased by this usurpation of their power.

There was another pause; Fenwood seemed to think he had perhaps gone too far with the "even Mr. Longfellow."

"Very well," said Donovan, in his best cold, deeply offended voice. "If that is all, I really must not keep Mr. Becker waiting any more."

"Yes, of course. You understand, I'm only doing my job."

"Yes, Mr. Fenwood. I understand entirely."

With a barely concealed sigh of relief, Donovan ended the call and returned to his guest.

iiiiiiiiiiiiiii

We were at the bus station, sitting in plastic seats facing away from each other, and he was telling me more about how magic works. I listened carefully, then said, "Why do you call it a grid when it isn't even in squares?"

I could see him fight the urge to turn around and stare at me. "Nick, I'm telling you that magic is real, that miracles are possible, that sorcerers walk among us, and you're worried that the language doesn't make sense?"

"Okay," I said. "Fair point. So, this stuff you do, you have to have a knack for it?"

"Yes, to feel and identify the grid lines. My theory is that it isn't magic as such, just something we don't understand yet. Clarke's Law and all that."

"Whose law?"

"Doesn't matter. But you can do it, or you can't. After that, it's a matter of aptitude and training, like everything else."

"What about you? Can you do it?"

"No," said Charlie.

Was there the least hesitation before he'd said that? I wasn't sure; I set it aside for later consideration. "How do people get the training?"

"The Mystici, or the Foundation."

"The Foundation?"

"They're the ones who are after us."

"Oh."

"So one group or the other, or else trial and error. Trial and error is a poor idea—it tends to create problems. Although there are a few who—no, that's just a distraction. Skip it."

"So, these groups. They're, like, enemies? Competitors?"

"Not enemies. Maybe competitors. 'Rivals' might be the best term, at least in some things. They both look for sensitives, and offer to train them, and sometimes recruit them."

"If I had the talent, would they find me, or would I find them?"

"Can work either way. They're always looking, and have various ways of finding you. But some sensitives will feel a grid line and follow it to a node, and they have people watching a lot of the nodes in case that happens."

"Node?"

"Where three or more lines come together. A lot of power there."

"Then how—"

"No, that's enough questions for now. You're set with the next name on the list?"

It isn't a name, part of my mind responded. *It's a person. Yeah*, said another part. *And a person I want to kill.* That was as much of a peep as I ever got out of my conscience.

"Yes," I said. "What do you have for me this time?"

He hesitated. "You don't like this guy much, do you?"

"No."

"Then you're going to like what I have. One thing, though."

"What's that?"

"Once you've used it, don't discard it. I'm going to want it back."

"This one can be used again? I thought that was impossible."

"It is impossible. That isn't why."

"Then—"

"I'll explain later."

"Whatever you say."

|||||||||||||||||

"What are you grinning about?" asked Donovan as he turned from his computer.

Matt shook his head. "Just, you know, how the universe works."

Donovan grunted.

Matt sat back on the sofa, stuck his arms out, and stretched his legs. "So explain," he said. "Who are the good guys? I mean, what do you do?"

Donovan rolled his computer chair the five feet from the kitchen to the living room, sat. "The main purpose is to study how magic works, what the limitations are, how it can be used. And to keep it secret. Mostly to keep it secret. Beer?"

"What kind?"

"Jesus. Picky motherfucker, aren't you? Rolling Rock."

"No th—oh, what the hell. Sure."

Donovan got one for each of them. There were six left. He handed one to Matt, sat down with his, and they made a sort of vague toasting gesture toward each other, drank. Donovan liked the beer more than Matt seemed to.

"What will you do to keep the secret?" said Matt.

"Let's cut to it, all right?"

"I thought that's what I was doing."

"We won't kill anyone. I mean, I won't, and I've never heard of anyone in the Foundation ordering it."

"Not killing leaves a lot open."

"Sounds like you're talking from experience."

Matt shrugged.

"Yeah, it does leave a lot open. But you've killed, haven't you?"

Matt shrugged again.

"And you've killed innocents?"

"What's an innocent?"

"I'm saying, don't judge us."

"I'm not judging; I'm trying to find out who you people are. You said you're the good guys. I want to know what that means."

Donovan realized he had, in fact, been getting defensive. He nodded. "All right. My bad. Keep asking."

Matt crossed his legs, ankle over knee. "When was it founded?"

"Nineteen thirty-nine."

"Really? That recently? I was thinking, you know, thousands of years of ancient lore and all that."

"The group it split from goes back to the Middle Ages, if that helps."

"Oh. What's the group they split from?"

"A bunch of pricks."

"Really?"

Donovan tapped his beer bottle against his teeth and thought about how to answer. "They protect each other, help each other, and at least some of them are total bastards."

"So, let me guess: They're the bad guys."

"Not this time. The bad guy is killing them."

"Oh. What do you mean when you say some of them are total bastards?"

"Well, let's see. Of the people whose deaths we're investigating, one of them was a racist asshole who got people beaten and maybe killed. Another made reporters disappear if they were going to expose something embarrassing to whoever was paying him. And the third was, at least, a corrupt State Senator."

"Really? It doesn't seem like killing them is such a terrible thing to do."

"I had that conversation with my boss not long ago."

"And?"

"It's bad because they pay me to think it's bad. That's the best answer I could get."

"How much do they pay you?"

"Minimum wage, plus a stipend, plus the apartment is free."

Matt looked around the room. "That doesn't sound like a lot."

"No. If it was a non-rent-controlled apartment in Manhattan, that would be different."

"Can you live on that?"

"Sure. Easy. As long as I also get in twenty hours a week or so doing medical billing."

Matt tapped his fingers against the beer bottle. "Why do you do it?"

"I can do it at home. It's very exciting work. I recommend it."

"I meant the other. Why do you do the investigations?"

"Oh. I ask myself that a lot between jobs. Maybe I'll get a PI license one of these days."

"So, you investigate when people are killed using magic?"

"Or when magic is used for crime, or anything else that might get noticed."

"How long have you been doing it?"

"Eleven years."

"How many times have they called you in?"

"Thirty-nine. This makes forty. Most of the time, it turns out to be a new sensitive playing around, someone missed by Recruitment, so we just turn it over to them."

"And the others?"

"Some are false alarms—someone picks up indications of magic, or hears a report, and it turns out to be nothing."

"And?"

"And sometimes it's a bad guy. Someone using magic in a way that could get discovered."

"What do you do when it's a bad guy?"

"Depends. Sometimes you can intimidate the guy into stopping. Threats. Shows of force."

Matt was staring, intense. "And if you can't?"

Donovan hesitated, then said, "There's a thing the sorcerer is trained for. It, like, pulls out the person's ability to sense the grid lines. Takes away his ability to do magic."

"You can do that?"

"We don't like to. It leaves the guy magically dead, completely, can't even trigger an artifact like normal people can."

"An artifact?"

"Never mind."

"So, Marci's done that?"

"No, but her predecessor had to a few times."

"What happened to her?"

"Him. He got old and retired."

Something about that must have struck Matt as funny, because he started to smile but stopped himself. "Is there a pension plan?"

Donovan had another swallow of beer. "Yeah, but it sucks."

"Health care?"

"Yeah, that's pretty good, actually. Like, ten-dollar co-pay, twenty for dental. Pretty sweet, really."

"So, you've never taken a life?"

"Me personally? No."

"Your team?"

Donovan looked at him, looked at his beer, looked up again, and nodded. "Twice. Susan once, the sorcerer once. Not the guy we were after, guys that were backing him. Like, say, what you were doing. We like killing people even less than we like de-sorcelling someone."

Matt laughed. "'De-sorcelling'? That's the term?"

Donovan felt his lips twitch. "That's what I call it. There's a technical term that everyone else uses."

Matt nodded and became serious. "So, what are you going to do with me?"

"I told you. I'm going to let you go."

"Then why are you answering all my questions?"

Donovan shrugged. "You seem like a decent guy for someone who tried to kill me. I don't know. Why does it matter?"

"If secrecy is such a big deal—"

"Like I said before, who will you tell? Me, I think they're a bit paranoid about it. It would take something really fucking huge to convince the public that magic was a thing. But, hey, I'm just a hired grunt."

"I want to help."

"I heard you. But the only thing I know for sure about you is that you took five hundred bucks to kill a complete stranger. I mean, that's not all that much of a recommendation, right?"

Matt nodded.

"Ever done that before?" said Donovan.

Matt shook his head. "First time. It just, I don't know, it fell into my lap, and I said what the hell."

Donovan waited, looking at him.

"Okay," said Matt after a moment. "A couple of months ago I needed some dental work I couldn't afford, so I knocked over a couple of stop-and-robs. I never thought of myself as being that guy, but I did it. And then this . . . shit. You know how they say sometimes you have to hit bottom before you can work up again? Well, everyone has a different bottom. I kind of think taking money to kill someone is mine. I want to start working up again. I want to be a good guy."

If Marci had been there, she could have told if he was lying. Sometimes you can tell if someone is lying by following his eye movements, but Matt's eyes weren't giving anything away. Donovan's Uncle Gary had said that you develop an instinct for when someone was lying, but Donovan was still waiting for that instinct to kick in.

"All right," he said. "I'm going to believe you. I'll send your name up to Recruitment."

Matt finished his beer, set the bottle on the end table. "Where's the head?"

Donovan indicated it with his chin.

When Matt came back out, he said, "What about working with you? On this? I mean, I'm already involved."

Donovan shook his head. "Yeah, sorry, but my team is pretty set. We have Hippie Chick to be the tough guy if we need it, and Marci handles the magic."

Matt sat back down on the couch. "What do you do?"

"Investigate."

"You any good at it?"

"Which came first, playing guitar, or collecting comic books?"

Matt stared at him, then looked at his fingertips, nodded, smiled. "Yeah, Mom was always on me about washing under my nails. You got training in that?"

Donovan nodded. "My mother's brother. He was, like, genius level. Sometimes he'd scare me he was so smart. He got a scholarship, full education, then became a fed. Mom was so pissed."

"Why?"

"Seriously? A fed? When I told them I was going to go live with him and learn how to be a PI, Dad smacked me across the face. Mom didn't invite me for Christmas that year. They didn't get over it until he—Uncle Gary—died."

"Killed in the line?"

"No, cancer. He'd quit the feds by then."

"Why?"

"He wouldn't talk about it. I got a suspicion he found out

Mom and Dad were right about 'em, but he never said so. He wasn't big on admitting he was wrong."

"What was he like?"

"My uncle? He had, like, an on-off switch. He liked to sit around in his underwear, drink beer, and watch ball. But, man, then he'd start to teach me something, and he just got ice in his veins. He could make you feel two inches tall just by the way he looked at you, and he'd stay on you with shit until you had it perfect, and then he'd grunt like he was saying, 'Took you long enough.' Then you'd be done he was all slapping you on the back and, 'What do we eat tonight, Donny? You make some of that Hawaiian bread, and I'll do a pot roast.' Weird motherfucker." He shook his head. "Man, you're bringing back memories."

"You get along with your folks?"

"Now I do, yeah. Don't see 'em much. They live in Philly."

"That's not that far, is it?"

"Not in miles. Tell me, other than hit people and shoot people, what can you do?"

"Back to me, huh? I was trained in interrogation."

"Yeah, me too."

"I know."

Donovan smiled a little. "What else can you do?"

"Talk down a drunk before he gets aggressive."

"Oh? What's the technique?"

"Shake his hand."

"Yeah?"

"Shake his hand, put your other hand on his shoulder, look him in the eye, shake your head, say, 'Yeah, man, I know what you mean.' You'd be surprised."

"That doesn't come up that often in what we do, but it might be useful in my personal life. What else you got?"

"I can get hit a lot and keep going."

"That isn't something we need. I hope."

"Some demolition. I'm not an expert."

"I'd like to believe we won't need that."

Matt sighed. "So, sounds like I'm confined to the titty bar."

"Sorry. And sorry to leave you on the wrong coast."

"I'll get by. And, well, you know, I did sort of try to kill you."

"I don't take that personally."

Matt nodded. "One more beer for the road?" he said.

"Sure," said Donovan, and headed for the fridge. He had the door open when Matt said, "You know what? Skip it. Maybe I'll see you around."

Donovan nodded, returned from the kitchen and opened the door, stepped aside. "I'll send your name upstairs. Maybe you will."

|||||||||||||||||

Sometimes it seemed like Susan put as much effort into doing nothing as she did into training. Thirty minutes before her own official *Game of Thrones* start time, she did a quick pickup of the apartment: She put her *gi* into the hamper, put the plate and glass into the sink, and put her artifacts into the closet. There were only three artifacts she carried with her: a smoke bomb (with an enchantment to prevent dispersal) in the form of a golf ball; an earring that would improve all of her senses; and her belt buckle that would generate a field of magic protection when she gripped it and said "velociraptor." Of these, the belt was the only one she ever used. She just never seemed to remember the others until after the point she should have used them. Nevertheless, they all went into the closet along with the other gifts from the Burrow that she never used. Then she double-locked the closet.

Twenty-five minutes to go.

She got out the ice bucket, filled it, opened the wine, and set it in the bucket next to her chair. Then she cut up the celery and spread cream cheese on it, put that on a plate, added some carrots and some exquisite little pickles acquired from the Russian Deli. She brought the plate along with what had become her official *Game of Thrones* wine goblet (acquired at King Richard's Faire outside of Chicago when she was nine) and set these next to the ice bucket. Then she used the bathroom; then she gave the computer the traditional you'd-better-not-go-off-for-the-next-hour glare, picked up the remote, and sat down.

Still five minutes to go.

Sometimes she wished she had someone to watch with her. Even a dog. Maybe a dog. Be nice if it was a guy, but she hadn't yet met a guy who could stand to be around her for more than a week. It wasn't just that she was so intimidating; there were boys who could handle that, even liked it. It was the secrecy, all the things she couldn't share, the way she might have to just run off with no notice, and wouldn't say why. And every time—every goddamned time—she could see, *Are you secretly a call girl?* in their eyes, and that would do it. If they'd asked, *Are you a call girl?* it would have been different—she'd have said, *Sweetie, if I were a call girl I wouldn't hide it.* But no, they'd thought it, and it made her want to break their legs, which was really no basis for a long-term romantic relationship.

She and Laughing Boy had hung out together a few times, talked about it. He'd even braved the wrath of Oversight a couple of times and visited her, staying on her couch. They'd talked about how hard it was to find anyone who could deal with the lifestyle. In Donovan's case, sometimes girls thought he must be some kind of secret agent. The ones who thought that was hot turned out not to be the ones Donovan wanted in his life.

How did Marci do it?

She shook her head.

It was time. She turned on the TV, fiddled with the TiVo, and settled in. Damn, those pickles were nice.

|||||||||||||||

Camellia Hortense Morgan pushed her chair back from the long glass table, and decided she needed to be patient and diplomatic. It was already getting dark, and it was way past her dinnertime, so it was difficult, but she had to. She spoke English, because that was the only language they all had in common; it gave her an advantage because she was a native speaker and could perfectly express the nuances she needed.

"You are," she said patiently and diplomatically, "all idiots."

Hodari Nwosu twitched his lips at her. "You are charming as always, my dear," he said in his Oxford accent. "Care to expand on that?"

Camellia barely nodded to him. Hodari was perhaps the sharpest person in the room; he'd jumped in to smooth things over before the others got annoyed because he knew her, because he would have realized that she wouldn't have let herself say that unless there was something going on far more important than whose feelings got hurt.

"The rumors of Mystici presence within our organization have been going on as long as we have existed, and we have yet to find a shred of proof. Nevertheless, I do not propose to dismiss them, as Madeleine has implied. Nor do I wish to panic, as Sir Thomas seems to think we should. Yes, there have been murders, and yes, this is a threat. But we are investigating it as we always do. That is what the Ranch is for. If every time this happens we throw away the systems we have built up exactly to deal with it, we may as well abandon everything else we do at the same time, because nothing will survive."

She looked around the table; the three men and three women

were all focused on her, even Fat Harold, who lifted his head—it had been drooping onto his chest as if he were sleeping—and said, "You contend, then, that these events are ordinary?"

Camellia avoided making eye contact with him, because this wasn't the time to remind him how much he irritated her just by existing. She studied the glass table while she let the annoyance wash over her. *I really need to get rid of this stupid thing and get something nice, like cherrywood. Something less antiseptic, less corporate, more real. And replace those goddamned fluorescent lights.* She raised her head and stared at the far wall, with its plaque listing, in Latin, the Three Laws that they all ignored.

"No, Harold, I am not claiming the events are ordinary. In fact, they are quite *extra*ordinary. Having been the one to bring them to your attention in the first place, I am not in the least suggesting that this is business as usual. What I am contending is that there will be consequences if our response throws away seventy-five years of protocols and systems that we've put in place for exactly this."

"If I may," said Nwosu.

Camellia hesitated, then nodded. Nwosu rose to his feet—he knew damned well how imposing he was, how he took over the whole room when he stood. Worse, he was unpredictable; there was no way to know what position he was going to take. She kept her face expressionless and listened closely, ready to shut him down if necessary. If possible. He nodded back to her, then turned to the others.

"I would put it this way," he said. "No one denies the seriousness of what is happening. It has exactly the earmarks of something big, organized, and, obviously, well funded. But what we do not yet know is why it is happening, who is behind it.

If we react to it by throwing aside our security protocols, are we doing exactly what those behind the attacks are hoping we will do? Ms. Morgan is proposing we discover the answer to that question, and, in the meantime, carry on the investigation in the usual way."

He sat down while the others thought about it.

Yes, he was exactly right. What he hadn't said, and perhaps hadn't considered, was that the security protocols had been a mistake from the day they were implemented. And what she couldn't say was that she would love to see the idiotic, paranoid compartmentalizations thrown into the dustbin where they belonged. She didn't say this, because there was one thing she didn't know: Was this the best possible time or the worst possible time to do so? She imagined the looks on their faces when, after the crisis passed, she walked in with a proposal identical to the one Ursine had just introduced, and had to keep a smile off her face.

"Mmm," said Harold to Hodari. "Ten minutes ago you were ready to approve the motion; now you sound like you're against it."

"Yes," said Hodari. "I have changed my position. She convinced me. That will happen, sometimes, when reasonable people speak with reasonable people."

"All right," said Betty Ursine, nodding her head slowly, her pink New England skin looking somehow unhealthy between Hodari and Nailah. Betty's fingers were tapping on the table as she studied Morgan. *Careful*, thought Morgan. *Careful. She's no fool.* Then Betty nodded. "All right. I'll withdraw the motion for now."

Camellia nodded back, keeping the relief off her face. "Then unless someone objects, I'd like to hear a short—I repeat: a *short* report from Grants and Acquisitions, after which what I really want is lunch and a strong drink. You can get your own lunches, but the first round of drinks is on me."

The motion was passed by acclaim.

||||||||||||||||

To Marci the grid lines were an instrument; she played them that way. Each line had its own vibration, its own tone. She would give herself to the line so that she could take from it, shape it into something beautiful; the final effect was merely an afterthought. It wasn't about the result; it was about the process—working the lines, the patterns, shaping them, exploring them; testing her abilities, filled her with a euphoria like nothing else. What could she do with magic? The question was more what couldn't she do, because that question led her to try things, to fall into it until she felt she wasn't so much an actor as a conduit between the power she touched and the matter she manipulated. It was a problem in three-dimensional mathematics, where the numbers were tangible and the operations excited the sensations. Marci didn't practice meditation, or, really, know anything about it; but when she heard about the serene joy of vanishing into one's own head, she thought she might understand just a little of what that must be like. What can you do with magic was, at this point, not even the question.

"What can you do with magic?" she'd asked Sam, one of her instructors, years ago, at the beginning of her training.

"What can *I* do?"

"No, no. You know, I mean—"

"What can be done with magic?"

"Yeah."

"Anything that can be done without it, and nothing that can't be done at all."

They were in one of the large practice rooms. It had a high unfinished ceiling and concrete walls. There was a rectangular table with three chairs to one side, where judges sat when someone was being tested, but it was unoccupied. The room felt more than anything like a gymnasium with the bleachers and basketball hoops removed—it even had the same echoes. All it needed was the musky smell of locker room instead of the faint antiseptic smell and she'd have been convinced she was back in high school. Marci had been assured that there were spells all around it to make sure none of the students could do any damage to anything past the metal doors.

"I don't understand," she said.

"What can be done with muscle? With brain? With muscle and brain working together, along with the materials the Earth provides?"

"Well, anything, I guess. I mean, anything that, uh, that doesn't violate natural law. Depending on, you know."

"Depending on what, Marci?"

"Well, on how much muscle, how much brain, what kind of materials."

"Well, there you go. The grid lines and points and nodes provide the muscle; the skill of the user provides the brains. The materials you have to find, but they're all around you, and can often be transformed into something else."

She caught herself playing with her hair, and stopped. "Transformed?"

"The technical term is 'transmutation.'"

"Like, lead into gold?"

"That would be atomic level, not molecular. There have been a couple people able to do that, but it's a fluke talent. And even for them it was slow and hard. How are you on physics and chemistry?"

"A little. I have the math background, but haven't actually studied them much."

Sam sat on the floor, cross-legged. Marci sat down facing him.

"You'll need to learn more," said Sam.

"I need physics and chemistry to be a sorcerer? That's—"

"Not 'need,' exactly. But the more you understand how things work, the easier it is to manipulate them."

Marci put her elbows on her knees, rested her chin in her hands. "So then, the more I understand natural laws, the better I can violate them?"

"Actually, that isn't a bad way to think about it, for now. Of course, there's a lot more than knowledge that determines what comes easy, what comes hard, and what's impossible for you."

"Like what?"

"Do you sing?"

"You know I'm tone-deaf."

Sam nodded. "And no matter how much you studied the techniques, you probably still wouldn't be very good at it."

"So there's talent involved."

"Yes. A mix of talent and knowledge and willpower."

"How much of each?"

"It varies with each person."

Marci started tracing circles on the floor with her finger as she worked on that. Sam let her think. After a moment, she said, "So, then, you're saying that underneath it all, natural law is still natural law."

"Yes." He looked at her. "Are you starting to understand?"

"Sort of. Can you give me an example? Something practical."

"All right. Suppose someone is shooting at you."

"I'd rather not."

Sam's lips twitched. "Work with me, Marci."

"All right."

"If you had some stone, and some stone-shaping tools, and the muscle and skill to build a wall, you could build one that bullets couldn't get past, right?"

"It'd take a while."

"Yes it would. My point is, magic can do the same thing, only faster. And with the added advantage of it being invisible, so the shooter will freak out a bit."

"Faster than a bullet?"

"Well, it's best to have the shield up before someone starts shooting."

"It's best if no one starts shooting."

"Well, yes. That is its own skill. To manipulate the will, the feelings, the emotions, of another."

"That seems kind of . . ." She fell silent.

"Morally dubious?"

"Yeah."

"It is. One difference between us and the Mystici is that, as a rule, we don't hold with that. We feel it is a violation, and only to be used in an extremity, or in the case of a subtle effect we are certain will do no lasting harm."

"And they don't agree?"

Sam frowned, as if looking for words. "It isn't that, as much as it is they don't think it's their business to tell anyone what's right and what's wrong."

"Okay. How about immortality?"

"No."

"Extended life?"

"Yes and no."

"Hmm?"

"Certain diseases we can cure, others not; some we're working on. But in general, magic can't be used to extend life, but we can do better than that."

"Oh? I can't wait to hear this."

"There is a spell—a very recent one, perfected by the Eggheads—that causes organs to fail all at the same time, within two or three weeks."

"Wait. How is that—"

"You don't understand—you can't understand, yet, and really, neither can I. But one of the worst aspects of growing old is how you grow old in pieces—eyes, memory, kidneys, who knows? The spell ties all of your major organs together, so you remain, in all important ways, young, until your body fails and you die."

"That doesn't sound all that good."

"Not to me, either, but I'm only forty. I'm assured that some-day it will."

"All right. I'm more interested in that shield spell. Can you teach it to me?"

"A shield spell? Why? Planning to join I and E? I'd figured you for research."

"No, it isn't that; it's just, I don't know." Who would not want to know how to do a spell that could stop bullets? I mean, it wasn't as cool making lightning shoot from your fingertips, but she didn't have the nerve to ask for that. Yet. "I just figured it'd be a good example," she finished.

"Sure," said Sam. "We can do that. It won't work if you're on water, though. Or, at least, without adding a spell to freeze the water first. But dirt will work, sidewalk, most floors."

"Show me!"

"All right." Sam stood up, Marci did the same. Sam reached out to the empty air with his hands, fingers moving like he was playing an invisible piano. "We'll use the floor here. Now, to start, touch the node and feel your way into the floor. Eight or ten inches should do it. . . ."

|||||||||||||||||||

Manuel Becker left work every day, including Saturday, at 8:01 PM CET, having shifted his schedule somewhat to accommodate his North American contacts, and took the bus across the river, then walked to his home on Calle Juan Pérez Almeida. It was a good ten-minute walk—actually a bit more, as he usually stopped for groceries—and one he took every day, regardless of weather. He didn't own an umbrella, so when it rained he got wet.

During the bus ride, he always thought about grid lines, and points, and nodes; he couldn't keep himself from wondering if he was crossing any. Once he would have been able to feel them. Now he refused to look at the maps on which they were marked, but he couldn't stop himself wondering. This was why he preferred not to travel. What he did not think about was work. If there were an emergency, he'd be informed; if not, he would think about it again tomorrow morning.

He arrived home and removed his coat, his tie, and his shoes and socks. Walking around barefoot comforted him. Then he put on music—today it was Strauss's Horn Concerto No. 1 in E flat Major, Opus 11, performed by the Philharmonia Orchestra, Galliera conducting, Dennis Brain as soloist, because it had been a difficult and vexing day; he wanted something triumphant. He sat in his favorite chair and did nothing except listen until the end—the touch of hunting horn and the strings coming in leaving the piece not so much unresolved as hinting that the story went on.

He got up then and made dinner: chicken paella, accompanied by brown rice with lemon, followed by *leche frita*. Like so many Englishmen living in Spain, he'd become more Spanish than the Spaniards he knew, so many of whom had become Anglophiles. But after all, Spanish food was better. He ate like he'd listened to the music: with his full attention. When he was done, he put the leftovers away for tomorrow's lunch, then washed the dishes, wiped the table and the sink, and sat down at his computer, where he worked on a jigsaw puzzle, this one a picture of the Himalayas. He had the border pieces done, and a lot of the obvious sections, so he was at a slow point. After exactly forty-five minutes he closed the puzzle, checked his email, deleted some spam, and shut down the computer.

He spent an hour with a novel by Julio Llamazares, then put it down, marking his place with a bookmark from La Fugitiva.

Then he went into his room and pulled open a drawer of his bedside table, removing an old and beaten folder that contained the notes he'd made in his efforts to perfect a spell to create a technical-magical interface for prosthetic limbs. He read over the notes until the tears came, then put the folder away.

He took off his shirt, knelt beside the bed, took the flogger from the bedside table, and whipped himself until he was ready to sleep.

CHI-TOWN | 6

Margaret Laurel "Peggy" Hanson was born in 1983 in Nashville, Tennessee, where she attended public school, graduating from John Overton Comp in 2001. She studied archaeology at Belmont University until her junior year, when she received an email signed: "Julia Ramirez." A week later, Peggy dropped out of the university and, to the amazement of her friends and family, and with little explanation other than "a good offer," she moved to Madrid, Spain, and started work in March of 2005. Her work, for the first four years, included a lot of education; the Foundation helped her get her degree, and paid for a great deal of post-graduate study; that may have been what sold her. It wasn't until 2009 that she actually became a full-time researcher.

Peggy spent a lot of her time on the Internet, and much of the rest of it at the Biblioteca Nacional de España. The research librarians there knew her, and liked her, and would sometimes call her if they came across something they thought she might be interested in. They didn't really know what she was interested in, but Peggy appreciated the effort.

She read the *American Journal of Archaeology* cover to cover, and every paper the Society for Historical Archaeology published. She would use satellite photos to study sites and compare them to reports. She corresponded with curators of museums throughout the world, and studied the pictures they sent her with a magnifying glass. Oh, and history, especially Central European history from 1100 to 1350? Don't even talk about it. She spoke and read eleven languages, only five of them in contemporary use, and she could find the one unusual fact in a nine-hundred-year-old document like no one else at the Foundation. It was tedious and repetitive and she loved it like she loved her cat, and considerably more than she loved her boyfriend, who kept insisting she learn to dance.

Her unstated and even unconsidered basic axiom was *nothing can happen without leaving traces*. It was her job to find the trace and deduce what had happened. Or, to put it another way (which she never did), she was a storyteller, building a tale out of hints and pieces and bits of dialog left behind by a non-existent author.

She had discovered previously unknown artifacts—items that a sorcerer in the past had imbued with a spell, set to be triggered by anyone who knew the correct phrase or gesture—five times in six years. It was an astonishing record. In three of those cases, the team had been able to deduce the word or gesture required, which was even more remarkable.

Most of the time, she worked in an almost meditative state— no rush, no urgency. The goal was never to *find something* in the paper or the document or the picture; the goal was to absorb it, to understand it thoroughly—so thoroughly that anything interesting just sort of leapt out at her. Deep down, she couldn't understand how anyone else could miss something—it was right there, plain as day.

She was also, quite naturally, pleasant to work with. She liked the environment of the office when she was there, and she liked her co-workers, and the very fact that she concentrated so fully made her easily interruptible: She could break off from her reading and share a joke, or hear who in the office had just broken up with whom (James was best for that—he heard everything first), and then get right back to where she was without so much as a ripple on the wide, calm lake of her concentration. Weather permitting, she took long lunches on the Paseo del Prado, sitting beneath the trees.

But then, when she did hit something—when a couple of random facts came together to fill her with the conviction that *there was something there*—everything changed: She'd lean closer to the papers, or to the computer. Her eyes would narrow. Her lips would part. Her teeth would clench just a little.

Her co-workers would look at each other and say, "Peggy's on the scent," and stop talking to her. Even Julia would keep her distance. From then on, they'd just bring her tea with lemon in paper cups and leave sweet rolls and *mantecados* on her desk like offerings at a shrine. She'd eat them—and her lunch—slowly and mechanically, without ever looking at the food. Once she'd bit into a hard-boiled egg she'd packed herself without realizing it was unpeeled. That pulled her out of her work and made her so angry she glared at it as if it had made an improper suggestion and threw it across the office. No one said anything.

When she was in that state, she was the last one to leave the office, and the first one in, and she would pull all-nighters as often as not. Whereas she was usually deferential in asking favors from co-workers, when she got like this she'd snap, "Molly. Find the paper on the Turkish site 8 AG 227. Look up everything that dates between 1230 and 1280," and Molly would be off to do it as if Peggy were Camellia Morgan herself.

In the past, this stage had lasted between three and eight days. This time, it lasted four days, twenty-one hours, and seven minutes, at the end of which time she suddenly sat back in her chair, blinked, smiled, and looked over at the desk next to her. "Hey, Herberto. How is your dog?"

"Fine, Peggy. It was just a cyst."

"Good," she said, and nodded. Then her head rocked back and she fell asleep.

||||||||||||||||

The East Coast felt different. Things were closer together, the streets were narrower and straighter, and the style of houses was all wrong. But it took a few minutes of just walking down the street to make Matt realize it wasn't any of those things so much as it was the mix—industry with houses with apartments with warehouses with stores with motels, and railroad tracks and bridges that seemed to come out of nowhere for no reason and go in random directions. There was something fundamentally *untidy* about it. He was most surprised, after walking a mile or so, to discover that he liked it—there was an odd sense of belonging, as if some part of him had always lived here.

Magic? he wondered. And, No, he decided. *Too bad, though. It'd be pretty cool to cast spells and shit.* This immediately brought up the question of whether he believed what he'd been told, and, if he didn't, how to explain what Marci had done to his throat, the strange transport, and the way he'd been confined to the chair with no rope or chain. He had no answer to any of this, so he put it out of his mind with the same effortless efficiency he'd learned in training—if you can't control what your mind is doing, you can't control what your body is doing.

The training. That's what civilians could never understand. Basic training gave you an experience you'd carry with you all your life, and advanced training taught you things you'd never forget. But SF training made you a different person. Whatever happened afterward, whatever you did, you were someone who had gone through that, been molded by that, been turned into a strange hybrid of who you were before, and the machine SF training made you.

That thought came to him on the chilly New Jersey street, and he pushed it out of his mind, too. He had other things he needed to think about, like where he was going to spend the night, how to raise enough money to stay there, and, what felt more urgent (even if it clearly wasn't), who had hired him, and why, and what to do about it all.

He had done things, had Matt. He hadn't divided the world into good guys and bad guys since he was eight—even when using those exact terms in planning an op. He knew very well his eight-year-old self wouldn't be pleased with the things he'd done, and he also knew that, no, really, honestly, in the real world things were more complicated than his eight-year-old self thought they were. That might be an excuse, but it was also just the plain truth, dammit.

But shit. He'd done things.

What was that bit in *The Avengers*? Where Black Widow had said she had red on her ledger and wanted to remove it? That line came back to him now. Yeah, it sort of hit. But he knew he couldn't remove the red. Maybe he could remove a little of it.

The thought kept coming back. *Red on the ledger, just like in the movie.* Whether magic, or something else, there were big things happening, and he didn't owe anyone anything; he was free to splash around however he wanted, and it'd be really nice, if he was still alive in forty years, to think about having used his skills to do something where he could point to it and say, *I made that different, and the different is better, and no fucking civilian can tell me it isn't.*

Okay, decision made. So, what was the first step? Well, the second step—he'd taken the first step almost by instinct, before even leaving the apartment, when he'd realized that Donovan was answering too many questions too easily, which meant either he, Matt, didn't matter in the least, or Donovan was playing a game of some kind.

Matt stopped by a sprawling complex called Journal Square, surrounded by dollar stores and taxi stands, and planted himself on a bench, where he effortlessly fit in with the homeless who hovered nearby. No, this wasn't San Diego, but some of the people were the same, and some of the neighborhoods he'd walked through had a familiar feel. A bit of walking and looking and it'd be pretty strange if he couldn't identify someone who was carrying, and then he'd have a weapon, and maybe some money as well.

And after that, he'd see.

There was a game going on, and someone had made him a player; he wasn't going to get out now.

||||||||||||||||

I took United Flight 263, arriving in Chicago around a quarter to eight in the evening. I checked into the Hilton Chicago O'Hare Airport, where they had my reservation all set and paid for—Mysterious Charlie was always good on the details. I gave them a credit card for meals and incidentals and relaxed in my room watching *Pacific Rim* until sleep took me.

The next morning I had a good overpriced breakfast, then took a shuttle downtown. This was my first visit to Chicago, so I spent some time just looking around. It was cold after San Diego, but not too bad as long as I kept moving; I found it more pleasant than otherwise.

Kind of odd, isn't it? I'm waiting for my chance to kill a complete stranger, and to kill him in an ugly and gruesome way, so I fill in the time by checking out local architecture and museums. How did I become this person? Well, put that way, it was simple: Some son of a bitch had destroyed my life, and he just didn't give a shit. To him, I'd been another chance to climb a ladder, add zeroes to his bank account, have more people calling him sir. To him, that's what mattered. Maybe there really is no satisfaction in revenge, but I can tell you one thing for sure: There's no satisfaction in letting someone get away with ruining your life, either.

And the Museum of Science and Industry is as good as the hype, so there's that.

Around one in the afternoon, I had a Belgian waffle at The Florentine. After lunch I walked around a little more. I stopped in a bookstore called After-Words thinking I'd pick up a book, but I couldn't concentrate well enough to decide on one.

Eventually I made my way to the Willis Tower and spent some time on the Skydeck. That relaxed me a little. I've always liked heights. Maybe I should have been a mountain climber. Around four o'clock I went downstairs and crossed Franklin, taking a position near the parking garage. I didn't expect him until five, but he might leave early, after all.

They aren't kidding about the Chicago wind, by the way, but that was a good thing, because I didn't get a second glance for having a scarf around my face or my hands in my pockets.

I fingered the polished carnelian and waited, reviewing things in my mind: I would hold the stone in my left hand, make a fist, and bring it to my shoulder three times as if doing a curl, and then, my eyes fixed on my target, I would say, *Darin-lick leerin den jall.* The sounds didn't come naturally to me, so I'd practiced it a great deal—not holding the stone, of course. I felt pretty good about my ability to say it, but there was some nervousness, too—if I screwed it up, I might not have another chance. Charlie had explained that sometimes getting the command wrong would do nothing, but sometimes the power in the artifact would be drained away. I rehearsed the words silently.

At exactly 5:11, Benjamin Lundgren came out, walking almost directly toward me. He stopped and waited for the light. After a minute, it turned green.

〃〃〃〃〃〃〃〃〃〃〃

Matt felt better with sixty dollars in his pocket, a Smith & Wesson M&P in his belt, and a heavier jacket with a backup weapon in it. He stopped at a convenience store and picked up a burner phone, also automatically checking out the store in case he wanted to come back and rob it later. *No. Stop it.* He went off to find a place to eat.

An hour later, fed and warm, he was sitting in the Coach House Diner, drinking coffee. He pulled out the new phone and punched in a number from memory—the only number he had memorized. It answered on the first ring, but there was only silence on the other end.

That was all right. He pulled out his earbuds, plugged them into the phone, put one in his ear, and waited.

〃〃〃〃〃〃〃〃〃〃〃

Most of the artifacts were polished semi-precious stones: turquoise, of course, and diaspore. Also black amber, opal, and obsidian. There were a few items carved from glass, which made Peggy realize that glass was an area she needed to study more—

off the top of her head, she had no idea what was used to color glass in thirteenth-century Turkey. She made a note to do more research.

But she had more immediate difficulties: She had to do battle with the translation. It was a dialect with which she was unfamiliar, and the writing was none too clear. The author was a mystic, sorcerer, and scholar named Izzet Ibn Karadag who, though clearly striving to be precise and meticulous, evidently saw no need to be consistent with either spelling or syntax, but did think it important to repeat his own name several times during the discourse, lest the reader forget to whom the debt was owed. He also changed the spelling of his name at least three times, which, Peggy supposed, was consistency of a sort.

She knew about the time-stop, and was able to determine that it had been set off by holding the stone loosely and then squeezing it rapidly three times. In addition, there was a device meant to freeze water, and another to part it. The rain of stones spell was set off by holding the stone in one hand while pumping the other up and down vigorously, though whether once or twice and whether it mattered which hand did which she couldn't say. One stone was intended to dissolve a man's skin slowly; she wasn't able to determine how that one worked.

In all, there were forty-four artifacts in the missing cache. She could tell what thirteen of them did, and in six cases she was confident she knew how the artifact was triggered.

She shook her head. It wasn't bad, but she could have done so much better if she'd had the original document and the additional notes from the anonymous sixteenth-century monk. Those, however, had been in the missing crate.

She organized what she had, and saved it. Then she stretched and stood up, feeling the pleased-yet-empty sensation that always accompanied finishing a task.

||||||||||||||||

Donovan had three keys. He kept them in his pocket on a key chain with a miniature LED flashlight that he'd never used, but which he was sure was a good idea to have. One key was to the main door of the apartment building and the laundry room. The second opened his apartment door. The third was to an Abloy PL 362 padlock, which closed a closet door that was far better built than anything else in the apartment; it would take power tools and at least a couple of hours to break into it.

Donovan turned the key, removed the lock, opened the door. He scanned the devices inside: the knotnots, a doeskin bag of marbles, a Louisville Slugger, an elaborate cut-glass decanter (empty), a simple glass jug (full of what seemed to be blue sand), a set of keys to a 1955 Dodge that didn't exist, a hammer, a black-jack, a can of spray paint (indigo), some disposable cigarette lighters with the child safety lock removed, a tiny plaster bust of Lincoln, and three pairs of work boots.

He removed a knotnot, the blackjack, the marbles, and a lighter, put them in his coat, and locked the door again, after making doubly sure the key was back in his pocket. Then he went back to his computer to call Susan and Marci, and told them there was work to do. Then he put on the Face and headed down to the laundry room.

||||||||||||||||

As always when investigating, Donovan arrived first. As always when arriving, he looked around to make sure he hadn't been seen, even though concealment was part of the spell that got him there. The place the slipwalk left him was dark and rela-tively secluded—a parking garage in the Chicago financial district; all was well. There being no crime scene to violate, which meant nothing he could learn before the others arrived, he just waited.

Marci arrived next. "Hey," she said.

"I didn't expect you so soon."

"It was either come right away, or start figuring out which bills not to pay, and if I'd started that I'd be at it until midnight."

"Gotten your first stipend yet?"

"No."

"Should be soon. It won't help much, but you know."

"Yeah. Every little bit. Hey, tell me something?"

"Sure."

"Why do you call Susan Hippie Chick?"

"Ever been to her place?"

"No. Have you?"

"A couple of times."

"Are you two a thing?"

Donovan laughed. "No, not hardly. The Foundation doesn't like hookups between team members."

"That would stop you?"

"Uh, no. But this life doesn't make it easy. And she's, I don't know. She's got her own things going on."

"All right. So, anyway, you were saying?"

"What?"

"Why do you call her Hippie Chick?"

"Well, for starters, she lives in Portland."

"And?"

"She roasts her own coffee beans."

"That sounds more yuppie than hippie."

"She orders them from somewhere called Peace Coffee. I mean, for real? Peace Coffee?"

"Is it good coffee?"

"I don't know. I suppose. Yeah, come to think of it, it was pretty good coffee."

"There you go, then."

"Still. Peace Coffee. Goddamned hippie."

"Speaking of," said Marci as Susan faded into view.

"All right," said Donovan. "Shield and all that, Marci. Let's get to work."

This time no one tried to kill them. As far as Donovan was concerned, this represented a significant improvement. Other than that, it was similar to the Manhattan investigation—a busy street near a large office building.

When Marci went into her thing, people in Chicago seemed a bit more uncomfortable than New Yorkers had—they hurried past and avoided looking at her, except for one middle-aged white woman with gold hoop earrings who stopped and asked Donovan if the girl was all right. He put on his charming face and said yes, she was attempting to reach the spirit of his mother, who had died in that spot many years before. The woman went on her way quickly.

Shortly after that, Marci opened her eyes and said, "Yes, there's something. It's going to be a while; you guys want to go somewhere warm?"

"Mar? Remember the part about people trying to kill us? Especially you?"

"Oh, right. Okay."

"Can you estimate how long?"

"At least an hour, maybe more."

"We'll live."

So they stayed where they were and got cold and ignored the people ignoring them. White people, in particular, either avoided looking at him standing next to Susan, or went out of their way to make eye contact and smile; when that happened, the Face would smile back. He was past letting shit like that bother him, but he never failed to notice. That was okay; noticing things was in his job description.

|||||||||||||||||

Peggy made a phone call, because she hated texting. She knew she must have woken him up, but there was no trace of sleepiness in his voice.

"This is Becker," he said.

"This is Peggy Hanson from A and E."

"Ms. Hanson. A pleasure to hear from you. How can I help Artifacts?"

"Mr. Becker, you put in a request a few days ago regarding time-stop."

"Yes, I did, Ms. Hanson."

"Then I believe I have some information for you. Shall I put it in the form of a memo and email it?"

There was a pause. "Ms. Hanson, it is after one in the morning."

Her heart raced. "I'm sorry, Mr. Becker. I was told to call anytime, when it was done."

"You are correct. I am merely wondering if you have been working all night."

"Yes, sir. I found it this afternoon, and I've been putting the report together since then."

"I am very impressed. Yes, please, Ms. Hanson. Send it at once. Email will be fine. Kindly make it a separate attachment, suitable for printing."

"Very well, Mr. Becker."

Peggy Hanson disconnected, took a deep, shuddering breath for no reason she was aware of, and turned to write the email.

||||||||||||||||

Conscience? No, it wasn't conscience. We've been over that already. But the fact is, I couldn't stay for the whole show. He was on the ground, writhing, his head going back and forth, eyes squeezed shut, making the most horrible sounds, and I couldn't watch anymore.

Yes, he was a son of a bitch. He'd done things far worse than what I was doing to him, and he was between me and Whittier, so he had to go. I was hard enough, determined enough, to do what I had to, but not to watch it happen.

I stumbled away and into a nearby pizza joint. I paid for coffee I didn't drink; instead I drank water. I wanted a shot of bourbon so bad I could taste it on my tongue. But I was afraid of it. I hadn't had a drop since the divorce, because I had the feeling that once I started I wouldn't stop, and I had something to do first. After, I promised myself. After Paul Whittier was dead, I'd treat myself to a double shot of the best I could find, something top-shelf, maybe Basil Hayden's if I could find a place that carried it. And then, if I just went down into a spiral like Kent and Billy had, well, that could happen. But not until I was done.

I squeezed my eyes shut, and instead of thinking about Ben Lundgren writhing on the ground, I thought about Paul Whittier, alive, holding that stupid pipe with the silver bands around it, looking at me, frightened, and then smirking.

"Who sent you?" he had asked, reaching into his coat pocket. I don't know what he had in there, maybe a gun, more likely a phone. I didn't wait, though. For once in my life, at a time when I had to do something instantly, I did the right thing: I flung my gun at his head and ran as fast as I could, out the door and down the two-lane Connecticut road. When I heard sirens I stepped off into the trees and slowed down a bit, snow crunching under my feet and leaving an obvious track, but I kept moving as fast as I could, sure, *sure* that any second there would be lights in my eyes and a voice over a bullhorn. I didn't really believe I'd gotten away until the plane was in the air and I was on my way back to Denver, beat, so numb with failure that I couldn't even formulate the question: How had he survived four .357 slugs to his head at point-blank range?

After a while, I was ready to drink the coffee, but it had gotten cold. I gave the waiter an apologetic smile when I asked for another. He smiled back, but also gave me the *Wait, are you a bum?* once-over. I guess I satisfied him, because he came back with the coffee. I ordered food—I don't remember what—and drank the coffee. When the food came I didn't eat any of it.

My brain shut itself down eventually, and that was good. I didn't want to do anything to wake it up again, so I just stayed there. It was after nine when I finally pulled myself up, left a big tip, paid, and went out to find a cab to take me back to my hotel.

||||||||||||||||||

When Marci was finally done with the investigation, Donovan decided that getting warm was more urgent than getting home, so they found a pizza place on Jackson. The others ordered food, but Donovan explained that if he was hungry he'd go next door to McDonald's before polluting his body with anything a Chicagoan would call pizza. The others smiled indulgently, and Donovan's stomach growled. He growled back, then changed his mind and ordered a sandwich. But not pizza.

It was a matter of pride.

Marci had tea; Susan had coffee. When the drinks had arrived, they all looked at one another a little uncomfortably. "So," said Marci. "Um. How is everyone?"

Donovan smiled. "Now y'all tell me how smart I am."

Two pairs of inquiring eyes turned his way.

"'Donovan,' I says to myself, 'we are liable to be in Chicago for as long as we were in Manhattan, but it's even colder there, and them ancient legends say it's got some kind of wind. So,' I continued to myself, 'when we're done, we ain't going to want to stand outside talking about it like we did in Manhattan, and we won't have a nice warm place to hang out like we did in whatever-the-fuck Ohio.' 'Why, that's a true fact, Donovan,' I answered myself. 'We'll go to a nice restaurant where they have coffee and such. But then we'll be surrounded by people, and even though none of the aforementioned people will be paying a rat's whiskers' worth of attention to us, we still won't feel like gabbing away at our private business.'"

Susan saw where he was going, and said, "Yes, Donny, you're very smart. What do you have?"

Donovan pulled out the BIC lighter and flicked it in all four directions. Abruptly, the noise of conversation around them diminished.

"*Now* y'all can tell me how smart I am."

"Brilliant," said Hippie Chick. "You have such amazing foresight, from now on I'll call it fivesight."

"Very smart," said Marci. "But I could have cast the spell myself."

"You take the joy out of life, girl. You are a joy-out-of-life taker."

Susan made a snorting sound, then turned to Marci and said, "So, fill us in?"

Marci nodded. "Well, I'll tell you first of all, I don't think the medical examiner will ever figure it out."

"Oh?" said Donovan.

"Caisson disease."

"I don't think that's ever come up in my medical billing job."

"Decompression sickness," said Susan. "The bends."

Marci nodded. "They won't find it in a post-mortem without looking, and they won't look, because the guy probably wasn't diving anytime within the last couple of days."

"So," said Donovan, "there is a spell that just does that to someone?"

"So it seems."

"Damn."

"That's an awful sudden manifestation," said Susan.

Marci nodded.

"What would the symptoms be?" asked Donovan.

"I don't know. There are a whole catalog that could have happened. What finally killed him would probably have been an arterial embolism or damage to the spine. I think. I'm not an expert; I just learned about it when I went diving with my family one summer."

"Joint pain," said Susan. "Arms, legs, maybe both. Maybe a skin rash, maybe dizziness."

"But," said Donovan to Marci. "You can tell that's what it is?"

"Yes."

"That," said Susan, "is pretty amazing."

"Painful?" said Donovan.

"A case bad enough to kill? Oh yes," said Hippie Chick.

"More painful than drowning beneath a layer of ice?"

Susan looked at him quickly. "I don't know how you can measure something like that, but certainly more drawn-out. Why?"

"Progression," said Donovan. "I need to get back home. I have some things to check, and then a Skype call to make." He stood up. "I want to run. Hippie, can you get the check and expense it?"

"Sure."

"The sound protection should stay up for half an hour or so.

I'm leaving now so I won't hear you talking about how smart I am."

He headed out the door and back to his arrival spot in a deep shadow of the parking garage, there to take him home. *Well. A goddamned clue. About fucking time,* he thought.

COMMUNICATION

7

onovan was still awake, trying to work things out, when the phone rang. He glanced at the caller ID and answered.

"Hey, Donny. Is this a secure line?"

"Uh. No."

Jeff's chuckle came through the phone. "Yeah, that was a joke. There's no such thing."

Donovan felt his mouth twitch. "Did you learn something, Jeff?"

"Yeah. Lawton-Smythe used Verizon. They don't keep their records more than a year. But Blum had T-Mobile, and they keep their records for more like seven years."

"Sweet. Could you hack in?"

"No."

"Shit."

"But I managed to forge a court order and give them a dummy email address to send the records to. It was easier."

"Really? Easier?"

"In this case, yeah. They don't look at those too closely any-more, because of how many they're getting. You just sort of digitally show up, wave it, and say, 'Gimme.' I couldn't create a 'gov' email address, but I figured if I made a 'usa.gov.' one they wouldn't look too close. And I am now, by the way, part of the 'Department of Justice Interstate Highway Intervention Task Force.' In fact, I'm all of it."

"You are a smart, smart man. What did you find?"

"Two calls from Lawton-Smythe to Blum. First one April 9, 2011, second one February 23, 2015. Each one lasted about ten minutes."

"That's what I needed! You are a god among criminals."

"Does that mean I get paid?"

"If I have anything to say about it. Email me your bill and I'll kick it upstairs and prepare to make a stink."

"You the man, Donny."

"You can put that in the email, too."

"Can you give me a hint what this is about?"

"They were both murdered, and I haven't found a connection between them."

"Until now."

"I still haven't. You have."

"Well, there you go. Now what?"

"Now I have two more names."

"How about if I wait until I've been paid for this one?"

"Jeff—"

"Jesus Christ, Don. You know I can get arrested for this? The authorities have no sense of humor about people forging court orders. How much of this do you want me to do for nothing?"

"Yeah, okay. That's fair. I'll get on it."

"Cool. Talk to you soon."

Donovan disconnected, and composed an email to the Black Hole. He had certain skills, but they did not include finding the right note between demanding and pleading when submitting a requisition for a third-party payment. It took him more than two hours, and when he was done he poured himself a drink.

"Shit," he announced to the empty room. Then, "I should get a cat." It wasn't the first time he'd had the thought.

As he drank his vodka, he mentally worked on putting things in order—in other words, on what he was going to tell Becker. Becker would want answers he didn't yet have, but part of the job was keeping the boss informed, and a lot of it had come together in the last few hours.

There were still too many unanswered questions when he received a phone call. His first thought was that it was awfully quick work for Budget and Oversight, but it was Becker. When Becker used the phone it meant he wasn't at work, and if he wasn't at work that meant something had happened.

"Good evening, Mr. Becker. I'm not ready for you yet."

"I have news, Mr. Longfellow. I've gotten an answer from Artifacts and Enchantments."

"An answer? What was the question?"

"Are there any traces of an artifact that can perform a time-stop."

"Oh, right. That. And the answer is 'yes,' or you wouldn't have an answer."

"That is correct."

"All right. It's good to have confirmation. Are there details about its history and all that?"

"They'll be along."

"Good. I'll have something solid for you soon. Now, about our victim."

"Benjamin Lundgren, thirty-six years old, married, one daughter, eleven. He deals in insurance instruments. Please do not ask me to explain what an 'insurance instrument' is; I have no idea."

"Is he a sorcerer?"

"Very minor. In 2010, he committed vehicular manslaughter while driving under the influence, yet nothing ever came of it. We are fairly certain he used his skills to accomplish that, although he may have done it with nothing more than money. We also know that he regularly uses sorcery to seduce women."

"That is, like, really creepy, Mr. Becker."

"Yes, it is."

"All right," said Donovan. "Give me some time to sort it out, and I'll call you back."

"I'll be here."

"What time is it there?"

"Two AM."

"Mr. Becker, I'm going to go to bed early, and rest my brain, then get up tomorrow morning and work this shit out. How about you do the same."

Pause, then, "Very well, Mr. Longfellow. It is important we don't waste time on false trails. A little extra time to ensure we're going in the correct direction would not be amiss."

"Thank you, Mr. Becker," said Donovan, wondering if the irony came across on the phone, and if it would matter if it did.

"Good night, Mr. Longfellow."

|||||||||||||||||

Matt pulled the earbud to give his ear a rest and to think. *Well,* he told himself. *That is all very interesting. I'm starting to think old Donny didn't lie to me. Strange.*

If Don was going to bed, he, Matt, would do the same, as soon as he figured out where. A hotel room would be nice, but the money in his pocket wouldn't cover it. He glanced at the cash register, but shook his head: not someplace he'd been hanging out for hours. And, *No. Stop it. You don't do that anymore. Good guy, remember? Good guys don't terrorize poor bastards who work in restaurants.* He frowned. *Drug dealers, now. Drug dealers are another matter.* He felt just a hint of quickening of his heart, and the bitter taste in his mouth as he thought about being in action again.

He put a few bucks on the table, got up, paid the check, and stepped out into the night like he owned it.

||||||||||||||||

Chicago was rough, no question. It got to me; I admit that. But once I was back in my room, it hit me how close I was to my goal. Just one more between me and Whittier. Just one. I wasn't supposed to be thinking about that—I knew it was important to concentrate on one target at a time. But so close!

Next stop was New Orleans. I had twice been to the French Quarter with my—on vacations, and it was wonderful. The French Quarter isn't New Orleans any more than the Strip is Las Vegas, but I'd loved it, and looked forward to going back.

Of course, with those thoughts going through my head it shouldn't surprise you that I had trouble sleeping that night— the first time since I'd started this.

After tossing and turning for most of an hour, I got up and looked at the file. I paged through it, studied his picture, read up on who he was. Then I put the file down and stared out the window. I could see planes landing and taking off. I'd be on one tomorrow, after another meeting with Charlie. Perspective is a funny thing. There was an airplane, over there, and here I was watching it. Inside were passengers staring out, seeing the lights of the Hilton. And tomorrow I'd be in one of those, maybe looking back this way at someone looking out at me.

I decided that, when my brain started doing that, it meant it was ready to shut down. I got back into bed and fell asleep.

||||||||||||||||

Camellia Morgan stared out of her office window. Below her were tiny cars and tinier people and busses that looked like toys and the other buildings along the Paseo del Prado.

They had all gone home now—Hodari to Hong Kong, Fat Harold to Cairo, Sir Thomas to Prague—and she had carried her point. The challenge now was to make it work.

Technically, she had been elected to her position six years ago, when Yamauchi retired. In fact, the election was a formality—Yamauchi had all but declared her his heir, and the board had never even considered anyone else. She had earned the position—no one questioned that. And now she had to keep earning it, every day: not to keep the confidence of the board, but for her own self-respect.

The investigation was running, yes—and in the hands of those best able to find answers. But.

But there were those things she hadn't told the investigators. At the top of the list was just how widespread the attacks were.

She sighed and watched the cars and the bicycles and the pedestrians, each one a bubble, the bubbles occasionally interacting, but fundamentally isolated, like each department, like each section of each department—the product of an organization that had been burned too badly by openness and trust, and now could never trust again.

There were nine pictures on the wall of the Executive Branch, taken right from the wall of the previous Executive Branch, on the top floor of the old Edificio de Oficinas Álvar Núñez Cabeza de Vaca in the financial district. The pictures were of varying quality, and showed four men and five women, with their names and the years of their births and deaths. The youngest had died at the age of thirty-one, the oldest at the age of seventy-one, and they had all died in 1944. And though cause of death wasn't listed, Camellia knew it very well: They had all died of trust. Trust in fellow sorcerers, trust in the good intentions of the Mystici, trust in the incredulity of Franco's secret police. They had died sacrificing themselves in a last effort to save the Foundation. It had changed things: The Foundation had been forced to reach out to other countries, especially the English-speaking world, and to fill its ranks with those who could protect it, and one another. It had worked—the Foundation had survived the war that had destroyed so many other institutions and people. But the effects lingered.

She and Yamauchi had spoken of it a great deal. He called it *hankon soshiki*—scar tissue. As he neared the end of his life, he'd said that her greatest task would be to determine when the Foundation had healed enough to replace the scars, and how to remove them. And now, when the attack was focused, not on them, but on the Mystici, and the protocols were actively interfering with the investigation, wasn't this the perfect time?

Unless Hodari was right.

Yamauchi had no patience for vacillation, or half measures. He had been slow, patient, and methodical, but when he determined a course of action he saw it through to the end. That was how the Foundation had survived the confrontation with the Church in '69, and how they'd rescued the Mystici from their own folly in '74.

So, yes, she would not rush into a decision. But a decision would have to be made, and it was her duty to make it, and then abide by the consequences.

She picked up her office phone and punched in a number.

||||||||||||||||

The call was answered after four rings with the word, "Camel-lia!"

She put the phone on speaker, hung up the receiver, and sat back in her chair and said in English, "Hello, Elsa. You're on speaker."

"Is anyone else there?" Elsa's accent was middle-class London slightly tinged with Yorkshire.

"No. How are you? How is your new hip?"

"Perfect. No pain, no loss of mobility. Of course, that wasn't all medical science."

"I'm pleased for you."

"Thank you, dear. And you? How is everything with my ancient enemies?"

Camellia no longer laughed when Elsa said that, but still smiled. "Better, I think, than with you."

"Yes," said Elsa, her voice suddenly serious. "The murders. You are following up on them, I trust?"

"That is what you don't pay us enough to do, dear."

"Camellia, is this about money? Because if it is—"

"No, no. I just can't resist putting in a dig now and then."

"Then how can I be of service to the Foundation today?"

"All of the attacks are directed against operatives or associates of the Mystici."

"Yes. We are quite aware of that."

"Then help us out. Do you see a final target? Can you get an idea of motive? Anything?"

"You know I'm not permitted to give you any details of our personnel, clients, or activity."

"Yes, but this time it's different, don't you think?"

"How?"

"Scale."

"By definition, that is a difference of degree, not kind."

"At some point, quantity transforms into quality, Elsa. This is big. This is stretching our resources. We need help. And I shouldn't have to remind you that this is in both our interests. The Foundation is not the enforcement arm of the Mystici, and if you treat us as if we were—"

"I cannot release confidential information. That has been the agreement since we started funding you. If there is something you wish that does not require releasing confidential information, name it and I'll see what I can do."

Camellia stood up and stared out the window. The shadows from the trees of the meadow cast complex shapes onto the plaza. Sometimes she imagined the patterns formed codes that revealed the true nature of the universe. She was not altogether certain they didn't. She turned back to the phone.

"As a matter of fact, there is one thing you can do."

"Yes?"

"Swear to me, Elsa Jane Merriweather, swear to me by both your power and your powers, that these killings aren't your doing, that the Roma Vindices Mystici are not behind this, and that you don't know who is."

There was a pause, then, "I so swear, by both my power and my powers."

"Thank you."

"Camellia, I don't know how you could think . . . we're the non-violent ones, for heaven's sake!"

"And also the ones ready to lend a hand to anyone with enough—no, sorry. We won't go there. Thank you for the assurance. I'll be in touch."

Camellia hung up the phone, then went back and stared out the window some more. *Well then*, she thought. *At least there's that.*

||||||||||||||||

Well, damn, thought Matt. *One guy supplies magic, the other uses it, and they're going around killing people.*

He took the earbud out, disconnected the cell, and stood up. The motel was cheap—though not inexpensive—but it had been warm, and he'd slept better than he had expected. It was just after 10:30 in the morning.

He showered and dressed in the same clothes he'd worn yesterday—the only clothes he had. Had he gotten enough from that drug dealer to at least get new socks and underwear? He had. *Good.* He'd do that first, even before breakfast. But then, breakfast. A lot of it. Eggs over easy, hashed browns, bacon, French toast, *and* a waffle. He was going to eat a big breakfast. Then he would—what?

Then he'd need to do some things he didn't know how to do. Well, that was okay; he'd find out. At least it wasn't dangerous. Public libraries were rarely dangerous.

He left the room key card on the dresser and headed out.

This city stinks, he thought. *Why do I like it so much?*

||||||||||||||||

"Good morning, Mr. Becker."

"It's afternoon here, Mr. Longfellow."

"Right. I've managed to put some of it together. Let me ask you something. Do we have any spies inside the Mystici?"

"No, Mr. Becker. So far as I know, we do not."

"Would you know if we did?"

"I very likely would not, but I do know a great deal about our resources, and I am fairly confident."

"All right. Do they have any spies inside the Foundation?"

"It is possible."

"Then I can't confirm what I suspect, but I would suggest, Mr. Becker, that we keep this information confined to only those who need to know it."

"That seems a good suggestion, Mr. Longfellow. What do you have?"

"One other thing first. Would you mind giving Budget and Oversight a kick for me? I've submitted a requisition for a guy who got me useful information, and won't give me any more until he's paid."

"How useful?"

"He established a connection between Lawton-Smythe and Blum."

"I see. Very impressive. Yes, I'll speak with them at once."

"Thank you, Mr. Becker. Here's the first thing you need to know: We're after two of them. One is a man; we don't know about the other, but he or she is the more interesting, and dangerous, of the two."

"I'm listening, Mr. Longfellow."

||||||||||||||||

T. Rex was such a cliche. But so what? Susan stood across from that magnificent jaw and stared. "Hello, Sue, I'm Susan," she murmured as she always did. Then she turned her back on Sue and continued through the Field Museum of Natural History. She had grown up in Cook County, and as a child had lived for family trips to the museum, and when she was old enough to travel herself had visited it at least twice a month. Walking through the echoing halls felt like a homecoming.

It wasn't the power that drew Susan in; it was the sense of age, of time. It humbled her, filled her with awe. It was the same awe that, she was sure, astronomers felt when considering the insignificance of Earth in the cosmos. These things walked, lived, ate, shat, mated, died, decayed for such a long time, and so long ago, that not just her lifetime, but the life of her species, was insignificant. Seeing them, so close she could touch them, made them real.

She had long ago stopped trying to understand why the powerful assurance of her insignificance was so calming, but it was.

After a few hours, relaxed and happy and pleased to live in a world where the Field Museum of Natural History existed, she made a call to her parents, and arranged to spend a day with them before she headed back to the parking garage where the slipwalk would take her back to Portland.

||||||||||||||||

Marci sat in the kitchen drinking herbal tea and listening to Pink Floyd, very softly. *And he calls Susan a hippie*, she thought. She glanced over at the clock. Four thirty. Lawrence needed to be up in two hours. She reflected on the last week. She didn't especially want to, but she did anyway.

Someone had shot at her. Actually shot at her. This was her life now. And Lawrence was in the bedroom, sleeping. *Jesus*.

She had a mad desire to call William and scream at him, say, *You didn't tell me it would be like this.*

Except that he had. He hadn't hidden anything from her. "It'll be scary sometimes," he'd told her when she'd first announced her desire to go into fieldwork. "Your life is liable to be threatened. There will be times when you'll need to be at your best just to stay alive."

She'd nodded as if she'd understood. She'd thought she'd understood.

But then he'd looked at her and said, "You'll be fine," and she had been. When it mattered, she had been. She remembered Donovan looking at her when the bullets sparked in front of her face—inches in front of her face—she'd seen them stop, and fall to the ground. And Donovan had looked at her and said, without words, *You're fine. You'll do.*

William knew she could handle it. Donovan knew she could handle it. Why didn't *she* know she could handle it? She could almost hear William's voice answering her: *It doesn't matter if you think you can handle it,* he would have said. *It matters if you handle it.*

Recruitment and Training—they called it the kiddie pool, though she'd never met a trainee younger than twelve and most were much older. Awareness of the grid seemed to emerge at different times: In many, it was late puberty. In others, it was when the cerebral cortex was about done growing, around the early twenties.

At first, they had her practice finding the nodes—laughably easy and fun, as it often involved visiting scenic areas, or interesting spots in different cities; she had gone to Chichen Itza, Rome, Vienna, Budapest, Hong Kong, Cairo, and Delhi; she had seen Victoria Falls, the Great Sphinx, Stonehenge, the Grand Canyon, Parícutin, the Temple of Artemis, the Great Wall of China. All in a month. It was amazing and wonderful and still gave her glorious Technicolor dreams from time to time.

Learning to find grid points—where two lines came together—was nearly as easy, but, alas, didn't require as much travel. And finally, the lines themselves; once her teacher had explained what they felt like, they also came naturally and easily to her.

Then they tried to teach her to shape, to cast, to form what she could touch, and it was like trying to sprint through water—so much exhaustion for so little result. But she'd done it. She'd learned. She'd been driven. She was sixteen then, and what sixteen-year-old doesn't dream of standing high on a mountain casting fire at a balrog, or blasting into a castle to have a magic duel with an evil overlord? Yes, there was a great deal she'd never be able to do: The trickier transmutations were closed to her, and the easier ones quickly made her too cold or too hot, and working with light just confused her.

But her teachers didn't give her time to dwell on what she couldn't do. They taught her how to find the remaining energy of a spell, and use what was left to determine what was done— tell a story by the words that hadn't been used. The part of her brain that loved mathematics as a gourmet loved food at once latched on to it, and, as with mathematics, she fell in love with the process, the diving in, constructing, deducing, concluding, diving deeper, over and over until she had it all. Each new technique they taught her fed her hunger the way a dry log feeds a fire. How to tell if someone was lying, how to tell if someone was watching with a hostile attitude, how to read intent in result and determine content from shape.

It was during that time, when everything was wonderful, that she met Lawrence, an American exchange student whose father had lost his job and could no longer afford to keep him at MIT. They'd had a year together, though, scrimping and sharing food and sneaking him in and out of her flat, and when her training was done the Foundation had given her permission to move in with him. Then one day a tall, athletic woman had come up to her in the middle of class and said, "Hello, Marci. I'm Susan Kouris. I'm with Investigations and Enforcement, North America. We're looking for a sorcerer. Would you like to work with us?"

Marci had asked questions, and Susan had answered everything clearly, fully, with a precise economy of language, and Marci had been given training in Sensitivity Removal Protocol—

how to remove someone's ability to detect the grid, to use sorcery, which was the nuclear option for fieldwork. And then, twenty-four hours later, Marci was telling Lawrence about their new apartment in Boston, at Dudley and Albion, paid for by her new employer, whom she couldn't name.

And six weeks after that, Donovan called.

And now she was being shot at. Her mother would have said, *Buck up, kiddo. It just gets worse from here*, and then given her that Mom-grin.

She hoped she'd be able to get back home soon and introduce Lawrence to her family. She couldn't afford to travel, but Susan said that once in a while the Foundation gave bonuses.

She looked at the time, and started coffee for Lawrence. Since she was up anyway, she might as well do something useful.

A GOOD SORCERER
IS HARD TO FIND

8

Donovan stood up from the computer and started pacing—kitchen, through the living room, to the bathroom, and back. The shooter, the man with the shotgun. What was his game?

By now, Donovan was convinced of two things: First, the Mystici were not the target as such—there lacked any relationship with importance in the organization. And second, that everyone killed had been a member was not coincidence.

So, if not the Mystici, then what, or who? It felt like vengeance—particularly the way each death was more horrific than the last. But what was the connection? The phone call, months ago, between Blum and Lawton-Smythe must have meant something, but what? No professional connection; one was a teacher who practiced sorcery on the side, the other a recruiter. Assuming a connection with the others, one was a State Senator, and the last—so far—an insurance investor. The Senator had no sorcerous skill whatsoever; her only connection to the Mystici was taking money from them for some relatively minor peccadilloes that helped them in California. The insurance man, like Lawton-Smythe, had some abilities but little skill.

There was a reason, a pattern. If he couldn't see it, it was either because he was being dense, or because he didn't have enough information yet.

He stopped pacing, sat down on the couch, stood up, and started pacing again.

Then he stopped and stared at the couch, frowning. He went back and dug his hand under the cushion, fished around, and pulled out a cell phone—a Nokia Lumia 630. The kind Matt had been carrying. It was on, set to silent, and the battery was almost dead.

"Son of a bitch," he said.

||||||||||||||||

Half an hour using the computer at the library provided Matt with a list of three phone numbers. He recognized that it should have taken him a third of the time, but computers just weren't his thing.

He got up and stepped outside into the March weather— snowy, nasty, and cold. There were definitely things he preferred about San Diego. He found a coffee shop, ordered a plain, black coffee, and punched in the first number on his list. The answer came quickly.

"Hello?"

"Santino. You'll never guess who—"

"Jesus Christ. Matt."

"Yeah."

"Where the hell are you, man?"

"New Jersey."

"New Jersey? Why there?"

"Long story."

"God. You know we've been back since December?"

"I know."

"You should have gotten in touch."

"You know why I haven't."

"Man, no one blames you."

I do would have sounded obnoxiously self-pitying, so he said, "I need some help."

"You got it, bro. What do you need? Money?"

"Money wouldn't hurt; I've taken to ripping off drug dealers."

"Holy shit, man."

"It's temporary. But that's not the main thing. I'm following up some stuff that might get kinda hairy."

"What sort of stuff?"

"I don't want to say, Santino."

"That bad, huh. What, is it Company shit, or private sector?"

"Private sector."

"Money in it?"

"Better than that, man. I'm going to be a fucking hero."

"Jesus, Matt. You know what that means. That means you're gonna get lit up."

"Might could. Not the plan, though."

There was a pause. Then, "If you need backup, Howie got out."

"Yeah? How?"

"Didn't re-up. He was there before the rest of us."

"Oh yeah, that's right. What's he doing now?"

Santino's snort came over phone. "Getting treated for P.T.S.D. like everyone else."

Matt chuckled. "I don't have his number; you got it? I don't think I'll need it, but you know."

Santino gave it to him and said, "What else? I've got about fifteen hundred bucks set aside."

"Naw. But thanks. Main thing is, you got any travel connections? This is going to involve a lot of T.A.D., and no way I can pay for it out of my own pocket."

"Foreign or domestic?"

"Mostly domestic, a little foreign."

"Covert?"

"Open. If I can go Space A on a commercial flight, that would work as well as anything else."

"I know a few people. Got an email address? I'll send you a list."

"And put in a word?"

"Sure."

"Thanks, buddy."

"You gonna brief me when this is over?"

Matt hesitated. "I don't know if it's ever going to be over. But when you're out, I might draft you. If you want to be a hero, I mean."

"Shit," said Santino. "Who wouldn't want that?"

||||||||||||||||||||

Our meeting this time took place in the locker room of the YMCA, after hours. I don't know how he arranged for the door to be open, but I'd stopped asking those questions long before. I followed his instructions, sitting on a bench in the middle of the second row, facing the third row.

"I'm here," I said.

His voice echoed oddly from beyond the lockers. "There's a problem," he said.

Those three words chilled me in a way that I hadn't thought I could be chilled anymore. I managed to say, "What?" but it was an effort, like I was forcing speech past a closed throat.

"We are being investigated, and it's happening faster and more efficiently than I had expected."

"They might stop me?"

"They might."

"What do I have to do?"

"Nothing."

"You're going to handle it?"

"No, I mean we have to stop. We have to delay for a while."

"How long?"

"I'm working on something. I can't give you an exact time or date."

"Charlie, I'm so close!"

"I know. I'm sorry."

"You know who is doing the investigating?"

"Yes. He's very good."

"What if—"

"No. Don't even think about it, Nick. You aren't in any position to do that. Even I might not be able to pull it off—I've failed twice already—and I have considerably more resources than you. And, Nick, I don't think you want to be that guy anyway, do you?"

"Jesus, Charlie. I have no idea who I am or who I want to be anymore. All I know is what I need to do. What now, do I go back to Denver and sit on my ass for I don't know how long? I'll go crazy. I don't even know where I'll stay; I've probably been evicted by now." I heard the whining in my voice and hated it.

"I'm sorry," he said again. "I'll put you up at a hotel. I'm going to try to figure something out. I hope it won't be long. I have made preparations for this possibility."

"What preparations?"

"You don't need to know; you don't want to know. Whatever happens or doesn't happen is on me, and that's how I want it. Let me do this. Please."

"I don't know how long I can wait without going crazy."

"Yeah. Remember, I want this to happen as much as you do. But it's better to wait than—"

"All right, all right," I said. "I'll wait."

"Thank you, Nick," he said, like I was doing him a favor.

||||||||||||||||

Becker was sometimes—rarely—referred to as the Ramrod. He was unaware of his nickname, because not only would no one dare use it to his face, but no one liked using it in the same building he was in, and when people did use it their voices tended to drop a little. That said, there had been, here and there, some speculation about where the name came from: The obvious explanation was that he was, after all, a senior manager in Investigation and Enforcement, aka "the Ranch." But some suggested it had more to do with the way he walked, talked, and interacted with those above and below him: He didn't have a lot of bend. And there were the obvious comments about where the hypothetical ramrod was, or should be, placed—but these were even more rare, and delivered more quietly, shoulders hunched, head down.

Manuel "Ramrod" Becker made his way from his cube, past the other small, close-packed cubes that contained his staff and his colleagues, and to the elevator. He punched in the number for the top floor, the tenth, the Executive Branch, traditionally referred to as the Twelfth Floor for reasons Becker knew well and cared about not in the least.

When the elevator doors opened, he took himself to the office of Ms. Camellia Morgan. Before reaching Morgan, however, he had to face the obstacle of her secretary, Florencia Trujillo. Three facts are worth mentioning with respect to Florencia: She was roughly the same age as her boss—that is, early fifties—she was the only individual in the Foundation, including her boss, who was not intimidated by Becker; and Becker couldn't care less about either of these circumstances.

"Good day, Florencia. I would like to see Ms. Morgan, if she's free."

"I will inquire, Mr. Becker."

Trujillo rose—she preferred to ask in person with someone waiting, rather than permit half of her conversation to be overheard—and vanished into the bowels of the Executive Branch. Becker rarely needed to wait for anything, but when he did he stood stock still, hands at his sides, eyes straight ahead, giving the impression that he would continue in that attitude for five minutes, five days, or five years, whatever it took.

It took under a minute. Trujillo returned, resumed her seat, folded her hands, and said, "Ms. Morgan will see you."

"Thank you, Florencia."

He went back to the big office. Morgan pointed to a chair; he sat.

"What is it, Mr. Becker?"

"Something of a development in the Mystici murders."

"Go on."

"My lead investigator pointed out a few things. First, all four killings have been in America—in the continental United States, in fact. Yet, most of the Mystici are concentrated in Western and Northern Europe."

"Go on."

"Maybe it's a vigilante starting there, planning to move on. But maybe not. Second, he's used a different form of attack with each killing. First was a time-stop permitting an attack with a firearm—"

"Americans," said Morgan.

"The second was a very subtle manipulation that stopped the heart. The third was freezing water in a swimming pool. The fourth was the infliction or simulation of a disease that fills the body with nitrogen bubbles."

Morgan frowned. "Why so different? If he can stop time and shoot someone, then why not just do that?"

"Exactly. Third, the attacks on our people, both of them, were work for hire, amateurs, for not much money. No magic used at all."

"Interesting."

"Yes."

"It occurred to Mr. Longfellow that maybe the attacker is using artifacts, that he has no sorcery of his own. Each artifact, of course, can be used only once, so it would explain that. I asked Artifacts and Enchantments to look into it. I got this last night. And, in passing, I must commend the department for fast and excellent work."

He carefully removed the memo from his inside coat pocket, unfolded it, and presented it to Morgan with something of an air of ceremony.

Morgan read it, then nodded. "Yes," she said. "I see. What do you suggest as our next step?"

"We need to determine what else was in the cache, and, if possible, recover it."

"Do you have a suggestion as to how to do that?"

"Mr. Longfellow hypothesizes that there are two individuals—one supplies the devices; the other uses them. If we can capture the second alive, he may be able to lead us to the first."

"And to capture the second?"

"Figure out his pattern, determine his next target, beat him to it."

"And to do that, Mr. Becker?"

"There are resources we need."

Her mouth twitched a little. "Resources. You mean money."

"Among other things. Mr. Longfellow was able to find a link between the first two victims by going to an outside source. If the—"

"Outside source, Mr. Becker? Is there a security risk?"

"I trust Mr. Longfellow implicitly."

Morgan nodded. "Very well, then I will, too, for now. Continue."

"The source will continue to be useful, but only if paid. I am therefore requesting that you instruct Budget and Oversight to release this and future payments."

"I see," said Morgan. "Is the amount substantial?"

"Roughly four thousand, five hundred at the current exchange rate."

"All right. I'll see to it."

"Thank you, Ms. Morgan."

"Is there anything else?"

"Only one more thing. Ms. Morgan, I don't know where this is going. There is a great deal I don't understand. Therefore, I don't know what we may require. But it is very possible there will be unexpected demands on the resources of the Foundation, and not a great deal of time in which to gather them."

"Are you asking for carte blanche?"

"No, Ms. Morgan. Not at this time. I am merely informing you of the possibility, so you can consider the matter."

Camellia drummed her fingertips on the desk. "We do not like the idea of the existence of magic being generally known. It would put us all at risk. That said, the Foundation has other tasks, performs other services, not just yours."

"I understand that, Ms. Morgan."

She nodded. "I will consider it. I appreciate the heads-up."

"Very well, Ms. Morgan."

"There is something else, Mr. Becker."

Becker had half stood up; he sat down again and waited.

"Do you know Vasily Vasilyev?"

"I do not."

"Russian, of course. Part of I and E, Black Sea area. Used to be Ukraine, but he's Jewish, so he got out after the coup. He's the sorcerer for a good team. He's a tracer."

"I'm sorry, a tracer?"

"A fluke talent. Give him a good feel for the actions of an artifact, he can tell you where the artifact is, and sometimes, where it was before."

"I see. Yes. That might be worthwhile. It is unlikely to lead us directly to either the shooter, or whoever is behind him—people who commit crimes with artifacts tend not to hang on to them once they've been used. But getting our hands on one could be useful. We might even get a fingerprint."

"Yes. I'll email you his contact information, and ask him to cooperate with you."

"Will I need a translator?"

"His English is good."

"Thank you."

"Of course."

Becker stood and gave a nod, turned, and walked away. Morgan gave a barely audible sigh and relaxed a little.

||||||||||||||||

From what Donovan could tell on Skype, Vasily Ilyanovich Vasilyev seemed to be in his midthirties, with shaggy, curly hair that could have been blond or light brown and a wide forehead that made him look smart. His first words were, "You must be Mr. Longfellow, yes? Mr. Becker said I should expect your call. Very happy to speak with you." He made the "v" sound with just the least hint that it wanted to be a "w" and the "s's" were pretty hissy, and "Becker" was kind of close to "baker," but other than that, Donovan detected little in the way of accent.

"Thank you for speaking with me, Mr. Vasilyev. Mr. Becker told me of your talent. Can you explain a little more how it works?"

"Please," he said. "Call me Vasily, if we are to work together."

"Vasily. I'm Donovan, then."

"Of course. To answer your question, it is very simple: If I am in an area where an enchanted artifact was used, I can sometimes tell whence it came."

"Tell how? I mean, how does the location manifest to you? Do you point to a spot on a map?"

"A direction, and a sense of distance. Sometimes a close sense of distance. Once I came within half a kilometer from over a hundred kilometers away."

"But you need to start from where it was used. I mean, you need to be there yourself."

"Yes, naturally."

"How long do you have after it's been used?"

"Well, of course, it will depend, yes? On the nearest grid line or point, on the exact spell. In general, it will last as long as if the spell had been cast as you would say normally, by sorcerer casting it, or sometimes a little longer. Can you tell what this is about?"

"A whole cache of artifacts was found in Turkey, sent to the British Museum, and vanished en route."

"What sort of artifacts?"

"We're pretty sure one was a time-stop."

"Bo—my god. That is, that is remarkable."

"Yes."

"When was it used?"

"A week ago."

"A week ago, I could not detect it."

"There was also one used to give someone a disease. That one is less than forty-eight hours old."

"Oh? That is possible, then, though I would not wish to guarantee anything."

"Yeah, I don't expect guarantees. But it sounds like it's worth a try. Hey, Vasily: You ever wanted to visit Chicago?"

||||||||||||||||||

Here's a question that doesn't come up often in either basic training or advanced, or in training for any specialty offered by the Armed Forces of the United States: How do you find a sorcerer? It isn't like they advertise. In fact, it seems like they go to a lot of trouble to make sure no one knows they exist. From what he'd picked up, Matt had the distinct impression that, in fact, keeping magic secret was the thing both organizations cared about the most. Don had as much as said that no one cared what was done with magic as long as no one did anything that risked detection by the public—by *civilians*, as they said. Matt didn't care for how that word tasted. Was that why he was getting involved in this? Just to avoid being a civilian?

Red on the ledger. Shit.

Matt sat on a bench outside the library and lit a cigarette— his first since he'd left the service. He wasn't sure why he was smoking again, but there it was.

One in a hundred thousand. That meant that, in the continental United States, there were between three thousand and thirty-five hundred, minus however many were off at whatever training base the two places had. Big country to find one of three thousand people in. Maybe they had a message board.

Actually, not that funny—they probably did. But finding it would be at least as hard as any other way of searching.

If I were a sorcerer, what would I do? That's easy. Get rich. How?

Well, the first and most obvious answer would be: conjure up big wads of cash. Would that work? If he understood more of this, he'd know; but then, if he understood more of this, he wouldn't need to go find someone to ask.

Well, let's suppose, for the sake of argument, that between the paper, the art, sequencing serial numbers, and all that, it was impossible, or so difficult it wasn't worth the trouble. And then, of course, there was the danger of detection; not using magic to break laws seemed important to these guys.

So take that off the table. Limit it to things that you could legally do without magic, but that magic would make easier, or better.

Easier. Maybe that was the key. Of those three thousand or so people, there had to be some who weren't crazy obsessed with making as much cash as they could, but were just satisfied with getting by while they played video games and watched reruns of *Seinfeld*. If so, then what he was looking for wasn't someone with a huge income, but with an income out of proportion to the work he put in.

Yeah, that would make kind of a tough Google search, though.

He put his cigarette out and went back into the library. A quick check of the Bureau of Labor Statistics revealed something like eight hundred different occupations. He could eliminate the vast majority of them at once—whatever this mythical sorcerer was doing, he or she was self-employed. Something not requiring work with anyone else who could see the sausage being made. Something taking some degree of skill or training or knowledge, probably, where he could get a reputation for good, fast, cheap work and keep customers coming back, while actually doing a whole lot less than it seemed.

Several hours later he had a list, a plan, a headache, an

appetite, and a mad desire for sleep. He'd come back tomorrow and get started. It shouldn't take more than a few days to go through the ads in the fifty biggest cities.

Ads. Shit. The son of a bitch might not advertise at all—he might want to keep a lower profile than that, just finding customers through word of mouth. If so, there'd be no way to find him.

Somewhere out there, Matt was sure, was someone who could sit down at a computer, type in a few keywords, and have the answer come spitting out in five minutes. This computer whiz would pick a suitable business, and look for a drop-off in commercial businesses over, say, the last few years. He'd set it up, and run it in fifty cities at once. Well, no, probably not—probably no way to do that. But, shit, there had to be something. There had to be traces somehow. And there had to be someone who could figure out how to find what he needed.

It was good to have friends, and friends of friends. And friends of friends who'd do favors without asking questions.

Matt pulled out his cell and punched in a number.

Twenty minutes later, someone he'd never met, or even heard of twenty minutes before, said, "Well, you know, if he's fixing cars he's got to dispose of a lot of oil, right? And maybe batteries, too? A lot of places keep track of that. Give me a couple hours, I'll get back to you."

It was good to have friends.

A DAY IN THE PARK

9

Susan answered at once. Donovan explained why they were going back to Chicago, to the scene of the last attack, and Susan said that she had no problem going, but wanted five minutes for a shower. He couldn't reach Marci on Skype, but she answered her cell fast enough. She was twenty minutes from her apartment and the slipwalk, out with her boyfriend, but would drop everything and go.

"Sorry," Donovan said.

"It's all right. He knows this kind of thing is liable to happen. I'll see you there."

He opened the closet, filled his pockets, and shut it. He started to leave the apartment, caught himself, and went back into the kitchen to put the milk away.

||||||||||||||||

Some people thought Susan worked out so much because she was dedicated. Others thought her "goal oriented," which might mean the same thing—she wasn't sure. Occasionally an idiot would hit on her by explaining that she was "sublimating," as if she were likely to respond, *Gosh, you're right; I never realized that. Fuck me right now.*

She had occasionally tried to explain that it wasn't like that at all, it was more like addiction. Or maybe "habituation" was closer. All she knew was that if she didn't work out for a day her body felt funny. If she went two days, she had trouble sleeping.

That, and there was something pleasantly hypnotic about the process. Swimming was her favorite, but the pool was five miles away, which too often seemed like a pain. So she ran, did weights, stretched, hit the bag, and, above all, practiced kata. She loved her kata like a junkie loved the prick of the needle: the feeling of every muscle behaving, doing exactly what it was supposed to do. It was a high. She didn't dance, but she understood dancers.

She was in the middle of stretching when her computer notified her of a Skype call. She stopped, spoke with Donovan, and jumped into the shower.

Clean—or at least not stinky—she threw on her Portland Community College sweatshirt, a pair of brown capris, and her knee-high red and white stripey socks with Ariel on them. *That's right. You've just gotten your ass kicked by a girl wearing* Little Mermaid *socks.* She put on her flat-heeled doeskin boots, closed the apartment, and ran up the stairs to the top floor of her building, then down the hall to apartment 409.

No one lived in apartment 409—it was a storage unit shared by everyone who lived there, according to an agreement with Mr. Sloan, the landlord. But it did have a bathroom.

She reached into the shower and turned the hot up all the way, then down to half, then off, then one quarter on, then off; then she pulled on the divertor that would have started the shower if water were running.

A section of wall opposite the shower fixtures lowered. She stepped through it to a stairway leading up. She stated the same Chicago address as before, and started walking.

||||||||||||||||||

Peggy had a feeling.

Peggy did not base her conclusions on feelings, or instincts, or intuition. She didn't *get* feelings; she got answers. But now she had a feeling. *I'm not done. There's more here. I'm sure there is.*

It was the dig in Turkey, where some British archaeologists had uncovered and shipped to England (after paying the proper bribes, of course) three large crates of carefully packed thirteenth-century artifacts, one of which had gone missing. There was the inevitable broken pottery, and even a brownish-red jug that was whole save for a chipped handle. There was an anvil, and a piece of what was probably the tongs to go with it. There were curious copper disks with tiny holes to string them together that some were arguing were children's toys, some thought had religious significance, and others believed were coins. There were tools, buttons (there are always buttons), utensils. And there were a few semi-precious stones—agate, diaspore—that had been shaped and polished.

Bits and pieces of many things had come together to point that out: Turkish folklore, newspaper accounts, shipping manifests, papers in archaeology journals, records copied (read: stolen) from the Mystici. In the end, she had found what the Ranch had been looking for, and everyone was happy; Julia had shown her a memo from Ms. Morgan complimenting the department. That was winning. Once you've won, you can stop, right? Right?

She pushed aside her current research—the kind she liked most, where she wasn't looking for anything, just looking—and brought up her notes labeled "Agri Cache." She read them over, each line a conclusion, each conclusion bringing back memories of how she'd reached it.

She couldn't have made a mistake. It was all there, all the pieces, fitting together—

Fitting together so perfectly.

She'd had many reactions over the years to success, failure, or discovery, but this was the first time she had ever felt herself flushing.

She opened the Foundation directory, found a number, punched it into her phone.

"Hello?"

"Mr. Becker," she said, forgetting how scary and creepy he was.

"Yes, who is—"

"Peggy Hanson from the Burrow. We have a problem."

||||||||||||||||

Donovan offered Vasilyev his hand and said, "It's a pleasure to meet you in person."

"And you, Donovan." The Russian's handshake was a little too strong, almost painful, but his smile seemed pleasant.

"I thought," said Donovan, "that the plan was to let me and my team show up first, so we could secure the area."

The Russian shrugged. "I hate waiting."

Donovan felt his lips twitch. "Yeah, I hear you. The others should be along."

"All right," he said. "Tell me, is it as hard as they say, being black in America?"

Donovan laughed, couldn't help it. "I love Europeans. You guys are the best."

Vasilyev frowned. "I do not understand. I didn't mean to give offense."

"No, no. It's cool. But no American would ever, ah, anyway, I don't know. I don't know what they say. I mean, it's a thing. The more money you have, the less of a thing it is. I'm not saying I want to trade places with a homeless white guy. But it's still a thing."

"I'm sorry. Can you explain?"

Donovan thought about it. "Okay, I got this thing I call the Face. It's automatic now; I just do it when I go out, don't even think about it. I make my eyes just the least fraction wide, and I do a kind of Mona Lisa smile. And I'm never the first one to make eye contact, but I always nod and smile if someone else does."

Vasilyev shook his head. "Why—"

"It's so I look harmless. So no one gets scared and decides to shoot me."

The Russian's brows came together. "Someone would shoot you otherwise?"

"Probably not. It's more like—oh, here's Hippie Chick. Good timing; I was getting to the hard part." He made the introductions, then introduced Marci as she appeared. Then he said, "Well, it's across the street there. Let's see if you can get what we need."

"Eh, oh," said Vasilyev. "I got it already."

"You—"

"Yes, yes. Before you got here. Trivial."

"What if you'd been shot?"

"He's got a shield up," said Marci.

"Oh. Right. Sorcerer."

Vasilyev shrugged. "I'm sorry you had to waste your time coming. I could have done it myself. I believe your Mr. Becker was trying to prevent the embarrassment of me dying on your soil, yes?"

"Mr. Becker doesn't get embarrassed," said Donovan.

"Ah."

"But you're right anyway. So, where we headed?"

"West. Almost straight west, a little north."

"How far?"

"Sixteen and a half kilometers."

"What's that in miles?"

"I don't know."

"About ten-point-three," said Marci.

"Math Girl," said Donovan.

"What—oh, is that my name now?"

"Unless I think of a better."

Marci and Susan exchanged eye rolls. *Team building*, thought Donovan.

"Come up with a different one," said Marci. "That makes me think you're saying 'Meth Girl,' and I don't do that anymore."

"Okay. Can't stick you with a nickname you hate."

Hippie Chick snorted.

"Someone have a map?" said Donovan.

"I have a phone," said Susan. "Welcome to the twenty-first century."

"Um. Right."

"Okay," she said a moment later. "Veterans Memorial Maywood Park."

"Good," said Donovan. He turned to the Russian. "Thank you for your help, Vasily. You'll be heading back now?"

"Back? No, no. How can I miss the last act of the play? Besides, I have not yet had the famous Chicago pizza."

"There is no Chicago pizza," said Donovan.

Vasilyev started to speak, but Hippie Chick cut him off. "No," she said. "Don't argue religion with a fundamentalist; don't argue pizza with a New Yorker."

"I'm from New Jersey," said Donovan.

"A distinction without a difference, in this case," said Susan.

"Use your superpower," said Donovan. "Find us a cab."

Chicago traffic reminded Donovan of home; it took a lot longer than he'd have expected for a midwestern city. But they reached the park. Donovan paid the cabbie and got a receipt, which he carefully tucked into his wallet next to nine others he hadn't yet turned in.

There was a van parked there that said: "Maywood Police," and a Dodge Charger, and another cop car; he looked around and spotted the PO-lice station across the street and down the block. In the park itself, there were a few kids playing on the swings with a few bored parents watching them.

"Okay," said Donovan. "Let's start with the pavilion."

They had taken three steps toward it when Donovan's cell phone beeped the 911 beep.

"Hold, everyone," he said.

He answered the phone. A few seconds later he said, "Everyone stay alert. Marci? Check the area."

He continued speaking into the phone for another minute, then disconnected. He looked at Marci.

"Something," she said. "The pavilion."

"Hostile?"

"No, someone or something is blocking me. I can't get a read on what's inside the building."

"Well, shit," Donovan said, and pulled the bag of marbles from his pocket. Susan was scanning the area. Vasilyev had the look of a greyhound before the bell; he was leaning forward a little, shoulders up, his hands clenching and unclenching, eyes straining toward the pavilion door as if he was trying to see through it, which was quite possible.

"Fill us in," said Hippie Chick. It was always astonishing how she could look so relaxed and feel so full of tension.

"The whole thing is a trap," said Donovan. "The Burrow figured out that they'd been meant to find the artifacts, which means someone wants us to be here looking for them, and it probably does not indicate they want to invite us in for tea and borscht."

"So," said Marci. "Does that mean we leave, or that we go ahead?"

"I vote for going ahead," said Susan.

"When did this turn into a democracy?" said Donovan.

"All right," she said. "Then what do you say?"

"Same as you."

"I hope," said Vasilyev. "We can avoid trouble. Have you a plan?" Maybe it was tension, but his accent was noticeably stronger than it had been a minute ago—that was definitely a "w" sound in "avoid," and the "r" was rolled, and whatever vowel sound made the "a" in "plan" didn't occur in English.

"Marci, see if you can pick up anything at all. Is there a spell waiting for us when we open the door?"

"I'm still not getting anything," said Marci. "Except the sense that I'm being blocked."

"All right. Marci and I will check around the back. You two wait here."

Donovan took them a long way off to the side, past the playground, almost to the baseball diamond before curving back.

"Think they know we're here?" said Marci.

"Best to assume they do."

"Yeah."

They reached the other side of the pavilion.

"Well?" said Marci.

"Well what? What are we going to do? I figured we'd stand here like idiots for a while. Is anyone staring at us?"

"Uh, not that I can see."

"Good. You do have a shield up, right?"

"Of course."

"Good. I don't expect anyone will shoot at us, but I'd feel pretty silly if I was wrong."

Marci's eyes were fastened on the door; Donovan looked around, at the kids on the swing set, the trees blowing, cars going by, the parking lot. It was a trap. You don't walk into a trap. *Ah, shit.* There, some soccer mom holding a toddler's hand. *Ten to one they're heading for the toilet. Fuck, fuck, fuck.*

His phone rang. He glanced at it. "Hippie Chick," he said, and answered it. "Hey. Getting bored over there?"

"You see the civilians."

"Yeah. I see them. All right. Go on in."

"Just like that?" she said.

"Yeah. We'll go in this way."

"Just walk in the door?"

"If we blow it up, it'll get noticed. So just go in, only a little more carefully, and stand to the side."

"All right. Going now," she said, and disconnected.

Donovan nodded to Marci and started forward. He reached the door and took hold of it. It wasn't locked.

||||||||||||||||||

Donovan opened his eyes. "Where am I?"

"You're in a hospital unit in the Madrid headquarters building, Mr. Longfellow."

"Mr. Becker? Where are you?"

"I'm right here, Mr. Longfellow."

Donovan opened his eyes. He kept his voice even as he said, "I'm very sorry to hear that, Mr. Becker."

"You've been unconscious for nearly a full day, Mr. Longfellow."

Donovan opened his eyes. "How's my team?"

"There were no fatalities on your team, Mr. Longfellow, although it was close. The Foundation has some excellent sorcerous healers, however. You should regain your sight fully, though it may take a few days."

"How's my team, Mr. Becker?"

"Ms. Sullivan was struck by the same sort of spell you were, Mr. Longfellow, but not so hard. She remained conscious, and she will also recover her sight, but there were burns as well. The prognosis is for a full recovery. Ms. Kouris received only superficial injuries, and was released after treatment."

"And Vasily?"

"Mr. Vasilyev was killed, I'm afraid. He was gone by the time we reached him."

Donovan was silent for a while, staring at black and purple crisscrossing patterns. "I'm on drugs, aren't I?"

"A relatively mild pain medication. I can find out which, if you'd like to know."

"It doesn't matter. My head's a little fuzzy is all. Tell me what happened."

"First, I must inform you that I took the liberty of telling your team that you would want them to report to me. They were reluctant to report to anyone but you. I hope I have not crossed a boundary, Mr. Longfellow."

"It's fine. Tell me what happened."

"There were four of them, two shooters, two sorcerers. You and Ms. Sullivan were the first ones through the door, and, according to Ms. Sullivan, struck with a spell intended first to strip away magical defenses, then to simulate a high-intensity explosion directly in front of you. As you may be aware, neither of these spells is simple, both can be blocked, neither was entirely successful."

"And then?"

"There was something of a melee. The shooters were ineffective, as both Mr. Vasilyev's and Ms. Sullivan's defense spells remained at least somewhat intact. I am told the matter went on for a long time—nearly twenty seconds as Ms. Kouris described it. Eventually, Mr Vasilyev's shield went down, and he suffered a fatal gunshot wound to the forehead. Immediately thereafter, Ms. Kouris disabled the remaining sorcerer and the gunmen."

"Disabled. Where are they?"

"Three of them are here, Mr. Longfellow, being questioned. One of the sorcerers was killed by Ms. Kouris."

"Poor Hippie Chick."

"Ms. Kouris seems to be holding up well, Mr. Longfellow."

"I shouldn't have gone in."

"I disagree, Mr. Longfellow. It is unfortunate about Mr. Vasilyev, but it was still a good decision. You recovered the artifact, which we can now use to get a better idea of its source. We now know considerably more about who we're up against. We have three prisoners to question, any of whom may give us a valuable lead. And a very immediate threat was contained."

"Excuse me, threat?"

"Mr. Longfellow, that was a pavilion in a public park, with civilians and children present. There were two gunmen there. Yes, they were waiting for you, but have you considered the potential for something to have gone wrong, for someone to have made a catastrophic mistake?"

"Mr. Becker, this is the first time I've known you to be concerned with the lives of innocents."

"Mr. Longfellow, there is little that I care about more."

Donovan grunted. "I want to see my team."

"Please rest for a while. Perhaps when you wake up, Ms. Sullivan will be able to speak with you as well; right now she is sedated."

Donovan exhaled slowly. "All right. But, Mr. Becker."

"Yes?"

"I don't like your interrogation techniques."

"Yes, Mr. Longfellow. I am aware of that."

"We'll talk tomorrow."

"Two days from now, Mr. Longfellow. Tomorrow I must travel to Odessa to attend a funeral."

⁣⁣⁣⁣⁣⁣⁣⁣⁣⁣⁣⁣

The pilot's name was Berghoff, and Matt couldn't believe how many dirty jokes the man had never heard. I mean, had he been living in Antarctica before he enlisted? By the time he set the C-27J Spartan down at Whiteman Air Force Base, there were a lot fewer Berghoff hadn't heard, and Matt felt like if he'd wanted he could have drunk free for the next week.

But he had other things on his agenda.

He caught a shuttle to Kansas City, arriving in the early afternoon. He found a cab and gave the address, getting out in a low-income residential neighborhood not far from the river. He felt a little naked without his weapons—he'd ditched them in what he hoped was a secure hidey-hole in Journal Square—but he figured he could probably handle any trouble unarmed.

He knocked on the door, and it was answered by an elderly woman in a flowered housedress who made Matt suddenly, for the first time in years, nervous about his appearance. She didn't seem frightened or upset, though; she just asked what he wanted.

Wishing he had a hat so he could take it off, he said, "Good afternoon, ma'am. I'm Matthew Castellani. I'm looking for Victor Everson."

She nodded and turned her head. "Victor!"

Victor appeared, about Matt's age, very long hair with a cupid tattoo on his cheek and grease under his nails. "Hey," he said.

"Hey. Matt Castellani." Matt held out his hand.

Victor took it. Victor's grip was limp. "So, uh—"

"You don't remember me," said Matt.

"No, sorry."

Matt wasn't surprised that Victor didn't remember him, seeing as they'd never met. "That's okay. It was a long time ago. You got a car?"

"Yeah. Why?"

"Take us someplace you like. I'm buying."

"What's this about?"

"You know stuff I want to find out about, and I'm going to ask you questions, and keep buying as long as you answer."

"What sort of questions?"

"Auto and small-engine repair."

Victor nodded. "Drinks or food?"

"Let's start with drinks and see how the conversation goes."

"Let me get my coat. I'll see you in back."

Victor's car was a 2002 Mazda with a cracked passenger window and a front bumper held on with wire, and it smelled like oil, but it ran smooth (which was worth noting—most auto mechanics Matt knew had cars that barely ran) and got them to a place called the Stardust that wasn't terribly busy at this hour. Victor didn't bother locking the door. They found a quiet corner. Victor ordered a Miller; Matt went along with it.

"So, what do you want to know?" said Victor.

"You got a nice place there," said Matt. "Is that your mom? You're taking care of her. That's pretty cool."

"Uh."

"Here's the thing, Victor. You don't have a job, and you're paying the mortgage on that house, and supporting your mother."

"Hey—"

"Relax and drink your beer, Victor. I'm not planning to do anything to you, or threaten your income. I'm just explaining how I know enough to ask the question I'm about to ask."

"Wait, what?"

There were two guys at the bar, both white, both probably retired. The bartender was almost certainly the owner's son, or nephew. He'd rather have been working somewhere with flashing lights and loud music. Matt looked back at Victor. "Just work with me. Now, you have no income, but you spend a lot. So, where are you getting it? Drugs? Oh, hell no. Not you. That is *so* not your scene. I don't think you want to have anything to do with anything that might involve violence. In practice, it isn't that easy to turn magic into money, is it? I've figured out that much. You can't change probabilities; you can't predict the future. All the easy, big ways of using it to make a living come with risks, don't they? So, what's left? You fix things. Cars, small engines, lawn mowers. Sorcery could help with that, since you were good at it anyway, right? Fix things fast, cheap, maybe save a lot on labor, even more on expensive equipment you don't have to buy. The only advertisement you use is word of mouth, and you're paid in cash, so no taxes. Did I call it?"

"How—?"

"Good. I don't mean to interfere. So let me start with one question: Mystici or Foundation?"

Victor stared at Matt. Matt waited.

"We never really met before, did we?"

"No, I made that up to get you here. So, Mystici or Foundation?"

"I don't know what—"

"No, no, Victor. There's no need for that. Yes, I know, it's supposed to be secret and all that. But I already know about the two groups. I just need to get a few details straight."

"You a reporter?"

Matt shook his head. "Nothing like that. This is for my own use."

Victor shook his head. "Look, I—"

"Okay, you don't want to talk about the Mystici. Or the Foundation. Whichever it is. But you can tell me this, right? How many sorcerers are there who aren't in either group?"

Victor just looked at him, forearms on the table, shoulders hunched.

"Okay, seriously, Victor. It can't hurt to tell me *that*, can it? Just a general idea of how many, I guess you'd say independents— is that the right word?—are there?"

"Rogues."

"That's the term?"

"Yeah. Rogue sorcerers."

"Ah, okay. So, how many are there?"

"I don't know."

"Not even a guess?"

"From what I've heard, not all that many. And the ones who aren't in either usually can't do much. It takes a lot of training."

"Got it. Okay. And the two groups aren't even in size, as I understand it. One is much bigger than the other?"

Victor nodded.

"So why did you choose the small one?"

"The big one, and I didn't ch—. Fuck."

Matt shook his head. "Don't sweat it. Nothing bad is going to happen from you telling me anything. Trust me. Another beer?"

"Yeah."

Matt got him one and brought it back. "I came across the Foundation by accident, and I've been sniffing around since then. But your group, the Mystici, I don't know much about."

"If they find out—"

"They aren't going to find out, Victor."

"And you aren't going to jack me up?"

"For what? Fixing lawn mowers? Why do they train people, anyway?"

Victor was silent for a minute, staring down at the table. Matt waited. Whoever owned this bar sure liked the Royals.

Victor spoke. "Without training, you're liable to hurt yourself. And that way, there are people who will, you know, stand up for your brothers and sisters if something comes up."

"Anything ever come up with you?"

Victor looked startled at the idea. "Me? No. I'm not all that good, you know. I mean, I worked, but the things some of the others did were kind of amazing."

"Yeah, I suppose. There's—"

"Man, I really shouldn't talk about this."

"You haven't told me much I didn't know. And, like I said, nothing you tell me will go anywhere. I swear."

"Shit. You still buying?"

"Yep."

"All right."

"There's this thing I've heard about, where someone comes in and takes away your ability to use sorcery."

Victor shuddered. "What about it?"

"How often does it happen?"

"Not very. I don't have numbers or anything, but it's rare."

"Why do they do it?"

Victor looked around the bar, as if suddenly afraid of being seen. "That's a Foundation thing. We don't do it. But if you use sorcery to try to kill another member, they throw you out and strip you. Maybe for other stuff, but not often."

"Strip you?"

"Of your ability to use magic. I mean, completely. You can't feel the grid lines; you can't even trigger artifacts, which is usually something anyone can do."

"That's gotta suck," said Matt.

"No shit."

"The times it's happened—what do you know about them?"

Victor took a long, long pull of his beer, then wiped his mouth with the back of his hand. "Nothing. It was just mentioned during training, as 'don't ever do this.' Can we talk about something else?"

"Oh yeah. Sorry. Is there, like, a headquarters?"

"Yeah, in London. That's where they took me when my talent showed up. I'd never been out of the country before. It rocked. And the headquarters, it's a pretty cool place."

"With their name, you'd think they'd be in Rome."

"They used to be. They moved during World War Two."

Matt nodded, then pushed a napkin and a pen at him. "Got an address?"

"Um," said Victor.

Matt shrugged. "You don't have to, of course. I can find it. But it'll take longer and be more irritating."

"Yeah, I know. But if they find out I gave it to you—"

"Is that somehow worse than them finding out what you've told me so far? And I already said they won't find out from me. If you've trusted me this far—"

"Yeah, yeah. Okay." Victor wrote the address out, and passed the napkin back.

"Thanks. So, is the Foundation in London, too?"

"No, Madrid."

"Oh, I guess that makes sense."

"Yeah, it was Franco, you know."

"Franco? The dictator?"

"I guess. I don't know much about him. I don't know how it all went down exactly. It had something to do with Franco and the Church and a bunch of members being scared. The people in London offered to pull them out, but they wanted protection, and it became a thing, so they split off."

Matt nodded. "That makes sense. Had this happened before? In the past, where groups split off?"

"Huh. I don't think so. You know, they didn't actually teach us the history. We just sort of picked it up between juggling balls without using hands and making invisible stone walls."

"Can you do that?"

"I can do the juggling one. Three balls, never got the hang of four."

"So, why not be a stage magician?"

"That's one of the things they forbid. They're afraid someone will, you know, pick up on it."

"What else do they forbid?"

"Anything criminal. Really, anything that's likely to be noticed."

"How do they enforce that?"

"From what I understand, as long as you don't go after another member, I mean, with magic, then all they do is write you a letter saying you should stop. If you keep going, you get another letter threatening you with, well, I don't know what the term is.

We used to call it excommunication, but that was just kidding around. I really don't want to talk about that."

"Right. Sorry. That thing you were saying about artifacts. How does that work?"

"Oh, man, that was what I really wanted to do. See, well, there's actually two different things. The one I wanted is, some people, if they can cast a spell, they can, you know, stick the spell into a thing, so that anyone who wants can wave it or whatever and set it off, like a magic wand."

"What's the other?"

"Huh?"

Victor, Matt decided, either had a very low alcohol tolerance, or just wasn't very bright.

"You said there were two things and that was one of them."

"Oh, right. Well, sometimes people find things, you know, from hundreds or thousands of years ago, that still have spells enchanted in them. If you can figure out how to set it off, you can use it."

"Pretty cool."

For the first time, Victor smiled. "Yeah, it is."

"I've heard of an artifact that had a time-stop on it."

"No shit? Wow. Time-stop. That's some . . . Jesus."

"Yeah. But Victor, doesn't stopping time violate natural law? I thought you couldn't do that?"

"Uh, I don't know. I mean, it isn't like they ever taught us that spell. I've never heard of anyone able to do it. They talked about time a little."

"What do you mean?"

"I can't remember. One of my teachers. Something about time being a mode."

"I don't get it."

"Yeah, neither did I. But it was, like, something about how

it'd be possible to set up an area where you were outside it. I don't know. He was talking about some kind of crazy physics that I don't understand, and how it might be used in magic."

"Can you give me some examples of spells you can put into artifacts?"

"Can I have another beer?"

"Coming up."

One day toward the end of her training, Marci had been sitting in the cafeteria, off in a corner, and William, her favorite instructor, had walked up and sat down across from her.

"So," he'd said. "Want to tell me about it?"

"What?"

"Jolene told me there's been something on your mind for the last week and she couldn't get you to talk about it. Maybe you'd be more comfortable talking to me? I feel like we have a certain rapport."

"Yes," she heard herself saying. "We do. All right."

William smiled and sat down across from her. He had one of those smiles that made you think everything was going to be fine, no matter what. "Spill it, then," he said.

She opened her mouth and closed it again. Words were harder than numbers, because they could mean so many different things, and even more when arranged differently. It wasn't that she didn't know the answer; it was that she wasn't sure if there was a way to say it that wouldn't be offensive. But one of the things that made William a good teacher was his patience.

"Here's the thing that bothers me," she said finally, speaking slowly and choosing her words as best she could. "We're doing all of this research, right? Into curing diseases, and ways to improve infrastructure using magic, and all of that."

"Yes, that's right."

"Well, it bothers me that we're keeping it secret. That maybe we can cure myelogenous leukemia. How can we just keep that to ourselves?"

"Oh. Yeah. I know."

"It bothers you, too?"

"Yeah. Only, what's the alternative? We'd have to reveal what we can do. Then what happens?"

"I don't know."

"Yeah, neither does anyone else."

"They aren't burning witches anymore."

"I know."

"In all this time, someone must have, you know, revealed things. Or tried."

"Yeah."

"What happened?"

He said, "That's something that's supposed to come up a little later in your training, but what the hell. There's a division of the Foundation called Investigations and Enforcement. We call it the Ranch because they're a bunch of cowboys. They handle that sort of thing."

"Handle it."

"Yeah."

"How?"

"A sorcerer's ability to detect and tap into the grid can be removed."

"Oh," said Marci.

"You won't need to learn that unless you want to work for I and E."

After a moment, she said, "Do you think doing that is right?"

He shook his head. "I wish I knew."

|||||||||||||||

"Hey, Laughing Boy," said Susan. "How are the eyes?"

"Getting better. You, in particular, are a delightful fuzzy blur and I can tell you have black hair, which I couldn't have yesterday. And that must be Marci behind you."

"It's me," she said.

"How are you, Marci? Doing all right?"

"My vision's healing faster than yours, but I have some burns on my face and neck that are going to take a few weeks and that I'll have fun explaining to my boyfriend."

"Yeah. Sorry. Where are you staying?"

"They put us up in a hotel," said Susan. "Saved the expense of a slipwalk, since they knew we were going to be here anyway. When are they letting you out?"

"When I can see again. Probably day after tomorrow. Shame about Vasilyev. He seemed like a decent guy."

"Yeah."

"You doing okay, Hippie? I mean, with what happened?"

"Yeah," she said. "Let's just not make a habit of it, okay?"

"I'm good with that."

"All right. So. Theories? Hippie?"

"About what, Don? What happened? Pretty easy, isn't it?"

"Oh? Lay it out for me then."

"Whoever is behind this knows eventually we're going to be on to him, figures we'll pull in Vasilyev—"

"Stop a minute. How does he know about Vasilyev? How does he even know Vasilyev exists, much less what he can do, and that we'd call him in?"

After about ten seconds, Susan said, "They have someone on the inside."

"That's how I read it."

"Damn," said Marci.

"What do we do now?" said Susan.

"Now, Marci and I recover, and we hope no more bodies drop until we're ready."

IIIIIIIIIIIIIIII

This time the pilot wasn't talkative—or else was nervous about having done Matt the favor. They made the trip mostly in silence after the initial, "Hey," and, "How's it going?" At the end, Matt said, "Thanks for the lift," and that was that, and he stepped out onto the field at the Naval Air Station Joint Reserve Base Fort Worth. From there, it was a quick jump to Arlington, and a meeting with Sheila McKenzie. The meeting took place in her basement, surrounded by the various pieces of computer equipment she was putting in, taking out, repairing, or testing.

She got a little nervous when she realized he wanted information and wasn't a potential customer. He put on his best reassuring voice and, when she wasn't interested in drinks, offered her $200. She was reluctant to talk about the Foundation, but he managed to convince her that he knew so much already, there wasn't any harm in it. They settled on $250, and when Matt left he took with him a great deal of advice on virus prevention you could use even if you weren't a sorcerer, and an address in Madrid.

IIIIIIIIIIIIIIII

"I was relieved to hear from you," I told Charlie. "I was afraid we'd be done."

We were in a closed office building in Glendale and I hadn't heard from him in three days. We sat in adjacent stalls in the men's room, and it was only later that I realized how ridiculous it was.

"I am hoping I've bought us some time," he said.

"So we can continue?"

"Yes."

I closed my eyes as, well, emotions hit me. Then I said, "Good."

"I'll leave a bag in this stall, with your hotel info, plane tickets, and the artifact. Still going to New Orleans. I've got all the details written down."

"This one's big. I mean, for me. This is the key."

"For me, too."

"Once this is done, Whittier is open. Defenseless."

"Yes. And we'll have to move fast, before he realizes it."

"That suits me. Sooner the better."

"I know."

"All right. What is the artifact this time?"

"Nasty, Nick. It is very nasty."

"Good," I said.

||||||||||||||||

The first thing Donovan did when he got home was make a Skype call. "Hey, Hippie. Did I interrupt anything?"

"Nope. Did we catch another body?"

"No, just need someone to talk to. About the case, I mean— sorry, not having a personal crisis or anything."

"I know," said Susan. "To have a personal crisis, you need a personal life."

"Yeah."

"I wonder how Marci does it."

"Hate to be cynical, but the over/under on that relationship is six months."

"Yeah. So, anyway, what's up?"

"I've got this thing buzzing around in my head, and it won't settle down. It's one of those nagging, something-is-bugging-me-I-don't-know-what deals."

"I know the feeling. Let's hear it."

Donovan sat back in his chair. Hippie Chick was resting her elbows on her computer desk, hands steepled, listening. "All right," said Donovan. "We've figured there are two people, right?"

"Right."

"One civilian, and one guy supplying artifacts. Call him the supplier."

Skype revealed a smile from her. "If you liked him you'd be more creative."

"True. So, here's the thing. Why isn't the supplier using the things, too? Isn't bringing in another person adding to his risk?"

"Only if he's found. He's trying to insulate himself. You know what he's risking if he gets caught."

"What if he isn't?"

"Hmmm?"

"What if he's already been de-sorcelled?"

"That's not a word."

"Yeah, whatever it is. What if?"

Susan was silent; Skype showed him furrowed brows and a serious look. Finally, she said, "Maybe. That would explain some things. But wait. No."

"Hmmm?"

"If he can't use the artifacts, how can he tell what they are?"

Donovan nodded. "That's it. That's the piece that's bugging me. Good work."

"Answers?"

"Well, the mostly likely is that I'm just wrong about the supplier. If I'm not . . ."

Susan said, "What? If you're not, what?"

"Oh, sorry. If I'm not, it means there's another player. He's working with someone on the inside."

"Our spy."

"Yeah."

"Our spy might be pulling all the strings."

"Yeah, that's what I'm thinking."

"Shit."

||||||||||||||||

I arrived at Louis Armstrong New Orleans International on Frontier Flight 702. It was around four in the afternoon when I arrived at the Ritz-Carlton, right on Canal Street in the French Quarter business district. I wished it weren't in the Quarter itself—if there's anywhere in the world that screams "distractions!" more than that little bit of New Orleans, I don't know it. But it was where I needed to be.

I kept myself in the hotel; I didn't even go out for beignets, which is a major sacrifice once you've had them. But it was a question of focus. I didn't know what had gone wrong, or what Charlie had done to fix it, but it seemed like this would be a really bad time to get sloppy.

I was so close.

Just one more between me and Whittier.

The massive knot of betrayal I felt was all tied in with the rest of it—the sound of the door shutting behind Joan, the pile of un-opened bills on the desk, each one an accusing finger, watching them tow my car away while I imagined all the neighbors shaking their heads, the gradual realization that none of my friends had called in weeks—all of it tied into one lump of hate, with one name behind it. Who would I be when that was gone? Could I go back, start over?

Stop it, Nick. Get your head back in the game.

This would be, according to Charlie, the trickiest of them all, because I had to use two different artifacts: one, as usual, a polished stone, but the other, to be used first, took the form of a pair of cheap sunglasses. I would have to put them on, look at the target, touch the left side, and say, *What time is it?* Then I could use the other in a more usual fashion.

It didn't seem like it would be all that hard, but it was still two things instead of one, and that made me a little nervous.

I napped a little. I was surprised, when I woke up, that I'd managed to fall asleep. I went down and got more coffee, had a bite to eat. It was hard, doing nothing, especially with the Quarter right there, out the door and around a corner. But I was there to do a job, so I just waited.

Finally, around 9:00 PM, I had a light supper and went to the lobby to begin my vigil. I spotted the security camera and made sure I found a place to sit that was beyond its scope, and identified a path out so it wouldn't pick me up when I left after the excitement started. I picked up a magazine and pretended to be reading it as I sat there. What I was actually doing was going over the routine in my head. This one was easier than some, because there were no words to say; I just had to rub the stone briskly with both hands while focusing all of my attention where I wanted it to happen. The stone was a deep blue with hints of red, and unlike the others, it had been carved so facets were showing. As I sat there, I wondered about the person who, so long ago, had shaped it, polished it, and then loaded it with a spell like a bomb, carefully recording—for himself, or another?—how to set it off. Would he approve of how I was using it? Did he hate evil as much as I did, and would he be pleased that his craft was being put to good use? I wanted to think so.

Just after 3:00 AM, Alexander Young, dressed in a Hawaian shirt, shorts, and white loafers, came into the lobby, obviously drunk, which excited no notice on anyone's part.

Not that I had intended to show him mercy anyway, but the white loafers made it easy.

|||||||||||||||||

"It seems, Mr. Longfellow, that our friend has struck again."

"All right, Mr. Becker. What are the details?"

"The victim is Alexander Young, a New York native, on an extended vacation in New Orleans. The exact method is as yet unknown but resulted in Mr. Young burning alive. The time was this morning in the very early hours."

"But, I assume, a connection to the Mystici is known?"

"More than a connection, this time. He was one of their sorcerers, doing much the same thing as your Ms. Sullivan, although they aren't organized the way we are."

"He was good, though?"

"Very. He specialized in defensive and protection spells, against both sorcerous and mundane attacks. Whether that is significant, of course, we do not yet know."

"And yet, they managed to kill him."

"Indeed they did, Mr. Longfellow, unless you want to put an impossible amount of weight on coincidence."

"All right. What else can you tell me about him?"

"Pure mercenary, Mr. Longfellow. He had accumulated immense amounts of wealth, although we don't know how. He lived in New York, but traveled at least half the year. He owned two yachts, though he rarely used them—"

"You know a great deal about this one, Mr. Becker."

"Yes."

"Then perhaps you know this: Is there a connection between him and Mr. Lundgren?"

"In fact, there is, Mr. Longfellow. I was about to mention it. They're friends. They grew up together in Chicago."

"I see."

"And in looking into this, we discovered something else. Mr. Lundgren owns, in secret, considerable interests—especially real estate, in California."

"Let me guess: San Diego area."

"Exactly."

"You'll email me the exact address and so on?"

"I already have, Mr. Longfellow."

"Very well, Mr. Becker. I'll get back to you as soon as I have something to report."

He checked his email, then made the calls, reaching everyone with no trouble. He was pulling things out of the closet when his cell rang.

"Jeffrey, my hero. What's the word?"

"Lots of words, Captain, starting with 'thanks.'"

"You got paid?"

"Yeah, and the check didn't even bounce."

"They sent you a check?"

"No, direct deposit. I sort of meant virtually didn't bounce."

"Yeah. Anyway, glad to hear it."

"You'll like the next bit even more."

"Okay, I'm listening."

"All those names you sent me connect. All of them. Like a chain. Lawton-Smythe to Blum, then Blum to Wright, then Wright to Lundgren."

"What's the timing of the calls?"

"Starting with the one a few months ago, all of them within forty-eight hours."

"No shit?"

"No shit."

"So it's like moving up a ladder or something."

"Exactly."

"That is going to help, man. I don't know how yet, but that's huge. Send me a bill, and look up one more name."

"I will, and what?"

"Alexander Young, two-one-two area code."

"Okay, on it."

"Jeff, you are the best that ever was."

"Fuckin' A right, man."

Donovan disconnected, checked his pockets, locked his apartment, and headed down to the laundry room. Andrea from 204 was there doing laundry, so he had to wait and make pleasant conversation with her for twenty minutes before she wandered off and he could safely use the slipwalk.

IIIIIIIIIIIIIIIII

Marci stood up from her computer and shut it.

"Uh-oh," said Lawrence. "I know that sound."

"What?"

"When you shut the computer that way, you're going to do something mysterious."

She smiled. "You know me too well. You might become a security risk." She wrinkled her nose at him.

"I'm not sure," he said, "that that's funny."

She walked over to stand between him and the basketball game on TV. She leaned over and touched his forehead with hers. "Now you look like a cyclops," she said. "I would never let any harm come to a cyclops."

"You're going to protect me? Jesus. What about my fragile male ego?"

"You're on your own with that." She kissed him and grabbed her coat.

"Going to wear something green?"

"What?"

"Saint Patrick's Day."

"Oh, didn't even think of it. Uh, my coat is kinda greenish, isn't it?"

"Mmmm. I'd call it olive. Hey, Marci?"

"Yes?"

"When you got hurt, you scared the shit out of me."

"I know."

"This thing you do. It's really important?"

"Yes, my love."

"And is it . . . no, never mind. Just, be careful, all right?"

"I will."

She closed the door behind her and wiped her eyes. She went around to the back of the house and let herself into the shed. She took the hand rake and dug into a spot on the dirt floor, pulled back, exposing the trapdoor. She replaced the tool, then went down the door, closing it after her and turning on the light.

She said, "Exterior Seven-three-nine Canal Street, New Orleans, Louisiana, USA," and walked down the stairs.

|||||||||||||||||

Donovan's shoulders were tense. He looked around, and, yeah, so were Marci's. Hippie Chick was fine, but she was a freak. There were a few people in the lobby: a couple having a quiet conversation, a businessman working on a laptop, a little girl who seemed to be waiting for someone, two people in different corners talking on their phones. Nothing indicated that someone had died there earlier that day.

"You're a freak," he told Susan.

She didn't turn around. "Hmmm?"

"Never mind. So, why no crime scene tape?"

"Ruled an accident," said Susan. "This is New Orleans; they want it to go away as fast as possible. Remember Vegas? Look. See where it happened? You can see the scorch marks. But—nothing."

Donovan nodded. She was right, of course. "He ran outside, it seems. There isn't even any smoke damage."

They were getting a few curious looks from people in the lobby, but nothing untoward.

He walked up next to Marci and spoke softly. "Is it possible for you to do your thing less obviously?"

"Um," she said. Then, "Yes, I think so."

"Just, you know, people."

"Right."

She strolled into the middle of the lobby, Susan walking with her as if they were having a conversation. It wasn't a completely convincing performance: Marci's face went slack, and her eyelids drooped. But it was good enough that no one called security.

After a couple of minutes, they strolled back together.

"Okay," she said. "I think I have some of—" Her face changed. "Out," she said. "*Move.*"

She led them, or pulled them, or pushed them not out the door, but farther into the hotel, past the front desk.

Behind them, the lobby exploded.

A second, a minute, a lifetime. Not enough time to do anything, but too much to do nothing. What now? How long has it been? Seconds? Minutes? Heat of the lobby behind him; were those sirens? Call Becker . . . no, no time. Has to happen now. Pull it together, boy. You said you could lead this team, and they trust you. Pull it together. It isn't about the yelling, or the alarms, or the thick, choking smoke behind you, or people streaming out with the is this real? *look even though they can see it is. It isn't about any of that; it's about making the right move and nothing else. Pull it together now.*

Now.

"Marci. Generate some bomb fragments."

"Out of what?"

"Out of thin fucking air. I don't care. Where's the nearest grid? Find it; use it."

Marci said, "Someone just tried to kill us."

"Yeah. I know. I need bomb fragments. Convincing ones. Then you're going to go invisible, and you're going to put them somewhere that—"

"Jesus, Don. You really think we can fool an arson investigator?"

Susan was looking at him: calm, confident. He took a breath. "I think," he told Marci, "that an arson investigator is unlikely to believe in magic if given any alternative at all. Marci, don't argue. This needs to happen now."

She stared at him, then nodded. "I got it covered," she said.

"I know you do."

||||||||||||||||

"I know you do," said Donovan, and turned away and got out his cell phone. He was, no doubt, calling Upstairs, and saying, *Don't worry about it; I have my people on this. We can handle it, no problem.*

Well then, Marci figured, she'd better handle it.

Invisibility was the first step, and the trouble was, casting invisibility didn't come naturally to Marci. Bending light was a pain. Drawing from the grid was easy, but maneuvering the light around her felt like trying to scoop up water in a hand with splayed fingers. She knew others who insisted it was one of the easiest spells, but for her it was slow and laborious—and knowing that she had to hurry didn't make it easier.

There was a line right outside the door, and, thank God, a point less than a hundred feet away. She touched it, caressed it, held it.

In the end, she got about halfway there with the invisibility and decided that was good enough—there was plenty of smoke in the air, and that would do half the job, wouldn't it? And creating a filter for the smoke and holding it in place while creating the fake evidence was going to be a tough juggling act even without the light bending.

Air had a tangibility light did not; that part wasn't hard.

She moved into the area, and discovered there was still fire, or, at any rate, heat; she drew on the grid and pulled some of the smoke around her and made it into insulation—and was hit with a wave of dizziness. She stopped for a moment, let her connection to the grid stabilize. She'd be generating a lot of heat by now, but at least that wouldn't be noticed in all of this.

Where?

Jesus. What did she know about arson investigation? What would they look for? Well, wires and scraps of metal, maybe. Where to put them? She couldn't see well, and the smoke and the light bending she was doing didn't help. But, okay, somewhere around—there. Maybe it wasn't the actual center of the explosion, but it had sure been hit hard.

There was no shortage of carbon all around her, and there

was—*ah, yes!* A hole in the floor had exposed rebar. They'd have to tear the floor up anyway, right? So pull some rebar from a place that wasn't exposed; no one would notice. And she didn't need much. Just touch it, feel roughness—*hot*—and go deep. Deeper—

Flinging whirling speeding, match the motion, match the speed, hello my friends, talk to me come to me whirl differently now just a little and little more molding like wet clay with a form implied by shape, how the lines swirl around you, my friends, and turn turn turn to every atom there is a weight and a form to every molecule under Heaven I cast my loop here and no you haven't changed, not really, heat from my skin a growing hunger but such a little change to steel, and there's copper wire in that wall that they'll have to tear down anyway, shards of metal bits of wire cast around and let go let go before you burn up, the very grid point hot don't need it anymore, walk, you can walk, don't make Susan come in and get you, dammit, just walk—

She stumbled out of the smoke, coughing, into the arms of a bug-eyed monster who turned out to be a fireman. He asked if she was all right, and took her to a truck where they gave her oxygen and wanted to take her to the hospital for evaluation, but no, she was fine, really, just caught a bit of smoke, that's all.

Donovan and Susan were twenty feet away, looking at her. She winked and gave them a thumbs-up. Then a cop came up to her, wanting her name and asking if she was a guest, but she did her *these aren't the droids you're looking for* thing, and she was back with her team.

"You okay?" said Donovan.

"Yeah," she said. And, "I think I got it."

|||||||||||||||||

Donovan didn't let himself start shaking until he was back home and had a drink in his hand. Even then, though, shaking with nervous energy, he held it together; there was something that needed to be done now, because there might not be much time left.

He made another Skype call—one he hadn't made in close to a year. The face came on after about thirty seconds, so tanned he could tell over the distortion, and smiling.

"Hey, Grampa," said Donovan. "How's retirement?"

"Hey, Chump. It's great. I fish, I watch the Buccaneers, and I sleep like a baby."

"And you've grown a beard. Too lazy to shave?"

"Damn right."

"So, you don't miss it?"

"Yeah, I miss it. Every time I go to the bank."

"Check."

"You okay, Chumpy? You don't sound like yourself." The old man seemed to be staring intently at the screen.

"Yeah, had a bit of a rough time, but came through it okay. You know how it goes—you get shaky after you're safe."

Grampa may have nodded. "Got a replacement for me yet?"

"Yeah. A girl named Marci. She's doing good. You'd be proud of her."

The old man smiled wide enough that Donovan could see it. "Bet I would. So, you caught a case?"

"A tough one. Nasty. It's made the news twice."

"Oh?"

"State Senator in California drowning in her swimming pool?"

"Nope, missed that."

"Terrorist bombing at a hotel in New Orleans?"

"Oh! Yeah, I heard about that. Everyone's heard about that."

"Uh-huh."

"I thought they caught the guys who did it."

"They caught bullshit. They picked up two loudmouth skinheads and they're going to pin it on them so they don't have to admit they have no clue."

"We doing anything about that?"

"Not my circus, not my monkeys."

"Seems kinda shitty to just leave them there, Chumpy."

"I don't get to make that call. And, you know, skinheads. I'm not crying with sympathy."

"That's what I don't miss about the job."

"Yeah. So look, I'm kinda stuck. Can I run it down for you? Just give me anything that comes to mind."

"Sure. What's old age for if not dispensing bullshit and calling it wisdom? Let's hear it."

Donovan gave him chapter and verse, including speculation and stray observations. Grampa listened, probably nodding from time to time, until Donovan finished.

"So, that's the story. Anything?"

"Well, it's pretty clear that there's an endgame here. Maybe two different ones."

"Right."

"You're going to have to figure out at least one of them."

"Yep. The question is, how?"

"Okay, Chumpy. I'm gonna get a bit abstract here."

Donovan felt himself grinning. "I'm listening, old man."

"Sometimes the reason you can't make out a shape is that you've got all the lines, but they're blending into the background."

"Yep, you're right. That's pretty abstract. What's the background?"

"The Mystici. All of this is happening around and through them."

"So, you're saying I need to learn more about the Mystici?"

"Yep."

"What exactly do I need to learn?"

"If I knew that, I'd just tell you. But from what you say, that sounds like the thing you're missing."

"So, how do I find out?"

"One thing you've always been good at is irritating people. I don't mean in a bad way, I mean just, you know, staying on them, annoying them until they react. Then you use their reactions. Remember the card cheater in Atlantic City?"

"Yeah. So, your point is?"

"Go bug Upstairs until they tell you the shit they don't think you need to know. That's what you need to know."

Donovan felt himself nodding. "Grampa, you're the best."

"And don't you forget it, Chumpy. You'll let me know how it plays out?"

"Depend on it."

WHAT WE DON'T KNOW . . .

11

This time we did the church confessional again. I was going to say something about repeating tricks to see if I could pull another chuckle out of him, but he said, "There's a problem, Nick."

"Again, or still?"

"I suppose still. I took a shot at the people investigating us and missed."

"Damn."

"Yeah, it's my fault. They keep being a little better than I expect them to be."

"Damn," I said again. "So, what does this mean?"

"I've been honest with you from the start, Nick. What it means is we're going to go ahead, as planned, and just hope we can be done before they catch us."

"All right. I'm good with that."

"You need to know, if you get caught, you're on your own."

"I know that. That became clear sometime around when you told me why you wouldn't let me see your face."

"All right, just so—"

"Charlie, this is it. This is the one. This is the motherfucker who ruined my life."

"I know. He's your reward for everything you've been doing for me, and I owe you that. But I don't want you going in without knowing the risks."

"Yeah, I know the risks."

"Also, well, there was the last attempt. The first time you tried."

"Uh, meaning?"

"Whittier's increased his security, and he now has a bodyguard."

I suddenly felt claustrophobic in the little closet. "Shit," I said.

"Don't panic. It makes things more complicated, and a bit messier, but I still like our chances."

"All right. You have what I need?"

"Of course."

"The son of a bitch will suffer?"

"Yes."

"Good. Charlie, tell me something."

"What do you want to know?"

"When this is over, are you going to kill me?"

There was a pause, then, "Would you care if I did?"

"I don't know."

"That's what I thought. No, Nick. I'm not going to kill you. But there's a fair chance someone else will before this is done, and it's far from impossible that someone will kill me, too."

"Yeah."

"But in the meantime, we're both still alive. So let's get to this, shall we?"

||||||||||||||

Florencia's voice came over the phone's speaker preceded by a harsh buzz. "Mrs. Merriweather is on line one."

Camellia considered not taking the call, then considered making Elsa wait just because, but rejected both thoughts. "Thank you, Florencia," she said, and pushed the button for line 1, and for speaker. "Hello, Elsa. You're on speaker."

"Hello, Camellia. So are you. Is anyone there?"

"No, you?"

"No."

"Maybe our speakers can have lunch together. What's on your mind, Elsa?"

"Are you making any progress on the murders?"

"Elsa! My goodness. This is a first."

"Please, Camellia. Is there progress?"

"Why do you care all of a sudden? What aren't you telling me?"

"You know I can't answer that."

"I know no such thing. Precedent is that you give no information, but precedent is that you don't ask about investigations in progress. I should think they balance out, don't you?"

"Camellia, I've spoken with our financial people. We have decided to increase our contribution to the Foundation by two hundred percent beginning this quarter."

"I see."

"I believe I could make it four hundred percent if I could demonstrate that you are making progress on this case. They consider this important."

Good God. Is she frightened? Yes, she's frightened!

"Are you trying to buy me, Elsa?"

"If you're for sale. Please. I just want a progress report."

"Very well, Camellia. Then I can tell you that we've had a major breakthrough. I can't give you details, because we don't yet know exactly what the ramifications are. But, yes, a big break-through."

"So you think you'll have the affair wrapped up soon?"

"I believe so, yes. Probably within a couple of days."

"Thank you, Camellia."

"No, no," she said. "Thank *you*."

She disconnected, and pulled in all the reports from the Ranch. Then she pushed the intercom button. She started to punch in Becker's number, but stopped, frowned, and tapped her fingers on her desk. Then she pushed the intercom button. "Florencia," she said, "at nine AM according to his local time please get Donovan Longfellow on the line." *And thank you, Elsa, for giving us the major breakthrough.*

||||||||||||||||||

Becker was calling on Skype. *All right, Don-baby. Let's see what we can pry out of this sonofabitch that he doesn't know I'm prying.* He clicked answer and Becker's face filled the screen.

"What did you learn, Mr. Longfellow?"

Donovan said, "That's what I was going to ask you, Mr. Becker."

As usual, Becker either didn't notice the tone or ignored it. "I assume you mean what we've learned from the prisoners?"

"Yes."

"Much the same as those who made the earlier attempts—hired anonymously through email, paid via dead drops."

"But two of these were sorcerers, Mr. Becker."

"This fact had not escaped my notice, Mr. Longfellow."

"There must be records of them."

"No doubt the Mystici have such records. We have requested them, but have received no reply."

Donovan grunted. Becker was, as always, staring right at the screen, his eyes focused just a bit below the camera, so it seemed like he was staring at Donovan's collar. He never moved. "What will happen to them?" asked Donovan.

"The sorcerers will face Sensitivity Removal Protocol; the mercenary will be disciplined."

"Disciplined, Mr. Becker?"

"You have no need to know the details, Mr. Longfellow."

Donovan clenched his fist under the table and attempted to keep his face expressionless, grateful for once for the Skype distortion. "How will the Mystici feel if we do that to two of theirs?"

There was a pause. The area behind Becker was blank, empty, like he'd put up a dark-colored curtain or something just so there'd be nothing to look at. "I do not understand why you're asking that now, Mr. Longfellow. It isn't the first time it has happened."

"It's the first time I've been involved in it. And I want to know how they respond. How do they feel when we do that to one of their people? May I remind you that I'm the one in the field? I'm the one who has to deal with the consequences if something goes wrong."

"Mr. Longfellow, you must understand that we and the Mystici need each other."

"Need each other, Mr. Becker? How is that?"

"I know you were given at least the outline of our history, Mr. Longfellow. They came into being as an over-reaction to a decree by Pope John XXII. We split from them as an under-reaction to Franco. These events defined the organizations. The Mystici now fear doing too much, and we fear doing too little. They need us doing what we do—keeping magic secret. We need them doing what they do—using their resources to increase our understanding of magic and what it can do."

"And do they share these discoveries with us, Mr. Becker? Because it seems to me that we would have to act to keep magic secret whether they chose to cooperate or not, whereas they have no need to give us anything."

Becker actually shifted a little in his chair. Might he be uncomfortable? "It is part of their ethos that they do not interfere with anything their members do, including criminal activity, unless it becomes egregious, by which time it would often be too late. If we didn't exist, they would need to carry this on themselves. So, yes, they share their research results with us, although not always instantly."

"You know a great deal about them, Mr. Becker."

"Yes, I do. It is part of my job to know these things. Now, please fill me in on what you've learned."

Donovan was silent a little longer as he switched gears. Then he said, "They immolated the poor bastard. A fire spell."

"I knew the result. It was a plain and simple fire spell? Nothing deceptive?"

"No. As straightforward as it gets, except that it started with some sort of spell to weaken Young's defenses. He caught fire, screamed, ran outside, and kept running until he died, about thirty yards up the street."

"I see."

"Then they tried to blow us up. Marci caught it just in time or we'd all be dead. Oh, and speaking of Marci, she covered for us. I think we'll get away with it. They've already hung it on a couple of people."

"We have, indeed, gotten away with it. I heard about the explosion, and wondered if it was aimed at you. I've been monitoring the news stations. It's being considered a terrorist attack. Please extend my commendation to her. To your whole team."

"I will, thank you."

"I believe that is all then, Mr. Longfellow."

Donovan caught movement—like Becker might be reaching to disconnect, which would be unlike him. Donovan spoke quickly. "I will have to think about what you've said, and consider if it might have an effect on the investigation."

"I do not see how it could."

"Nor do I, Mr. Becker. But you must admit, it is a great deal of information. I wish I'd had it before."

"There was no need."

"It makes me wonder what else I don't know."

"About the Mystici? A great deal, no doubt."

"Yeah. Hey, tell me one more thing. I understand why they have more people than us—we're a little more selective, and don't recruit as aggressively. But why do they have so much more money than us? If I worked for them I'd be getting more than minimum wage."

"They wouldn't hire you, Mr. Longfellow."

"True."

"And to answer your question, it's because they are willing to do things for money that we are not."

"Like what?"

"They will, on occasion, sell sorcerous services. Not for anything illegal, you understand. But certainly for things that are morally dubious."

"You mean, to people outside of the Mystici? To civilians?"

"Yes, exactly." Then, after a moment, "Mr. Longfellow? Mr. Longfellow, are you still there?"

"Mr. Becker, did you have a good reason for not mentioning this until now?"

"Your pardon, Mr. Longfellow. I don't see what difference it makes."

"It makes all the difference, Mr. Becker. It changes the entire investigation."

"Can you explain?"

"The source of Alexander Young's wealth, Mr. Becker. I had not considered the possibility that he was making a fortune selling protective spells to civilians. That broadens the possibilities for—you know something, Mr. Becker? At this moment, I am not inclined to explain anything to you. I'll get back to you when I have something specific. Good night."

"Mr. Long—"

Donovan closed the call and set himself to invisible, then spent some time cursing softly under his breath. He was still cursing when his phone rang. He looked at the number. He didn't recognize it—it wasn't Becker—but he knew what country code thirty-four meant. "Well," he said to the empty room. "This is bound to be interesting."

|||||||||||||||

Becker frowned when his phone rang. Not many people called him on his personal number, especially during work hours, and none of them had blocked numbers. His first guess was that someone wanted to sell him something, and he considered letting it go to voicemail, but then mentally shrugged and answered the phone. "This is Becker."

"Manuel."

His first impulse was to look around the office to see if he were being watched—absurd. No one would care to whom he was speaking. His next impulse was to disconnect. Before he had time for a third impulse, the voice came from the phone again. "Hello? Manuel? Are you there?"

He swallowed and said, "Yes, I'm here. Hello, Charles."

"It's been a long time. I didn't expect you'd have the same cell number."

It's the only thing I kept. "What's on your mind?"

"Manuel? You sound, ah, different."

Becker suddenly felt hysterical laughter welling up—a feeling he hadn't had in years. *Different? Seriously? Different? Yeah, maybe just a little bit.* The feeling passed as quickly as it rose, like a sudden thunderstorm that leaves everything behind it feeling empty and silent. "How about you?" he said. "How have you been?"

"Keeping busy."

"What are you doing these days?"

"Promise not to laugh?"

"No."

"I own a string of Laundromats in Houston."

Becker didn't feel the urge to laugh, but he smiled and shook his head. "I don't know which is stranger, Charles. The Laundromats, or Texas."

"I know. How the mighty have fallen, right?"

"I guess."

"What are you doing?"

"I work for the Spanish Foundation."

There was a pause, then, "No shit? Do they know about you?"

"Of course," he said, maybe a bit sharply. "I'm working in Investigations and Enforcement, so my history—our history—was actually a bonus."

"Yeah, I guess I can see that. So, is it worse being on the sidelines than it would be to be out of the game entirely?"

"My goodness, Charles. A sports metaphor? You *have* gone Texan."

"I guess I have. There are worse fates. I think."

God. And now I'm just talking to him like, like back before. Is this bad? No, not bad. But strange. "To answer your question, I don't know which is worse."

"Yeah. So how is it? I mean, the Foundation. They keeping you busy?"

"Busy enough, yes.

"That's good."

"How about your Laundromats?"

"I'm up to the point where I can take vacations, which is nice. In fact, that's why I'm calling. I'm on vacation, and suddenly started wishing you were here."

"Oh? Where?"

"Orlando. Disneyland."

"Disneyland, Charles? You? Do you have kids?"

"No kids, just me and a sweet little redhead I'd love for you to meet. Hey, don't knock it. It's pretty cool, actually. Journey into Imagination. It's magic, Manuel."

"Only magic we've got left."

"Yep. Hey, Manuel. We were right, you know."

"I know."

"I wish it had worked. Failing that, I wish we hadn't been busted. But what we were trying to do. We were right."

"I know."

"Man, it's good to hear your voice. You ever get to the States? I'd love to sit down and have a beer with you."

"Yeah, let's do that. I can get some free time. Maybe meet you at Disneyland, and you can show me around."

"I'd love that. Got an email address?"

Becker gave it to him, and said, "Email me, and we'll set something up. But I have to run—work is calling."

"All right, Manuel. I'll be in touch. It was good to hear your voice."

"Yours too, Charles."

Manuel disconnected and frowned at his cell phone. He shook his head. Then he hit a button and said, "Mr. Horowitz? . . .

Would it be possible for you to trace the call that just came in on my personal phone? . . . Thank you. Get back to me when you have something."

Disneyland was in California; Disney *World* was in Orlando. *Charles, my old friend, just what are you up to?*

||||||||||||||||

Donovan stared at the phone. *Yep, that was interesting all right.*

He'd never before spoken to anyone in the Executive Branch, much less with Morgan herself. That, in itself, was interesting and needed thinking about. But first—

The head of the Mystici was scared because Alexander Young had been killed. According to Morgan, Young's death had frightened the person at the top of the largest and most powerful organization of sorcerers in the world.

Alexander Young was more important than they'd realized.

Well, okay. Young was a sorcerer. Specializing in defensive spells. Well, fine. Then . . .

He turned to Skype and made a call.

"Hey, Donny. Another body already?"

"Hey, Marci. No, nothing like that. Is this a good time?"

"For about fifteen minutes until the water boils. What's up?"

"Alexander Young was good at defensive and protection spells. Are there any that would be tied to him personally?"

"What do you mean?"

"Something he casts and then sort of maintains, maybe unconsciously."

"Oh, sure. The ones that are up constantly, the best ones, are like that."

"So, when he died, it might be that a bunch of protection spells went down?"

"Very possible. What are you thinking?"

"I'm thinking if someone high up in the Mystici, I mean, all the way at the top, suddenly became paranoid when Young was killed, we may have a clue about our guy's endgame."

"Oh," said Marci.

"Yeah. Okay, you go back to watching a pot boil. I need to think about this."

"Don't strain anything."

"Heh."

Donovan pressed the hang-up button, then paced around the room for a good half hour. He gave some thought to what it meant if Young had, indeed, been protecting high-ranking members of the Mystici, but he also had to consider the matter of Morgan having called him personally. He looked at that from several angles, but couldn't get away from it: Why do you avoid the proper channels? Because you don't trust the proper channels.

Becker was, at least in Morgan's mind, a suspect. And Morgan knew a great deal more than Donovan did.

He sat down and made another Skype call.

"Mr. Longfellow," said Becker in his usual cool and empty voice. "I'm pleased you called back. I didn't much care for how you ended our last conversation."

"I need the video feed from the hotel lobby."

"I'm not certain we can get that, Mr. Longfellow."

"I am."

"Mr. Longfellow, kindly watch your tone."

Donovan closed his eyes and took a slow breath. "My apologies, Mr. Becker. I was wrong. Mr. Becker, I understand the Foundation was built to preserve secrecy. That secrecy being turned inward has cost several lives, including that of Mr. Vasilyev. And it very nearly cost my team our lives. However, I was wrong to think it was your fault. It's the whole culture of the Foundation.

"But right now, Mr. Becker, we don't have time for that. They took another shot at my team, and they know they've failed. They might put the brakes on, but they might push on to their endgame as fast as they can. If my theories about why Alexander Young was killed are correct, that is exactly what they'll do. We do not have time to play nice, Mr. Becker. So, if you would, please talk to whoever you need to talk to, apply whatever pressure you need to apply, and get me those tapes, all right? Because if this ends up costing one of my people because you refused to get us key information, I'm not going to be at all happy."

There was a pause; then Becker said, "Very well, Mr. Long-fellow. I'll see what I can do," and disconnected.

Well, fuck, thought Donovan. *I think I just might have gotten through to the cold son of a bitch.*

||||||||||||||||

The buzzer went off, which was a sufficiently rare event that it took Donovan a moment to realize what it was. He got up from his breakfast—toast with blackberry marmalade and an orange— and went over to the intercom. He pressed the button and said firmly, "Uh . . . hello?"

"Hey, Laughing Boy. Can you buzz us in?"

Susan? "Us?" *What the—*

"Marci and me."

Um . . . "Sure," he said, and did so.

Five minutes later "they" were at the door. He opened it, and it was, indeed, Susan and Marci. They filed past him, Susan with a small tote bag, Marci with a suitcase. He shut the door behind Marci and began his careful inquiries: "What the fuck?"

"Hey," said Susan. "Do you feel like you're taking your life in your hands every time you get on that elevator?"

"Want to tell me what you two are doing here before nine in the morning?"

Susan shrugged as if it should have been obvious. "We talked it over, and decided we didn't want you to get deaded. So we're here for the duration. Got any coffee?"

Donovan stared at her, then elaborately looked around the apartment. "Just where, exactly?"

"Oh, come on. There's room. For sleeping, two in your bed, one on the couch."

"Seriously? This isn't—"

"It isn't what, Laughing Boy? Your life isn't threatened? All of our lives aren't threatened?"

"Shit. If you were going to do this, we could have done it at your place, which is at least big enough."

"Would you have come?"

"No."

"See?"

"Tell me you didn't both slipwalk here." He looked at their faces. "Shit. Oversight will have my ass. Or, worse, they might have yours. You know they can charge you for an unauthorized slipwalk? They can deduct it from your pay? Unless they get pissed off and kick you out. Jesus. I'm going to have to—"

"Shut the fuck up," said Susan. "Deal with it. This is what we have to do. The bad guys potentially know your address. In any case, they know who you are. You think we're going to let them take a free shot at you if they feel like it?"

"The only one of us who's been specifically targeted is Marci, not me."

"So," said Susan with the air of someone springing a trap. "Want to help us protect her?"

"Ah, shit." And, "Okay. I have one spare blanket, no spare sheets, no spare pillows except the ones on the couch."

"We'll figure it out."

He sighed. "Do you two play Hearts?"

||||||||||||||||

Becker walked down to the Paseo del Prado, to a place beneath the trees just in sight of the museum and out of sight of the Foundation. There he waited as he always waited, not moving, hardly even blinking, as if waiting itself were an activity requiring the most careful concentration.

After a quarter of an hour, an old man walking with the assistance of a black cane approached him.

"Mr. Becker," said the old man. "You haven't changed."

"Nor have you, Mr. Crosheck," Becker lied smoothly.

Crosheck laughed. "I'm not sure what this is about, but I appreciate it. I haven't had an excuse to slipwalk in over a year. I intend to see a bit of Madrid before I go back."

Becker nodded. "Shall we find a place to sit?"

"No, I'd rather stroll."

"As you please. Have you heard from Mr. Longfellow lately?"

"Chumpy? He just called me yesterday for advice on a case. It was flattering. He still calls me Grampa. Why?"

"I'm his handler."

"Yes, I know. That's why I felt comfortable giving him advice on how to handle you."

Becker's smile was quick, more of a formality than an indication of amusement. "Mr. Crosheck, I heard from Charles Leong today."

"Did you really! I take it for the first time in a while?"

"For the first time since our encounter with you, Mr Crosheck."

"We were all a lot younger then, weren't we?" They were walking slowly, and only now turning the corner around the museum. "This way," he said.

"All right."

"So, what did your friend Leong want?"

"I don't know. He lied to me about where he was."

"You're involved in the investigation of murders."

"Yes."

"And this is the moment he calls you out of nowhere."

"Exactly."

"So he's involved."

"It's hard to believe he isn't."

"And the question is, why would he alert you to that?"

Becker nodded.

Crosheck stopped beside a tree, pulled a leaf, held it up to his nose, and inhaled deeply. He closed his eyes, smiled, then let it fall to the ground. They continued walking.

"Why did you want to see me?" asked Crosheck.

"He said something, while we were talking. He said what we'd done was right. And I agreed with him."

"Yes, Mr. Becker?"

"What do you think, Mr. Crosheck?"

"What do I think? If I thought you were doing right, I wouldn't have worked so hard to find you, to catch you, to disable you, to perform what they call the S.R.P. on you. No, Mr. Becker, I do not think you were right. You took lives. And that wasn't the worst of it. You turned a man into a raving lunatic. You drove a woman to suicide. A young man, barely older than a boy, ran off and hasn't been heard of since, and is probably dead. The woman who took her life had a family. Did right?"

"Mr. Crosheck, does it mean nothing to you what those people were doing with their powers? How many people they were hurting? And what we were trying to do, to get the Mystici to use their gifts for something worthwhile? None of this means anything to you?"

Crosheck was quiet for several paces. Then he said, "Magic is an exercise of will."

"I remember, Mr. Crosheck."

"Then you should know that nothing is more vile than removing another's will—then forcing another to do your bidding. Whether that bidding is right or wrong, whether it helps or hurts, it is still wrong; it is a crime."

"We differ in this matter, Mr. Crosheck."

"I know that, Mr. Becker." Then he said, "If it means anything, I respect you."

"It does mean something, Mr. Crosheck. Thank you."

The old man nodded. "It is a terrible thing that I did to you. I think it was right, but that doesn't make it easy to live with. Of all the times I've done that, your and Leong's are the only ones I can't put out of my mind, that I argue with myself about." They walked a little farther. "But we are burning daylight. I think you didn't risk the wrath of the Black Hole to speak of matters of conscience and justice, no matter how important they might seem."

"I'm trying to understand what Charles—Mr. Leong—wanted. Why he called me, cast suspicion on himself."

"What comes to mind is that Chumpy—Mr. Longfellow—said there were two people involved."

"Yes, so he—ah. He is drawing attention to himself in order to draw it away from the other."

Crosheck nodded. "Or perhaps a third."

"A third? What third?"

"I don't know. But you know of two people involved in this. Is there a law that says there can't be more?"

"What you're talking about sounds like conspiracy."

"Is that so impossible?"

Becker considered that; Crosheck remained silent. They turned and began walking back the way they'd come.

"What might be the object of this conspiracy, Mr. Crosheck?"

"How would I know? I'm throwing possibilities out."

Becker smiled a little. "As far as eliminating possibilities, this isn't working as well as it might."

"Best to know them all before you start to eliminate them."

"Mr. Longstreet asked about the possibility that the Mystici have a spy among us."

"What did you say?"

"That it was possible."

"Well?"

"I don't know if they do. If they do, I don't know if the spy would be involved. I hate to waste resources attempting to find a spy for the Mystici if that has nothing to do with the case."

"If I understand correctly, I doubt the Mystici are behind the murders of their own people."

Becker nodded. "You're probably right. I think I won't take the bait. I'll keep Mr. Longfellow on his task, and arrange to meet Mr. Leong, if he actually wants to meet, which at this point I doubt—I suspect I won't hear from him again."

"You think he wanted you searching for a Mystici inside the Foundation?"

"That is my belief. I'll give it more thought. In the meantime, thank you very much, Mr. Crosheck. You've been extremely helpful."

"Entirely my pleasure. I look forward to seeing Madrid."

They walked a little farther, until they had returned to the museum. "I'll leave you here, Mr. Crosheck. I wish you a pleasant day."

"And you."

"Oh, and Mr. Croscheck?"

"Yes?"

"I hope you rot in Hell."

"Yes, Mr. Becker. I know."

Donovan accepted defeat with at least some measure of grace. Susan and Marci were on the couch; he was at the kitchen table, turned away from it, facing them. Donovan didn't have any wine, but Susan seemed happy enough with a beer, and Marci had tea. Donovan studied the condensation on his own beer bottle, and calculated that if they talked about the case they wouldn't have to deal with how the three of them were going to survive in his apartment without murdering one another.

"Here's how I see it," he said. "We have two people, X and Y. The shooter, and the supplier. There's also someone inside the Foundation, who is either a spy or the mastermind."

The others nodded, and waited.

"So we find the shooter, and hope he can lead us to the supplier, and hope the supplier can lead us to the mastermind, if he exists."

"That," said Hippie Chick, "is a lot of hoping."

Marci nodded.

"I know," said Donovan. "So, as long as you're here, see if you can help me figure out something better."

Susan and Marci looked at each other, shrugged, then turned back to Donovan.

"How are we finding the shooter?" Marci wanted to know.

"We have a lot of facts, and more coming from Upstairs. Once we have everything, I'm hoping we can put it all together enough to predict his next target, and be there ahead of him."

"More hope," said Susan.

"Yeah."

"Well," said Marci. "What about the artifacts? You call him the supplier, because he's supplying the artifacts. What if we find him through them? That'd cut out some steps."

"Sure, but how? Vasilyev is dead, and even if he weren't, that would mean waiting for another attack."

Marci looked down at the floor; then she looked up. "Did Becker give you a list of what artifacts are missing?"

"As many as we know."

"Show me."

Donovan turned around, opened up his laptop, and waited for it to come out of "sleep" mode. Then he brought up the file. Marci got up and read over his shoulder. Her hair smelled like cucumbers, which Donovan thought was pleasant but kind of weird.

"There," said Marci. "In the bottom right. 'A:ph.'"

"Yeah," said Donovan. "What does it mean?"

"When we'd get memos from the kiddie pool, they'd say: 'T' and a colon and two initials."

"T for Recruitment and Training," said Donovan, "and the initials of whoever wrote the memo."

Marci nodded. "The A means Artifacts and Enchantments."

"So who is 'ph'?"

"I don't know. Let's find out."

"We can do that. But what will it give us?"

Marci said, "What was the Burrow looking for?"

"The artifacts," said Donovan. "What they did, how to trigger them."

"Right. What they were not looking for is how they went missing in the first place."

"Yeah," said Donovan. "I figure the PO-lice are on that."

"But that's what we need to know. If we can trace the actual theft—"

"But how—oh. Damn, girl. Nice. I should have been on that."

"Call Becker. Find out who 'ph' is."

"No and yes, in that order. I don't want to talk to Becker about this. The bad guys have somebody on the inside."

"You think it's Becker?"

"Are you sure it isn't?"

"Then," said Susan, "do have another way to find out who 'ph' is?"

"Yeah. You guys wait here. Make yourselves comfortable; figure out how we're going to survive here. I'm going to make a lightning trip to Spain. If I don't get anything, maybe I'll find Fenwood from Oversight and punch him in the mouth just on general principle."

||||||||||||||||

It was a perfectly perfect day when Donovan stepped away from a perfectly perfect tree on a perfectly perfect tree-lined boulevard that would have been more at home in a romance novel than a major European city. Donovan only gave it the most cursory look, however, as he recovered his footing and looked around for the address.

Right across the street, of course. It was a big, off-white building full of shops on the lowest floor and manikins wearing elaborate

Renaissance garb on the second. Donovan found the proper door and went straight back.

A cheery receptionist met Donovan as he entered and said something with an upside-down question mark at the beginning.

"No habla español," he managed. "¿Habla inglés?"

"Of course, sir," said the young man in an accent that made Donovan think of West Virginia. "How may I help you?"

"My name is Donovan Longfellow, and I need to make a pickup in the receiving department."

The young man continued smiling. "I assume you mean the shipping department?"

"Usually, that's where it would be. But this is a special case."

The young man lost his smile and nodded abruptly. "How can the Foundation help you, Mr. Longfellow?"

"Where is the Twelfth Floor?"

"On the tenth floor."

Donovan kept his face straight and nodded. "Could you please tell them that I'm on my way up, and would like to see Ms. Morgan? Tell her it's . . . um, shit. What's the damn code?"

"Sir?"

"Tell her I love doing nothing."

"Sir? I don't—"

"Goddammit. Just tell her it's urgent. I've just slipwalked from New Jersey, where I work on the Ranch, and I know what Oversight is going to say about that, and I don't care. I need to see her. Can you tell her that?"

He nodded. "Go on up, sir, and speak with the receptionist. Mr. Longfellow, was it? I'll relay the message."

Donovan took the elevator to 10, stepped off, walked up to the nearest desk, and read the plaque. "Ms. Trujillo?"

She nodded and addressed him in mildly accented English. "You must be Mr. Longfellow."

"Yes, ma'am."

"Please go on back. It is left behind my desk, at the very end of the hall. There is no need to knock."

"Thank you, ma'am."

A minute later, he stood before the organizational summit of the Foundation. The office was huge and floor to ceiling window, with rows of plants set to catch the sunlight as it moved around. The desk wouldn't have fit into Donovan's apartment. A shelf held Japanese vases and Victorian dolls. Donovan wondered if she used magic to keep the sun's glare off her computer. She, herself, was between fifty-two and fifty-five, didn't care that her hair was streaked with gray, and she kept it short. Her clothing was business casual, not designer, but elegant. She favored violet, which matched either her eyes or the color of her contact lenses. She wore a gold necklace with a modest ruby set in it, and no rings. There were no pictures on her desk.

He said, "Ms. Morgan—"

She interrupted. "Camellia. Does Mr. Becker know you're here?"

"No."

Morgan nodded. "In that case, Mr. Longfellow, you'd better close the door."

"Donovan, then," he said, and closed the door, and sat down.

"So, Donovan. What can I do for you?"

"There's a memo from the Bu—from Artifacts. It was signed 'ph.' I'd like to know who 'ph' is."

"Why?"

"Because he or she may have information that will aid our investigation."

"What information exactly?"

"If I knew I wouldn't need to ask."

"Are you keeping secrets from me, Mr. Longfellow?"

"It seems to be the official Foundation pastime. I thought maybe I'd play, too."

Morgan considered for a moment, then nodded. "You are asking for information pursuant to your investigation."

"Yes."

"And you do not wish to reveal details, because you are uncertain about who might learn what, and what that person might do with the information, and you're afraid there may be an information leak."

"Yes."

"Is there any part of this you're comfortable telling me?"

"I intend to find everyone involved in this, and what their plan is, and thwart it."

"Thwart it."

"Yes."

Morgan nodded. "Her name is Peggy Hanson. I'll have the Burrow send her up and meet you in the conference room. Ms. Trujillo will point it out to you."

"Thank you."

"And Donovan."

"Yes?"

"Good hunting."

Donovan nodded and stood up.

By the time he'd gotten directions to the conference room and followed them, there was already a woman there, looking wide-eyed and young, fat, pretty, no makeup. She was wearing blue jeans and a brown button-up sweater, and Donovan was pretty sure she was wishing she'd worn something more businessy.

"Peggy Hanson?" he said from the doorway.

She nodded.

"Do you speak English?"

She nodded again.

"I'm Donovan Longfellow. Can we talk for a minute?"

She nodded a third time. She looked like she wished she had a purse so she could clutch it. *Jesus. What did they tell people about I and E? Or was it a race thing?* I assure you, Ms. Hanson, I hardly ever eat white people. *No, probably wouldn't hit the right note.*

Donovan closed the door and sat at the head of the table, Hanson on his immediate left. He said, "May I call you Peggy?"

She nodded a fourth time. Maybe she had a stutter.

"Thanks. Then call me Donovan."

"Am I in trouble?" Her voice came out like a squeak.

"Huh, what? No. Not at all."

She relaxed a little, but it seemed like she wasn't entirely sure she believed him.

"We're trying to get information on the missing Turkish artifacts."

"I've told Mr. Becker everything I found out!"

Donovan tried smiling again. "There is a man named Charles out there, Peggy. He's responsible for the death of one of our people, as well as several others. I'm pretty sure he's the one who stole the artifacts."

"You think that I—"

"Stop it, Peggy. I think you are completely honest. I think you are utterly loyal to the Foundation. I think you're very good at your job. I think you might know things you don't know you know. I think I want to ask you questions. I think if you sit there scared as hell, you aren't going to think clearly, and I need you to think clearly. Should I take you out for a drink? This is Spain, so they have good sangria here, right? I love sangria. I'm trying to figure out how to relax you, Peggy. I don't intend to hurt you, scold you, or even give anyone a report that will turn into a bad review. I just want to have a conversation. I want you to take me through the investigation, so I can figure out if there might be something in it that will help me. Okay?

"Why don't you stand up, take a walk around the building, breathe some fresh air, tell me a funny story about your cat, and—"

"How do you know I have a cat?"

"Please, Peggy."

"All right, Mr.—Donovan. All right, Donovan. Ask your questions. I'll do my best."

Donovan smiled again. "Now we're talking."

IIIIIIIIIIIIII

Donovan left Peggy Hanson in a better mood than he found her in at least. He left the executive wing and took the elevator down to 2, stepped off, and followed the signs to Budget and Oversight. He gave the receptionist his friendliest smile.

"Hello," he said. "Do you speak English?"

The nice young man shook his head and gave Donovan an apologetic smile. "Deutsch?" he asked.

"Señor Fenwood?" said Donovan.

The man nodded enthusiastically, and held up a finger. Then picked up his phone, pushed a button, and spoke in Spanish for a moment. Then he hung up the phone, smiled, and pointed to a chair. This part of the building was all actual offices instead of cubicles, and the chairs in the waiting area were comfortable. The first two magazines on the table were in Spanish—one showed someone's hands on a piano; the other depicted a woman in a short black dress holding a champagne glass and looking seductively into the camera. Donovan checked the picture carefully for clues. He was still doing so when he caught movement, and looked up to see Fenwood staring at him.

Donovan stood up. Fenwood took a step backward.

"Jesus," said Donovan. "Don't they feed you here? What do you weigh, twenty-five pounds?"

"Please, Mr. Long—"

"Oh, stop it. I didn't come here to punch you out. Though I can't deny the thought's crossed my mind."

Fenwood stopped backing up, but he still looked ready to bolt. "Then how can I help you, Mr. Longfellow?"

"Can we go back to your office?"

Fenwood hesitated.

"I promise," said Donovan, "that if I decide to kick your ass I'll bring you here first."

For some reason, that worked—Fenwood led him back. Fenwood's office wasn't in a corner, thought Donovan with a certain reprehensible pleasure. The desk was placed so there would be no view out the window. There were a few pictures on it next to the computer, but Donovan couldn't see what they were. There was a small bookcase beneath the window. The lower shelf had a few computer manuals, the middle shelf accounting books, and along the top were four intricate, detailed model eighteenth- or nineteenth-century sailing ships. There were two plain chairs facing the desk; behind it was an office chair that cost as much as Donovan's stipend for six months.

"Mind if I sit down in one of your guest chairs?" said Donovan. "You can go ahead and sit in your own very comfortable chair."

They sat down. Being in the chair seemed to restore some of Fenwood's confidence. "Well, Mr. Longfellow? How may I help you?"

I should have taken the desk chair. "It's pretty simple. I want you to do some checking within the Foundation."

"In the first place, you do not have the right to ask me for an investigation of any sort. In the second—"

"Oh yes. And keep it secret."

"Mr. Longf—"

"I'm hoping to find the source of a financial leak within the Foundation."

"Financial leak? There's no—"

"And I'm sincerely hoping it doesn't turn out to be you, on account of how well we get along. So can you check that for me?"

Fenwood's mouth opened and closed; then he said, "There is no way for any money to be 'leaked' from the Foundation, Mr. Longstreet. We have a series of checks and balances in place to verify the accounting. Any discrepancy would alert Ms. Molina, the department manager."

"And it's foolproof? There's no way some accounting expert and computer genius could fool your system into thinking everything balanced?"

"No, there isn't."

"You understand, by saying that, you're casting suspicion on Ms. Molina."

"That's absurd!"

"Well, the money's missing." *Or, at any rate, it's possible that there's some money missing.* "Suppose some computer wizard found a way to prevent the alarm from being given?"

"We check it manually twice a year."

"How long since the last check?"

"January."

"Check it now." Fenwood started to speak. "Please," Donovan added.

Fenwood sniffed and began working on his computer, using his mouse and typing occasionally. After about five minutes, his eyes grew wide. He looked up at Donovan and said, "Oh my God."

"How much?"

Fenwood stared at him, horrified. "Ninety-two thousand, four hundred, and fifty-five dollars and sixty-four cents," he said.

Donovan nodded. "Check into it, will you? And for now, keep this just between us."

"If I discover something like this, I'm supposed to—"

Donovan stood up, leaned over the desk, and dropped his voice. "Do this for me, Mr. Fenwood. Please?"

Fenwood hesitated, then nodded.

"Good man," said Donovan. He straightened up. "I'll be in touch."

||||||||||||||||

Susan had had another beer, and Marci another cup of tea. Marci had taken her shoes off and her feet were on the couch; Susan was lounging facing her. Donovan wished very much he could have listened to their conversation while he was gone, but there was no point in even asking.

"Did you get anything?" said Marci.

"Yeah. The name of the researcher is Peggy Hanson. I told her that we needed to find the supplier—the one who stole the crate of artifacts—so if we could figure out how it had happened, that it might give us a clue. There was a bit of back-and-forth, but in the end, we agreed that most likely the supplier had known about the cache of artifacts before it was sent, and made arrangements to have it vanish during shipping. So, how do you learn about the existence of artifacts just as they're being dug up? I asked how Peggy found out about the cache. That turned out to be a mistake. She told me. In detail. I was afraid I wasn't going to get out of there with my sanity."

"What sanity?" said Marci.

"Remember when you called me sir? What was that, two weeks ago?"

"I was a lot younger then."

"Yeah. Anyway, then I asked her how someone who hadn't known about it in advance would have learned of it, and that made her get all sorts of funny looks on her face. I'm going to have a beer. Anyone else? No? Okay."

He got one, opened it, sat down again in his desk chair, back to the kitchen table. "So, she said it had to have come from whatever archaeological dig unearthed the stuff in the first place."

"How?" said Marci. "Does the Mystici have the manpower to watch every dig going on everywhere, just in case something magical shows up?"

"No," said Donovan. "And whoever our mastermind is, he or she has even less manpower. So that isn't what happened."

"Oh," said Marci. "Good then. Uh, is there a spell that can do that? I've never heard of such a thing."

"That's just what I asked. Neither had she. I mean, she thought it would be great if it existed, and I could just see her wishing she had the ability to, like, go find magical artifacts. But, you know, when they're buried somewhere, they're just there. Buried. They don't give off a signal or anything like that."

Donovan looked at Susan, who gave him a *why are you looking at me?* look. He took a long pull of his beer and wiped his mouth with the back of his hand. "We knew the supplier was working with someone inside the Mystici, the Foundation, or both. I was betting on the Foundation, so I checked it out. And yeah, someone is siphoning funds out of the Foundation. That is not only evil in that it furthers their dastardly scheme or some shit, but more important, it puts our wages at risk, so, you know, now there's no fucking around. But anyway, I'm getting ahead of myself. Point is, there's someone on the inside. That's confirmed."

Marci shifted, putting her feet on the floor and leaning

forward. "I believe that," she said. "But that doesn't tell us how they got hold of the artifacts, or get us closer to finding him."

"Right. But keep that in mind. We know that the leak didn't come from the Burrow, because the Burrow didn't start looking into it until the artifacts were in use already. So if you want to steal magical artifacts, the first thing you need is to know they exist. How would someone find that out, other than the way the Burrow does it, which is a cross between happenstance and meticulous detective work. So I asked her to go over for me what happens on a dig."

Donovan stopped and pulled out a small notebook, consulted it. "I took notes." He cleared his throat. "So, archaeologists pick a site based on various methods—someone finds something and says, 'Hey, I found this in this-and-such spot,' or maybe there's a historical record of a city having once been in a certain location, or it's an obvious continuation of some previous dig, or it's a great place to put a city, or sometimes they even follow up on folktales.

"A team shows up and lays down a grid on the site. They go over the top level, picking up any obvious things, dating them if it's easy to do, and bagging and tagging them just like a crime scene. Then they gradually go deeper, keeping track of what layer things are found at. They keep careful notes, including who is on the site, weather conditions when things were found, and tons of other things. And it was right about then that Peggy sort of choked, stopped talking, and said, 'Hey, is there a magic spell that can read a book someone else has?'"

Donovan stopped and waited.

Marci said, "Well, I mean, it's possible, isn't it? There are clairvoyance spells, and spells for preventing clairvoyance, and it's a whole thing. Not something I ever got good at, because it involves manipulating light, and I . . . oh, wait. I see where you're going."

Donovan nodded. "The first possibility of discovering a magical artifact, if you aren't actually on the site, would come from reading the notebooks."

"I don't get it," said Susan. "How do you go from 'I found a really old coin' to 'wowie zowie there's magic here'?"

"Thanks for asking that. I feel better. When I asked Peggy, she looked at me like I was an idiot. Then she had to back up and explain things to me in the same tone I used when my niece asked me why people have to go to work. They don't go to these sites blind. I mean, they know something when they walk in, right? About the culture, the language, what they ate, that stuff. So, Marci, you do enchantments, right? I mean, you recharged my knotnots."

"I know the basics, sure."

"If I said, 'Hey, I need a device with a water-walking spell,' what would you put it on?"

"I don't know. Something easy to carry around, something that won't attract a lot of attention, but that also stands out. I mean, you don't put a spell on a quarter, because then you're digging in your pocket trying to figure out which quarter the spell is on, right?"

Susan nodded.

"Yep," said Donovan. "And that's how it was found."

"Um, explain?"

"If you know the culture, and you can read the journals, you identify things that stand out, that don't belong. Not 'don't belong' in the sense that would attract the tabloids—all things that are part of the culture. But odd. You know, just a little bit weird."

"Like," said Marci, "why are there a bunch of polished rocks here?"

"Yeah," said Donovan. "Like that. Some archaeologist writes in his notebook: 'Why are there a bunch of polished rocks here?'

Our guy reads the notebook, does some checking with folklore or his own records, and there we are. From there, he starts figuring out how to steal it."

Susan nodded. "Okay, I get it. How does that get us closer to the supplier?"

In answer, Donovan turned to his computer, brought up Skype, and placed a call.

Becker came on at once. "Mr. Longfellow," he said. "How can I assist you?"

"How are we doing on those security tapes?"

"There's been progress, Mr. Becker. I hope to have them soon."

"All right. There's something else. Do you know of anyone in the Foundation who is skilled at clairvoyance?"

"Several, Mr. Longfellow. Can you be more specific?"

"Someone who could find a notebook and read it, given a general location."

"And read it, Mr. Longfellow? From my understanding of sorcery, that would take a great deal of skill."

"That is my understanding as well. Can you find such a person?"

"I believe so. Yes."

"Then I suggest you speak with this person, or these people, and ask where we might find a criminal mastermind."

"I see. Can you give me the background?"

"It would take a long time, Mr. Becker. I'd rather we just got on with it, if it's all the same to you."

Becker looked away from the screen. Then he looked back and said, "I'll get back to you, Mr. Longfellow."

"I look forward to it, Mr. Becker."

Donovan disconnected.

"Security tapes?" said Susan.

"I'll explain when we have them."

"I thought you didn't trust Becker."

"I don't. I don't trust anyone who isn't in this room. But he's going to have to either answer the question, or identify himself as working against us."

Marci nodded.

"Got it," said Susan. "So, what do we do in the meantime?"

Donovan sighed. "I guess we figure out how to get you two settled in."

||||||||||||||||

Recruitment and Training made up the third floor. Recruitment was a small part of it—one corner containing the cubicle of the recruiter for the Mediterranean Region, another for the head of R & T, and a few desks for clerical staff. Manuel Becker walked up to the cubicle of the department head because he liked to do things in person when possible.

William Faucheux looked up, and said, "Mr. Becker. May I help you with something?"

"I need to borrow a pair of sorcerers, Mr. Faucheux. Whoever you have with the capability of subduing a hostile."

"Can you give me any more details? That is, if I know the exact nature of the probable resistance, I can be more precise."

"I'm afraid not, Mr. Faucheux."

"All right." Faucheux picked up his phone and pushed a number. "Doris? William. Please release Melissa and Heinrich and ask them to meet Mr. Becker by the elevator. Tell them this is not a training exercise, and that it is possible their skills will be needed. Mr. Becker will explain more." He disconnected, and nodded to Becker. "They are the best of the current class," he said.

"Thank you, Mr. Faucheux," said Becker, and headed back to the elevators.

The students looked nervous and excited; Becker approved. "You will follow me," he explained. "We are going to make an arrest. If there is any resistance, you will subdue the individual, but not harm him. Under no circumstances will you render him unable to speak. We will bring him to the basement holding cells with as little disturbance as possible under the circumstances. If he does resist, I do not know what form the resistance will take, so be ready for sorcerous or physical attacks. I repeat, subdue, do not harm. Is that clear?"

They nodded.

"Then let's go."

They went up the elevator to 6. The Research and Development department looked like a library, like a warehouse, like a mad scientist's laboratory, like the house of a pack rat. People—researchers—were scattered randomly about the floor, which was undivided by anything except support pillars and one cubicle in a far corner.

Becker walked toward the cubicle, Melissa and Heinrich flanking him, and looking around. Partway there, Becker stopped in front of a table behind which stood two men, one watching a computer screen, the other passing his hands over a thin piece of stained glass. There were a pair of wires leading from the glass into a USB port of the computer. "All right," said one. "Anything now?"

Becker said, "Christopher McCaan?"

The one who'd spoken looked up. "Yes, that's me. If you'd just give me a sec—"

"I'm Manuel Becker from Investigations and Enforcement. Please step away from the table and come with me."

"Huh, what?" The man looked surprised, and not in the least guilty. "What's this about?"

"Just some questions."

"Uh, all right. Can I finish—"

"No. Please step away from the table."

"Jesus! All right! Where are we going, anyway?"

Melissa and Heinrich fell in next to McCaan. Becker turned and headed back to the elevators.

|||||||||||||||||

From Dallas to Aviano Air Base in Italy, and then the train to Madrid. Matt decided he liked train travel. He thought about bumming around Europe taking trains everywhere, and it didn't seem too bad, what with one thing and another. The few words of Farsi he had didn't help any, and it was amazing how little he remembered of the Spanish he'd had in school. Three years of it, but anything beyond "Good day, mister" defeated him. He wondered what he'd do at night.

When he reached Madrid, he found a phrase book, and was able to memorize the most important phrase: "No hablo español. Soy canadiense." Fortunately, no one demanded he speak French and people were happy to direct him to a hotel where he was assured they spoke English.

They did. He took a room, ate a meal, and got some sleep. The next morning, the concierge, who spoke better English than Matt did, was happy to not only direct him to the Paseo del Prado but also compliment him on his choice of tourist destinations, waxing eloquent about its beauty. Then the concierge secured him a cab, sending him away happily.

At 9:00 AM local time, he stood opposite the headquarters of the Spanish Foundation and considered his next move.

|||||||||||||||||

It wasn't as bad as Donovan had been afraid it would be, at least for the first day. Susan ran out and picked up a couple of cheap pillows and a sheet and some extra food, and the whole thing crazily reminded Donovan of when he'd had sleepovers with his brother and cousins and blankets and a flashlight.

A couple of hours later, Becker called on the phone, meaning he'd called from home. "Mr. Becker," said Donovan. "Good to hear from you. Did you find the clairvoyant?"

"We did, and we've questioned him."

"And is he still in one piece, Mr. Becker?"

"He was very cooperative, Mr. Longfellow. There was no need for enhanced interrogation of any sort. Apparently he's a dupe, not conspirator."

"Go on, Mr. Becker."

"He did, indeed, spend occasional evenings over the past year reading archaeologists' journals, looking for potential artifacts, and reporting them."

"Who'd he report to?"

"He thought he was reporting to someone at Artifacts and Enchantments."

"But?"

"He was not."

"How did it work?"

"He sent it to an email address. It looked right—it was to our own server. He had no reason to believe it was going to anyone outside."

"Which means," said Donovan, "that someone inside had to set up the email address, right?"

"Yes."

"It also means—okay, I don't—" His uncle had given him the basics of this, but it was years out of date, and he'd never used it. "He has to, I mean, his computer has to do a thingie where it requests that email, right? So while he's requesting it—"

"Yes, Mr. Longfellow. I spoke with our computer people here.

A 'script,' as she called it, was put, or set, or started, to detect when our query checked his email."

"And?"

"Now we wait until he downloads his email again."

"Do we have any idea of when that might be?"

"In the past, he has connected over the weekend, presumably because there are fewer people here."

"And today is Thursday."

"Here it is the very early hours of Friday."

"All right. So, we're waiting. Is that what you called about?"

"No. I've acquired your security information. I've just emailed it to you."

"Thank you, Mr. Becker. Get some sleep."

"Yes, Mr. Longfellow. Thank you. I shall."

Donovan checked his email, and there was one from Becker. It had "security feed" as the subject line and just a URL for the body. Donovan said, "If anyone is interested in watching with me, I've got the tapes from the hotel lobby."

"Tapes?" said Marci.

"I don't mean *tapes* tapes. I mean a video feed, from the hotel."

"Oh," said Susan, getting up from the couch and hovering over him. "What for?"

"Identifying the guy who immolated Alexander Young."

"You think," said Susan, "you'll see him cast the spell?"

"Probably not, but it's possible. This is the first killing at a place with a security feed; it'd be stupid not to watch it. Worst case, I get something I can use next time."

Marci said, "Just seeing someone walk through the lobby from a grainy security feed, you think you'll recognize him later?"

"Uh, how do you do. I'm Donovan."

"All right."

They both hovered around him as he started running the feed

from a point eight hours before the killing, and fast-forwarding past parts where the lobby was empty.

An hour and ten minutes later, he stopped it and said, "Son of a bitch."

"What?" said Susan.

"That's him."

"Huh? Where?"

There were three people on the screen at this point, two of whom had their faces toward the camera. Donovan tapped one with his finger.

"Him?" said Susan. "He looks like a salesman who doesn't work out enough."

"Yeah, but that's our guy."

"How do you know?"

"I recognize him."

"From where?"

"He was in the restaurant in Chicago at the same time we were. He was in the booth next to the door, hunched over, drinking water and ignoring his coffee. Shit. He was shaken. I should have put it together. We could have had him right there."

"Are you sure?" said Marci. "How could you be that sure from just one glimpse?"

Donovan turned and looked at her. "In the booth behind him were a mother and daughter, white, midfifties and midtwenties respectively. The daughter worked around there; the mother was visiting from out of town, somewhere warm. At the table next to them was a guy reading the sports section. Black, midforties, corporate lawyer. At the next booth—"

"Okay, I get it."

Donovan turned back to the screen. "Son of a bitch," he said again.

"Well, all right, then," said Susan. "We have a face. Do we have any way to go from a face to a name?"

"There's Google face recognition," said Marci.

"I've heard of all sorts of government agencies that have more sophisticated versions," said Donovan. "But I don't know any way to get access to those."

"You could ask Upstairs," said Susan.

Donovan nodded. "They've all gone home now, but I'll do that first thing tomorrow. Worst that'll happen is they'll say no. In the meantime, Marci, try the Google thing."

||||||||||||||||||

Once upon a time there was a woman named Shveta Tyaga. Some would have said she was born a *Shudra* to very devout but poor farmers; others would dispute this, denying the validity of the term *Shudra* in her region of Tamil Nadu, if not in the entire subcontinent. That her family were farmers, and poor, and devout could not, in any case, be denied.

She discovered her sorcerous abilities at the age of twelve, when she found a small sample of *Combretum ovalifolium*, which her mother called the Heartflower, and Shveta wanted it to grow quickly, and it did—it grew from a seedling to a fully formed plant in under a minute. She tried it again, and it worked again.

She thought this was delightful, and wondered what else she could do.

She didn't *discover* the grid lines, the grid points; she simply became aware of her knowledge of them, as if it were something she'd known all along. Her ability to reach out to them, connect, use them, was remarkable, though certainly not unprecedented.

Throughout history, there have been those who had special, unusual, or unique talents; there have also been those who have been able to harness the energy of the grid and shape it to their will without training. Perhaps the latter is an example of the former. In any case, Shveta was one of these. In essence, she taught herself magic, learning certain limited but useful spells, mostly associated with growing things. Within a couple of years, her family, though not wealthy, could no longer be called poor. She kept her abilities a secret until her sixteenth year, when she was drawn to a node a few miles due east of Keelakunupatti. She left her home after dark, walking miles and miles until she reached it, and she was thus found by the subcontinent recruiter for the Roma Vindices Mystici.

For the first two years of her training, she amazed her instructors, who soon wondered if they'd be able to keep up with her, much less continue to teach her. It seemed she instantly mastered everything she attempted—defensive spells, observation spells, and especially attack spells. She could use magic to kill someone in 109 different ways—although, to be fair, more than half of those were either pointless or silly. Causing someone's blood vessels to burst doesn't much matter when you've had to boil the individual's blood to accomplish it, and puncturing someone's brain with his own hair is actually not all that painful and a considerable waste of energy.

In any case, she stayed with her lessons for two years, growing in ability and control and knowledge. She couldn't do everything—no one can—but those things she could do she could do very well.

Some said the trouble was that it had taken so long to find her; by the time the Mystici began her training, she had acquired the habit of independence, which naturally led to a resentment of authority.

Whatever the reason, she walked away from the Mystici at the age of nineteen, afterward traceable only by effect: an abusive wealthy husband robbed and murdered, a slumlord robbed and murdered, a brutal pimp robbed and murdered. See the pattern? Bad person with money becomes a dead person, and the money goes into Shveta's pocket.

Shveta's parents had been poor, and she didn't care for it. But it had always been important to them that she be a good person, and that, too, was ingrained.

She didn't kill often—every year or so. And then she'd live on the proceeds as long as she could. This made her very hard to find, for those who objected to her activities, and for those who might want to find her for other reasons.

Hard, but not impossible.

"Good morning, Shveta. Sorry to bother you so early."

"Hello, dear. What is it?"

"I need a favor."

"For you, anything. Almost anything. Some things."

"Would you mind heading to the States? I think our guy there may need some help."

"Um. I'm kind of involved in this thing in Warsaw. Remember? You wanted me to do it?"

"I know. But this trumps everything else. It's important. Please."

"All right. For you, this is one of the things."

"Thanks, sweetie. I'm emailing the details . . . now."

ASSUMPTIONS AND GUESSWORK

13

There was a long hallway with nothing off to the sides, then a desk, a man behind the desk, and an elevator behind the man. He was a young man, neat, looked like a business major. There was nothing on the desk except a computer and a telephone; Matt hoped he had some good solitaire games on the computer.

Matt approached the desk, smiled, and said, "Do you speak English, by chance?"

"Why, yes, sir. How may I help you?"

"I'd like to speak with Mr. Becker, please?"

Matt was watching for any change of expression; he saw none. "I'm sorry, I do not recognize that name."

"Um, is there a building directory?"

"Sir, I'm afraid this is a small set of private offices and apartments; we have no directory."

"I see. May I speak with anyone in the Spanish Foundation?"

The man never lost his smile, but he shook his head. "Are you certain you have the right address, sir?"

Matt knew when the best move was to husband his forces for

another attack. He matched the young man's smile and said, "Perhaps not. I'll go check. Thank you."

"You're very welcome, sir."

Matt went back out and across the street to sit on a bench, consider matters, and give the Spanish Foundation time to have a good look at him if they wanted to.

||||||||||||||||||

Donovan woke up next to Susan, who must have climbed in after he'd fallen asleep. He looked at her and shook his head, muttered, "Dayam," and got up. Marci was already at the computer. It was a little annoying to be unable to check his email, but he never got anything interesting anyway. And the smell of already-made coffee made up for it.

He threw on a robe and stumbled toward the bathroom, now overflowing with toiletry kits. The bathroom seemed a lot more cramped than it had yesterday. Go figure. Shaved, showered, dressed, and set for the day, he made straight for the coffeemaker, took some.

"I decided," said Susan, "that if we didn't leave you any coffee you couldn't be blamed for what happened."

"You are a good human being," said Donovan as she headed toward the bathroom. "I don't care what Marci says."

Marci turned and gave him a look, then went back to the computer. Donovan drank his coffee and made another pot. Once Susan was back, he came up behind Marci and looked over her shoulder. "What are you working on?"

"Since you were sleeping, I went ahead and called Mr. Becker and asked him about running the picture."

"Damn. Initiative and everything. Well done. First time talking to Becker?"

"No, no. We met in Spain, after the, after Chicago."

"Oh, right. What'd you think of him?"

"He's creepy."

"Yeah. What did he say?"

"He said yes, but they didn't get any more than we did last night. They ran the face through Interpol, and at least some of the Homeland Security files, and came up blank. So I've been organizing notes since then."

"So," said Donovan, "if his face didn't pop, we know that he doesn't have a criminal record. Or, at least, not for a major crime. He's not on a no-fly list, and probably no felony convictions. I don't think we can conclude more than that. So what else do we know?"

Marci looked at her list. "We know his motivation."

Susan, who had been pulling out eggs and bowls and milk, looked at her. "That's news to me," she said. "Okay, what is it?"

Marci looked mildly startled, as if she were being asked to explain how she knew when she was walking uphill. "Revenge," she said.

"For what?"

"I don't know," she said, frowning. "How could I know that?"

"Well," said Susan, "how do you know it's revenge?"

"Well, because. How he's been killing people."

"Uh. I'm not getting it."

Marci looked at Donovan, as if explaining the obvious was beyond her. Donovan nodded and turned to Susan. "The first one he just killed, right? The victim probably didn't feel anything. The second one was a heart attack, which has to suck. Then drowning beneath a layer of ice. Then the bends, which is horrible. And this last guy was burned alive. Each one gets worse, like he hates each one more than the last."

"Well, but—" said Susan. "Maybe he's a psychopath, and as he goes, he wants to hurt his victims more and more."

"That's silly," said Marci. "He can't just choose anything he wants. He has to pick from the things that were in the cache. So he has to pick what order to do them in."

"Jesus," said Susan. "You're right." She turned to Donovan. "You knew that, too?"

"Yeah," said Donovan. "Sorry. I should have made it clear earlier."

Susan drew her brows together, then raised her head and said, "It makes too much sense. You're right."

"So, okay," said Marci. "We have a face, and we have motive. We have connections among his victims. You'd think we'd be able to move forward from there."

"We also," said Donovan, "have a vague notion of how it all connects to the Mystici. They sell their services."

Susan frowned. "Did we already know that?"

"Not exactly. We knew that some of their agents might sell their skills on the side, like Blum did. But what Young was doing went beyond that. It's, like, official policy. From what I can put together, the Mystici find civilians who can use magic, and can afford magic, and they supply it. They avoid anything that might make waves, but that still leaves a lot open. Some of the money goes to the guy who casts it, some to the Mystici. I don't know how they divide it, but that's how Young got so rich. Defensive spells—like, a permanent bulletproof vest, or protection against maybe dying in a car crash or whatever—are going to be the perfect thing."

"Well," said Susan, "that's good. Rich people don't have enough advantages; nice to know they have access to magic, too."

"Whatever," said Donovan. "That explains where the Mystici get their money, and where Young got his, and why our shooter wanted Young dead—Young was protecting someone our shooter wants to go after. It means we could be looking for a guy who is, basically, a decent person, who's been badly fucked over by someone protected by the Mystici. Doesn't that fit?"

"It fits," said Susan. "But you're making a lot of assumptions."

"Such as?"

"Well, what makes you think our shooter is 'a decent person,' whatever that means?"

"Oh," said Donovan. "Right. Name all the victims who were killed at home."

"Um," said Susan. "Just one, the State Senator."

"Right. Now name all the victims who didn't have family."

"Oh. Yeah."

"Yeah. He's making sure that we don't have a kid coming along and finding Daddy's body."

"Well, damn," said Susan. "That might not help, but it gives me some idea of what 'a decent person' means, so thanks for that."

"You're welcome."

"But I still think it's a stretch to go from the killer having some basic human decency to concluding that therefore the ultimate victim doesn't."

"Then instead of a conclusion, let's call it a hypothesis."

"Sure," said Susan. "But how does that help us? I mean, if we're going to comb the world for assholes who have hurt non-assholes we're not going to get to a number we can examine in our lifetimes."

Marci leaned forward, elbows on her knees. "Well, okay then. Let's narrow it further. I like this game."

"Marci, never leave me," said Donovan.

Susan pulled her chair a little closer to the table. "Don, what could you tell from the picture?"

"Just what you said: He looked like a car salesman who never worked out a day in his life."

"You mean, a car salesman in particular, or was that a general thing?"

"A general thing. I mean, someone who needs to keep up his appearance for the public, doesn't do manual labor, picks out his clothes by reading *Dress for Success*."

Susan said, "Could you get any hints about where he's from?"

"No, not with the picture off the security camera. I couldn't see, like, a suntan, or a lack of suntan, or anything like that."

"But," said Marci, "you could tell he didn't work out?"

"His gait. His stride. He didn't walk like someone who exercised."

Marci said, "If our soon-to-be-victim could do something to this guy bad enough to make him want to give him a horrible death, then one thing we can conclude is that Mr. Victim-to-be has power, right?"

"Why do you assume 'Mr.'?" said Susan.

"Because he has power."

"So do Angela Merkel and Janet Yellen," said Donovan.

"So do I," said Susan.

"Statistically—"

"Let's not go there," said Donovan. "Keep saying 'he,' but we'll keep in mind he might be a she. Now move on. What were you saying?"

"That he has power, that's all."

"What does that even mean?" said Susan.

"It means he can force his will on another through violence, the threat of violence, or economic coercion."

Donovan nodded to Marci. "Good. So, he killed someone, he beat someone up, or threatened someone, or ordered the killing or the beating or the threat, or used money or influence."

"A loan shark?" said Susan. "That would fit all the bills."

"Maybe," said Donovan. "Let's not get ahead of ourselves."

"Back the other way," said Susan. "Anything else we can deduce about our shooter?"

"He can handle a shotgun," said Marci. "Any conclusions from that? Like, I don't know, a hunting background?"

Susan shook her head. "Anyone who's motivated can handle a shotgun."

"I can't," said Marci.

"If you want, I can show you in two minutes."

"Let's stay on track," said Donovan. "Gun lessons can come later. I'm going to call up the video again."

He did, and they huddled around him and watched. *Damn. He seems so harmless.* "Okay, it's unscientific, and it's unsupported, but this guy had to lose everything to get him steamed enough to do this. And that means he had something to lose. That coat he's wearing cost five hundred bucks new, and when it was new he'd never have worn it in this condition. I won't say he came from a long way up, but he's gone a long way down. I wish I could see his hands. I want to know if he has ring impressions and how he keeps his nails." He felt himself scowling at the screen and stopped.

He turned away from the computer. "There's so much I could be wrong about—you just can't tell a lot from a feed like that. But I'm going to bet that that man has never experienced violence in his life. Susan?"

"I don't see anything to contradict that. He's not, you know, hyper-aware, the way you get if you've been assaulted."

"Okay, then. Could be a family member, but my money is on something economic. Job, house, maybe all of that. Maybe a car he loved; he looks like the kind of guy who might pour everything into a Ferrari and have a breakdown when it gets repo'd."

"You know," said Marci, "half the country got killed when the mortgage bubble burst. If it's one of them, we'll never find him."

"I don't know," said Donovan. "How many of them would have the resources to trace his misery up the chain and find the one responsible?"

"The one? How many are there? The entire board of directors of, well, just about every financial institution in the country. How do you pin it on one person, not to mention finding him?"

"Yep," said Donovan. "That's exactly what we have to figure out."

Marci shook her head. "You're working on a whole lot of assumptions here."

"Just what I was thinking," said Susan.

"Maybe not as many as it seems. I mean, playing percentages. Some guy gets laid off, his house gets repossessed, maybe he loses his family—that happens a lot when money goes to hell; trust me on that. All this, and he just happens to be in a position to know who to blame. Unlike almost anyone else, he can put a name to his misery."

"How?" said Susan. "The Mystici might be able to tell him, but if they're the ones who are protecting the guy he's going after that'd be kind of a weird decision."

"Not because of the Mystici," said Donovan. "Because of his position."

"He's in the field," said Marci, "A low-level mortgage banker."

Donovan nodded. "Someone fucked over by the institutions and the company he was serving. Can you imagine the sense of betrayal?"

"Still a lot of guesswork behind that," said Susan.

"I wouldn't call it guesswork. I'd call it induction with some intuitive leaps. But the good news is, if I'm right, we can test it. We've gotten it down to a manageable number, and we have a face."

"That's a manageable number?" said Susan.

"Yeah. Because it's something a software geek could use to search on without devoting his life to it."

"If he had access to the information."

"Right."

"And if we knew the right kind of software geek."

"Right."

Donovan pulled out his cell phone and hit a number. "Jeffrey? Got another one for you. Good news: This one is legal."

||||||||||||||||

Matt gave up after a couple of hours, and wandered off. Across the plaza was a place with awnings and chairs outside. *Ah ha,* he thought. *My keen deductive skills tell me there will be food there.*

There was. He had something with rice and cheese and a meat he guessed was either mutton or goat, and there was certainly lemon in it, and a taste that was unaccountably similar to some of the things he'd had in Afghanistan. He didn't try to solve the mystery, however. He permitted himself one glass of wine, and was considering a second when two men approached his table. Neither one looked in the least threatening. One seemed small and pale and tidy to the point of obsession; the other was more relaxed, with shaggier hair and an easier gait. Neither one was able to handle himself in a fight. Matt remained seated.

The smaller one spoke in a precise, upper-class British accent. "I'm Manuel Becker; this is William Faucheux. We're with the Spanish Foundation. May we join you, Mr. Castellani?"

"Please do."

Neither one offered to shake hands, so Matt didn't, either.

"You understand," said Becker, "that we are careful whom we let into the building."

"Of course."

"There are security concerns. Frankly, Mr. Longfellow ought not to have told you where the building was."

"He didn't."

"Then, may I ask how you found out?"

"It was long, and it was difficult, and it was a pain in the ass, and I was sort of hoping it would show you how gosh darned clever I am." Matt gave what he hoped was a charming smile.

Faucheux's accent was middle American. "At any rate, it shows your determination. May I ask why?"

"Did you see *The Avengers*?" Faucheux nodded; Becker shook his head. "In that case, I'll just say that it seems like it might be a way to help, and I'd like to do that for a while."

"We did receive your information from Mr. Longfellow," said Becker. "I passed it on to Mr. Faucheux, who is in charge of personnel. For my part, I am, in fact, impressed with your determination. It is a rare thing."

"But the fact remains," said Faucheux, "that you did attempt to kill one of Mr. Becker's team, which casts some doubt on your altruism."

"Oh, you know about that, huh?"

"Yes. And about your dishonorable discharge, and the reason for it."

Matt nodded.

"Unfortunately, between them, I'm afraid we can't use you," said Faucheux.

Cutting through the disappointment was Matt's observation of a flicker, a twitch, from Becker. Becker had not been expecting that. Matt had the impression that a twitch from Becker was jaw-dropping amazement from someone else.

"I'm sorry to hear that," he said.

"We will," said Faucheux, "keep your information on file. It is possible that things will change."

"I hope they do," said Matt.

They both stood up, so Matt did, too, and this time they shook hands.

When they had gone, Matt sat down and finished his wine.

Okay, then. I wonder if the other team is hiring.

||||||||||||||||

Delta Flight 3571 arrived at LaGuardia at ten in the morning, which meant I had to wake up around 4:00 AM to make sure I got through security. I arrived in that curious state of tremendous excitement and bone-deep weariness. I don't remember getting to the hotel, but I did, and I even had my suitcase with me.

I tried to take a nap, couldn't sleep, thought about going for a walk, tried to watch TV, tried to take another nap, and succeeded, getting a solid three hours of nothing. I woke up groggy, of course, and my mouth tasted funny. I took a shower and stood under the hot water for a long time. My mind drifted to what I'd do after I killed Whittier, but, as always, came up empty—that moment was like the end of the universe. If there was something that came after, it was impossible to conceive of.

Dressed in my towel, I sat down at the desk and fired up my laptop. There was an email from Charlie: "We need to meet. Go to Aire Ancient Baths, 88 Franklin Street. Give them your name as Patrick Harper and they'll bring you to the right place. Be there by four PM."

I checked the time and cursed, then dressed as fast as I could and headed downstairs for a taxi.

I made it with ten minutes to spare. I gave them the name as I was told, and they gave me a robe and showed me where to change and I wondered if I could afford to actually use the place when we were done. I sat in the spa for a while, and got a massage, and was left lying on a table, facedown, covered in warm towels.

"Hello, Nick."

"You must be Lef-tenant Sharpe," I said.

I actually heard a smile in his voice. "You caught the reference, then."

"Yes. And thanks for the treatment. It was just what I needed. I'm ready for the bad news."

"Bad, not catastrophic. He's taking the rest of the week off and returning to his Connecticut home until Monday."

"Well, at least I know the place. What do you say? Do we wait until Monday, or take him there?"

"We don't dare wait."

"All right. What's the plan?"

"I've arranged for a town car for you. It will be at your hotel tomorrow morning. Allow two hours for the drive, in case of traffic."

"All right. What about his security? He has to have bumped it since last time."

"Yes. I'm afraid you'll have to be working with someone on this. I was hoping to avoid bringing anyone else in, but you need someone who can disable the alarms and put his private security people to sleep if that's how it plays out."

"All right. When and where do I meet this person?"

"Tomorrow, seven PM, Little Thai Kitchen on West Avenue in Darien. You'll be meeting a woman called Shveta. She'll be wearing a tan pants suit and a silver choker set with onyx."

"All right."

"You should eat there. I've heard it's good."

"Charlie, do you really think I'm going to be able to eat?"

"Another time, then."

"When it's done, am I going to hear from you again?"

There was a pause; then he said, "I'm not sure, Nick. It depends how things play out on my end. I hope so."

"In case I don't, thanks for everything."

"Remember I'm doing this for my own reasons, Nick."

"I know that."

"Then you're welcome."

||||||||||||||||||

Manuel Becker was, in fact, surprised by Faucheux's decision— he'd thought the ex-soldier might indeed be a worthwhile addition. But Faucheux had fallen completely for the security culture that had served the Foundation so poorly; so on reflection, Becker ought to have expected it. For now, he put the entire matter out of his mind, because, speaking of security culture, there was a larger problem to face.

He took the elevator to the "Twelfth Floor," which is to say the tenth, and spoke to Florencia Trujillo. "Good afternoon, Florencia. I wish to see Ms. Morgan. Is she available? I can wait."

Becker knew that Trujillo knew "I can wait" is code for "This won't wait." She, however, gave no hint of this understanding. She simply said, "Please wait here," and vanished into the rows of cubicles and offices. She was back in five minutes. She seated herself and said, "She will see you."

He nodded and went back and back and back until he reached the big corner office. The door was open. As he shut it behind himself, Morgan rose and gestured toward a chair, and they sat down at the same time.

"You have something?"

"I am coming to you with a possibility, Ms. Morgan."

"Go on."

"There are indications that someone may be working against us from within."

Morgan's brows drew together. "Explain."

"I heard from Charles Leong yesterday. We were unable to trace the call, but I believe he was lying about his current location, which he claimed was Orlando, Florida, in the United States. He also claimed to be living in Houston, Texas, and after some checking I believe he is lying about that, too. I then met with Kevin Crosheck, and—"

"You did!"

"Yes."

"Well. I confess, I am startled. You met with him in person?"

"I authorized a slipwalk for him, Ms. Morgan. I judged it important to be able to read his face and body language."

Morgan hesitated, then nodded. "Very well."

"I'm going to tell Mr. Longfellow, my investigator, about Mr. Leong."

"Of course. And about yourself?"

"I do not believe that information will be useful to him."

"Very well. I will accept your judgment on that. Is there anything else?"

Becker nodded. "It is possible that the source of the killings is somewhere in the Foundation. To discover this, I must ask you a question, Ms. Morgan."

"Go ahead."

"My knowledge is limited to North America. If there were similar killings going on elsewhere, I would have no way of knowing. Now I must ask if that is possible."

Morgan studied him for a moment. The moment dragged out. Becker remained stationary, patient. Eventually, Morgan gave a small nod, turned to her computer and used the mouse, then typed. It may have been possible for Becker to read some or all of what was on Morgan's computer in the reflection from the window behind her, but he did not attempt to do so.

Presently she turned back to him and said, "You now have access to all relevant files."

"Thank you, Ms. Morgan," he said. He stood, nodded, and went back to the elevators, and so to his office. He sat down at his desk, and the files that had appeared. When he finished, he went over them again, more carefully this time.

When he was done, he stood up and walked the forty feet to another cubicle, which was labeled with a simple sign that said: "Myra Kentspeth, Europe."

"Ms. Kentspeth," he said.

"Yes, Mr. Becker?"

"Conference room. Five minutes."

He walked away without waiting for a reply. He repeated this for Ms. Sutherland (Asia and the Pacific Rim), Ms. Mandere (South America) and Mr. Poulin (Africa). Then he walked down the hall to the conference room, sat down in the first chair he came to, and waited.

IIIIIIIIIIIIII

Donovan's apartment was not made for three people to live in. No one had yet blown up at anyone else, or even, really, gotten snippy, but they were all of them being careful, and staying out of one another's way as much as possible, which wasn't very. And yet, Donovan found he sort of enjoyed it. They took turns cooking. Marci had a meat loaf recipe everyone loved, and Donovan baked a loaf of bread that lasted under five minutes, but Susan really impressed them with a duck a l'orange with garlic-roasted asparagus.

Donovan and Marci cleaned up, more getting in each other's way than helping, each of them getting more irritated, and more determined not to say anything. It might have turned bad if

Donovan's phone hadn't rung. He looked at the caller, and answered gratefully, stepping as far out of the way as he could.

"Jeffrey. You're a lifesaver."

"You don't even know what I have."

"Don't care. If you hadn't called, someone was going to kill someone, and I don't like my chances in this crowd."

"Why? What's going on?"

"Eh. Company. Never mind. You find anything?"

"Got a name."

"No shit?"

"No shit."

"Well, damn. I didn't think that was going to work."

Donovan noticed there was now silence in the room—the others were clustered around him.

"Why? With all the info you gave me?"

"Well, most of that was guesswork."

Susan mouthed, *Ah ha*. Donovan flipped her off.

"So, what's the name?"

"Nicholas Raymond Nagorski, late of the Denver office of Augsburg Financial."

"I don't suppose you can tell me about this company?"

"Donny! After you made those mysterious spooks you work for pay me so fast, and then fed me such an easy search? Of course I did."

"Jeffrey, you are *so* my hero. I'm putting you on speaker. Okay, go."

"Hello, mysterious mystery people. My name's Jeff and I'm your host. Let's play 'Find the Bad Guy.' Or is he a good guy, Don? You never told me. Anyway, Augsburg Financial, where Nagorski worked until December of 2011, yeah, right before Christmas, happy holidays, is a holding company that specialized

in investments in—Okay, look, it was one of those places that
got fat off the mortgage boom, and was too small to be saved by
the bailout. They got gobbled up, and bunches of old shit
started coming to light, which Nick first tried to bring to his
bosses, then sent on to the SEC sometime in late 2009."

"Wait," said Susan. "So this guy's a whistle-blower?"

"Tried to be, but he was, uh, whistling in the dark."

"I see what you did there," said Donovan.

"It took a couple of years, but word got back and they fired
him. Then his house got repossessed, he got divorced—"

"Jeff, you've been working!"

"Hey, I'm the man, right? I'm like Mr. Universe in *Serenity*
without the getting stabbed part. Or the sexbot."

"Yeah, I gotta see that movie."

"You really do," said Marci.

Susan said, "It opens with this really cool—"

"Go on, Jeff. Quick."

"Right," said the phone. "He got divorced, lost custody, and
about a year ago he dropped off the grid. I've always wanted to
say that."

"Glad to give you the chance. So no word of him since then?"

"Last thing we have is a phone call to United Airlines on April
third of 2014."

"Where did he want to go?"

"No idea. All I've got is that the call happened."

"Okay. Good. You rock. I am hanging up and composing an
email to the people who pay you. I mean, right now. It'll be sent
before the echo of my voice dies in your ear."

"That's why we get along so well."

"Later, Jeff."

"Later."

He disconnected, and said, "Not now," to the pair of voices

that demanded attention. "Before we do anything else, I'm sending that email."

|||||||||||||||||

Becker left the conference and returned to his desk. There was
a lot to process, starting with the whole scope of what was happening. And the sudden appearance of Shveta Tyaga in the mix
was more than a little chilling. It was clear that Longfellow's team
could be in danger, and he needed to address that before doing
anything else. They were going to need backup, and none of the
other teams was available. That meant talking to Recruitment
and Training, and finding the best students, and finding who was
currently available on the short—too short—list of freelancers.

He opened up a new file and started a list of names. Once it
was done, he ran some searches on it and filled in contact information.

He printed the file, because he wanted a hard copy on which
to either make notes or, more likely, scratch off names. He took
the sheet, and was about to make his first call, when he hesitated,
considered, and, at the bottom, added a question mark followed
by the name "Matthew Castellani."

|||||||||||||||||

I figured Charlie must know me pretty well, because among the
things he left for me in a bag next to the massage table was a
bottle with a single Ambien pill. Maybe I'd find it easy to fall
asleep, but more likely not.

I returned to the hotel and forced myself to eat something,
though I didn't want to. Then I went back to my room and tried
to lose myself in a Will Smith movie, but I couldn't concentrate.
I paced around the room, then went out and took a walk. People
in New York are actually nicer than we in the West think they

are, but they're always busy. I watched them for a while, wondering if there was more neon in New York or Las Vegas, and if someone, somewhere, was getting a Master's Degree in something by studying the question.

I felt better after the walk, and, more important, it killed some time. I went back and watched the rest of the Will Smith movie. Then I took the pill and went to bed. I tossed and turned for a while, but the Ambien did its job.

Tomorrow I'd do mine.

INSECURITY THEATER | 14

The hard work was done.

Donovan had had his share of crap jobs, and one thing he'd learned was that when someone told him the hard work was done it usually meant there was a lot of boring, grinding bullshit left.

All of the information they needed was publicly available online—it just had to be dug out. Names of CEOs, major shareholders of publicly traded stock, all the stuff. Marci sat at the computer because she was better at it than the rest of them, but that still didn't make her fast. Donovan wished he could just bring Jeff in on things and have him work it, but that would violate protocol even more than he, Donovan, was comfortable with—not to mention the cow Oversight would have about it.

After several hours at it, Donovan was starting to get a bit punchy, and was thinking about calling it a night, coming back to it in the morning. That's when the email arrived.

"All right," he said. "We got something."

They turned to him.

"Not the shooter, but we have a name for the supplier. Charles Leong. Some years ago, before I started with the Foundation, he was de-sorcelled for committing a string of murders of—get this—evil sorcerers."

"For real?" said Susan.

"In effect. Sorcerers who were doing fucked-up things. He went on a killing spree until they caught him."

"Do we know where he is?"

"Probably somewhere in North America."

"That's helpful," said Marci. "So, do I switch to him?"

Donovan considered, then shook his head. "No. Keep doing what you're doing. I'm going to see if I can figure out a way to find Leong."

Marci nodded and turned back to her work. Donovan called Jeff, and left him a message asking him to locate a certain Charles Leong, probably living under an assumed name; to Donovan it felt like a pointless request, but, hey, Jeff had surprised him before.

An hour later, Marci sat back and said, "Okay, got it."

They huddled around her, looking at a half-profile chest-up picture of a man in his late fifties with distinguished gray hair, a firm mouth, and mild brown eyes. Donovan looked for the evidence of airbrushing, but it was hard to tell. Makeup, though, for sure. Lots of makeup.

"His name," said Marci, "is Douglas Winston Lowrey, and he is—"

"Not our guy," said Donovan.

They looked at him. "Uh, sorry, Marci. I shouldn't have interrupted."

"No," she said. "Go ahead."

"We're looking in the wrong direction. No, that isn't right. Not entirely the wrong direction, we just—okay." He squeezed his eyes shut, then opened them again. It was good to be able to see, but his eyes seemed to get tired and sore faster than they did before he'd gotten himself blown up. *Note to self: Don't get blown up anymore.* He said, "None of the people he killed worked for Augsburg Financial, or for any of the companies that bought up Augsburg Financial. That isn't who he's after. If it was, there would have been more bodies. Or at least different bodies."

Susan grabbed a kitchen chair, pulled it up to the computer, and sat down, leaning forward. Donovan just watched over Marci's shoulder.

"I wish," said Marci, "you'd said this before I spent five hours—"

"No, no. Don't worry. You didn't waste your time. We need this."

"So, then, what are we looking for?"

"We're looking for whoever betrayed our shooter. That's what's motivating this guy: It's that he lost everything because of someone he thought he could trust."

"So, a friend?"

Donovan shook his head. "You've got your guy at the top there, Mr., what's-his-name, Lowrey. Now go back down a little. Lowrey has hired someone in the last year for a high-power, big-money position, and it was someone who until then worked for the SEC."

Susan said, "Wait, for the—oh."

"Oh yeah," said Marci.

"Nagorski was a whiste-blower, turned the information over, got hosed."

Marci didn't speak; she was already at the keyboard.

"And I'll tell you something about the guy," said Donovan. "He's now rich, and he's not a sorcerer, but he knew someone in the Mystici. In fact, I'll tell you exactly who he knew: the late

Georgio Byrne Lawton-Smythe. What the connection is I don't know, but—"

"Cambridge," said Marci. "They were classmates at Trinity College, in England."

"No shit," said Donovan. "Damn. Well, now I feel all smart and shit."

Marci nodded. "His name is Paul Whittier."

"There's the target," said Donovan.

"Looks like," said Susan. "Can we verify it? I mean, come at it from the other direction, just to be sure?"

"What do you mean, the other direction?"

"The chain," said Marci. "The chain of bodies. How does everyone fit together?"

Donovan nodded. "I like that. Let's start with Whittier. Somehow, Whittier learns that there's someone who wants to kill him."

Susan said, "How?"

"I don't know. Maybe a sorcerer tells him?"

"How does the sorcerer know?"

Donovan spread his hands. "A disruption in the Force? How do you sorcerers find out stuff like that?"

"In my case," said Susan, "I read it in the newspaper."

"I get my news online," said Marci.

"People," said Donovan. "Let's focus, all right? It's late." He kept forgetting how young they both were. *Christ.* Sometimes it was like being a nursery school teacher. "Maybe that's what happened; maybe someone took a shot at the guy, and it made the news. Somehow, he learns his life in danger. He makes a panicked call—or maybe not a panicked call; maybe he was all ice cool—to his old buddy Lawton-Smythe, who he knows has connections to the Mystici, because Lawton-Smythe is the one who arranged for the spells that got him where he is, right? I mean, we're pretty sure he used magic to advance his position, and that fits in with Lawton-Smythe's skill set. That was the call in 2011: 'Hey, buddy, help me advance my position, and I'll slip you some bucks.'"

The others nodded. "Okay," said Susan. "Then what?"

"He wants protective spells."

"What?" said Marci. "He didn't have any? Someone like that is bound to be walking around with the magical equivalent of a bulletproof vest on, don't you think? I mean, if he knows there is such a thing."

Donovan moved around to the head of his small kitchen table, looking at the other two. "Maybe he did. Maybe whatever protection he had saved his life, and that's how he knew he was a target. That would make sense. But when someone actually takes a shot at you, whatever protection you have, no matter how good it is, all of a sudden doesn't feel like enough. Your mind starts working on you. You go, 'Well, that stopped him from killing me, but now he knows about it, I need something better.' So you call your old school chum, Lawton-Smythe, and say, 'I need more protection.' Lawton-Smythe doesn't do that sort of thing, so he calls someone he knows in the group: Nate Blum. He says, 'Hey, this dude is in danger; can we up his protection?'"

There were more nods.

"All right," Donovan continued. "Now Blum is in recruiting, right? He knows everyone, and what they're good at. So, who can cast the spell?"

"Alexander Young," said Marci. "He has exactly the right skills."

"Yeah, but why would he do it?"

"Money?" said Susan.

"Okay, sure," said Donovan. "Money. Young does it for money. I figure, a lot of money."

"Whittier can afford it, right?"

"I don't think," said Donovan slowly, "that that's how these people work."

Susan and Marci looked at him with identical *what do you mean?* expressions.

"I'm trying to come up with an explanation for what we know happened," he said. "And what happened is that Blum called Caren Wright. Why?"

"I give up. Why?" said Susan.

"Move, Marci. I need the computer. Susan, there's a corkboard at the back of the bedroom closet. Could you grab it, please? Put it on the table."

Donovan turned on his printer, plugged it into the laptop, sat down, and went to work.

An hour later, there were pictures of Nagorski, Lawton-Smythe, Blum, Wright, Lundgren, Young, and Whittier on the board with notes on the lines of how they connected. "Okay," said Donovan. "Whittier calls Lawton-Smythe asking for magical protection. Lawton-Smythe calls Blum, who knows who's good at that kind of thing. Blum, our guy in the MetLife Building, is the key to the whole thing, because he's in recruiting. When I say 'recruiting,' you think 'personnel' because that's the ticket; in the Foundation, recruiters are the ones who know what everyone does, so let's assume it works the same with the Mystici."

"Why?" said Marci. "I mean, why would a recruiter have that kind of connection?"

"Because they not only know everyone they've recruited, but they talk to each other, and they gossip, and unlike us, they're actually part of the organization. They're the ones with the connections inside, and outside."

"Okay," said Susan. "Yeah, that fits with what I know. So, Blum is the one who put it all together?"

"Yeah. I figure if Wright got her position in part thanks to magical help, then she owes the Mystici. So Blum calls in a debt. He says, 'We need you to call in a favor from Benjamin Lundgren.'"

"Wait," said Marci, looking at the board. "How does Wright connect with Lundgren?"

Donovan picked up his Sharpie and wrote under Lundgren's picture: "Rich as fuck, considerable real estate holdings in the San Diego area."

"Oh," said Marci.

"So, why Lundgren? What does he bring to the table?"

"Money," said Donovan. "He pays Young for the protection spell."

"And our shooter, Nagorski," said Marci, "then follows the same chain, killing them all in order, so by the time he's ready to take out Whittier, Whittier has no more protection, and maybe doesn't even know the others are dead. See? I was right. The chain of bodies."

"Your new name," said Donovan, "is Girl Detective."

"I'm currently working on an impotence spell."

"Point taken. So, is everyone happy we've got the guy?"

They both nodded.

"Good," said Susan. "Let's get some sleep."

||||||||||||||||

Matt had good eyes, and knew how to use them. But one thing he couldn't tell: Did the Brit soldiers parading through the airport at a trot, in fatigues, rifles at port arms, know how stupid they looked? As far as security was concerned, it was a pointless exhibit, "security theater," as the experts called it. But, watching their faces, he couldn't tell if they knew it. He was inclined to think they did, in which case, kudos to them for hiding it.

He watched them, had flashes of Afghanistan, and thought, *It could be worse. It could have been twenty years ago, and I could have been British, and been sent to Ireland.*

He stood next to a shop selling things that said: "BA" and wondered. What if he'd joined up, and been sent to do that? He'd heard stories—he'd spent a summer with an uncle in St. Paul, and there'd been a small but active community of "boy-os" who drank hard and listened to loud music Matt hated and sometimes talked about what they'd seen—though never, ever, what they'd done. Would he, Matt, have told his CO to get stuffed, rather than do those things? True, Matt had done some pretty ugly things in Afghanistan, but that was different because—

Because—

Fuck that. I came here to do something. Time to be about it.

He was setting off to check into ground transportation when his cell phone rang. It was a blocked number, but what the hell. He answered.

"Mr. Castellani? . . . This is Manuel Becker. I'm hoping you can do something for me. How fast can you return to America?"

"Uh, I'm at Heathrow, but on the wrong side of security."

"I'm booking you on a flight right now. Virgin Atlantic, departs twelve thirty. I'm texting you the information. If you leave your luggage behind, it will save time at Customs. This could be very close."

"I'll do my best, Mr. Becker."

"I have backup flights available if you don't, but try."

"I will."

Matt turned back toward the checkpoint. *Security theater. Son of a bitch.* He hoped he'd make it.

||||||||||||||||

For the second time, Donovan woke up next to Susan, and for the second time, he muttered, "Dayam," under his breath, and for the second time he stumbled out of the bedroom to find his computer was in use.

"Do you ever sleep?" he said.

"Sure. Two hours a night, whether I need it or not."

"Fucking kid. Back in a minute."

Shaved, showered, and teeth clean, he gave the bathroom over to Hippie Chick, who had the grace to at least look tired. He started coffee, grunting at Marci that he wasn't ready yet when she started talking. He put on tan slacks and was looking through his shirts to find a nice one when he realized he was only doing that to look good for Susan, at which point he gave himself a good talking-to and put on a T-shirt he'd picked up in Vegas and that had seen better days. Then he got some coffee and sat down at the kitchen table, next to Marci and the computer. "All right," he said. "Let's hear it."

"I got a bunch of background on Whittier. He's been working with the Mystici for a while. They aren't just protecting him. If you look at how he rose up, how he got his money, the whole thing, they've been helping him all along."

"If he went to school at Cambridge," said Donovan, "he didn't start out poor."

"Poor? No. Not really rich by these people's standards, but certainly not poor. He started out as the son of a high-level Mystici operative."

"Well, shit."

"Yeah. His mother was one of their operatives for, like, thirty years. Recruitment and Training manager, like William. She passed away in March of 2011 from pneumonia and heart failure, aged eighty-six."

"That," said Donovan, "provides another missing piece. He

got his sorcery from Mommy, and then she died, and he suddenly needed more. That's why he placed the called to Lawton-Smythe, who then made the first call to Blum. How'd you learn all of this?"

"Got some names, then I called Mr. Becker."

"Again? Damn, girl."

"Now I'm trying to figure out where Whittier works. He's got two different offices in two different buildings in Manhattan, and I have no idea how to predict which one he'll be at."

Donovan frowned. "Well, it's a safe bet that Nagorski does. How would he know?"

"Maybe he doesn't," said Susan. "Maybe he plans to take him at his home."

"Does he have kids?"

"No."

Donovan grunted. "Maybe, then."

"That's where he tried before," said Marci.

Donovan almost spilled his coffee. "What?"

Marci nodded. "He took a shot a couple of months ago. Broke into the guy's house in Connecticut, shot at him from point-blank range, and ran off into the night."

"How do you know that?"

Marci looked smug. "Detective work, Detective. Once I knew where he worked and where he lived, I started doing newspaper searches. The previous attack was written up, and the attacker fit Nagorski's general description. Close enough that I'm convinced, at least. Hey, you're the one who called it."

"Did the newspapers describe how he missed at point-blank range?"

"They just said he missed. I figured the point-blank range because, well, that seems to be how Nagorski does everything."

"How did Nagorski get away?"

"I don't know. He drove, or ran, or some combination. It's a big, wide area, and it took them a while to get the search organized. He just got past them."

"Well, damn. That probably means he won't try it there again."

"Probably," said Susan. "So, Marci, we need you to figure out where Whittier is. Can you track him?"

"No," she said. "But why don't we just call him?"

Donovan stared at her. "Um. Yeah. Think you can find a phone number?"

"I could find a corporate number, but I don't know how I'd get through to him. People at that level have buffers."

"I suppose," said Susan, "your Jedi mind tricks won't work over the phone."

"Uh yeah, no."

"Try to reach him," said Donovan.

Marci made several phone calls, then finally turned and told them what they already knew: "Either they're lying to me, or he's out of the office this week."

"Well then," said Donovan, "there are four places he might be. We deliver four messages. If we can convince him to get somewhere safe—no, wait a minute. What the fuck are we thinking?"

"Trying to save his life?" said Susan.

"Yeah. Why? I don't give a shit about this asshole's life. That isn't our job. Our job is to catch the guy trying to kill him."

"Jesus, Don," said Susan. "That's cold."

Donovan shrugged. "It's our job. And, seriously, do either of you think the world wouldn't be a better place if that guy got blown away?"

Marci shuddered. "I don't want to be the one to start making those decisions."

"We're not. I mean, we do want to save his life. But not by

sacrificing our mission. We have a job. I propose we do it. Does anyone object?"

Marci opened her mouth, then closed it.

"Go ahead," said Donovan. "What is it?"

"My boyfriend doesn't know what I do," she said. "But he knows it's important to me."

"What's your point?"

"When I was leaving, he started to ask if I was doing good. If I was on the right side. But he stopped, because he was afraid I'd be insulted if he asked."

"You afraid you're not?"

"I don't know. Letting someone die—"

"The plan isn't to let him die."

"I know that. But we can save him."

"This time. What if we don't get the guy who's trying to kill him? Will we be able to save him next time?"

Marci looked down. "Maybe not," she said.

Donovan looked around. "Susan? Look, I'm being straight with you. I don't like this prick, and I won't shed a tear if he goes down. But I think the best thing we can do for him is to do our job, all right?"

After a moment they nodded—Susan firmly, Marci with more hesitation.

"All right, then," said Donovan. "Let's be about it."

"So," said Hippie Chick. "Where are we going?"

"Marci?"

"He has a condo near Central Park, and the house in Connecticut."

"If we were told the truth, and he isn't in, that probably means he's gone to Connecticut," said Susan.

"We should confirm it," said Marci.

Donovan nodded. "How are you with clairvoyance?"

"Not great," she said. "What are you thinking?"

"We know what he drives?"

"Um . . . yeah, a BMW."

"Then see if there's a BMW parked outside the Connecticut house."

Marci nodded and closed her eyes. Her fingers twitched spasmodically. Donovan got up and opened a window. Marci started shaking her head, as if to say she couldn't get it; then she opened her eyes and said, "Yes. He's in Connecticut."

"Then," said Donovan, "that's where we're going, too."

|||||||||||||||

When I couldn't wait any longer, I checked out of the hotel. I put my suitcase in the car, though part of me wanted to just leave it—to make a dramatic gesture about the finality of the day. But if all went well, and I did what I meant to, I'd be really annoyed about not having any clean underwear tomorrow.

The thought made me laugh a little. I set the GPS and headed out. I'd never driven a car that nice—it was quiet and smooth and fun. Joan would have liked a car like this. She'd probably never have let me drive it. *Shit.*

By the time I was out of the city, I was nearly there.

|||||||||||||||

"Your timing, Mr. Becker, is either excellent or terrible. We were just setting out."

"All of you? To where?"

"Bus to the PATH station, train to Connecticut."

"Then you've found him?"

"We believe we've found his target. We're hoping to trap him."

"Stay where you are. I'll have a rental delivered to you. I can have it there in . . . ten minutes."

"If it's urgent, we could slipwalk."

"For a place an hour's drive away? With all of you there? Oversight would have our ears."

"I suppose. Uh, Mr. Becker? What's going on?"

"Is Ms. Sullivan there?"

She bent over Donovan's shoulder. "Right here, Mr. Becker."

"Ms. Sullivan, we have reason to believe that the people behind these killings have Shveta Tyaga working with them."

When Marci didn't answer at once, Donovan looked at her. His eyes were a little wide.

"Okay, Mr. Becker," said Donovan. "I think maybe you'd better fill us in."

"Yes," said Becker. "Would you care to begin, Ms. Sullivan?"

Marci nodded. "She's a rogue sorcerer. She's—very good. They've been looking for her for years. She's one of the examples they use when giving us training for I and E. That's why I know about her."

"Why am I just now hearing about her, Mr. Becker?"

"We have never before had reason to think she was on this continent."

"Ah yes. Secrecy and compartmentalization. How's that been working out for us lately?"

"Very, very badly, Mr. Longfellow. But as much as I agree with you, we don't have time for that conversation. I've ordered the rental."

"So," said Donovan, "this call was just by way of warning?"

"Yes. That's all I can do at this point. And we don't know she's there; I've just learned of the possibility."

"But if she is, we won't have any fun, is that about it?"

"Yes."

"Can you get us any help?"

"Text me the address you're heading toward, and I will have someone ready with an emergency transport, and there will be medical teams standing by in our infirmary."

"What about some hitters or something? You know, so we don't need the medical teams?"

"Apparently," said Becker, "our European team, our South American team, our Asian team, and our African team are all involved in other cases."

"Are. They. Really."

"Yes," said Becker.

"At exactly this moment."

"Yes."

"And you just learned this."

"Yes."

Donovan nodded. "Compartmentalization," he said. "Got it. Of course, the good news is, she can't be everywhere at once."

"Yes."

"Any contractors, or just spare sorcerers we can find to back us up?"

"I'm checking on that, Mr. Becker. So far, there's no one available outside of the kiddie pool, and Mr. Faucheux says none of the trainees are ready."

"Perfect."

"I'm trying to bring someone in, but he's overseas, and I don't know if he'll arrive in time."

"All right."

"Of course, Mr. Longfellow, you have the right to call off the operation."

"Yeah." He turned around, got the sense of his team, and said, "We'll go ahead with it."

"Then may I suggest you hurry. The car should be there."

"Good-bye, Mr. Becker. I'll let you know how it goes."

He disconnected, and turned to look at his team. He said, very long and low, "Fuck."

MR. NAGORSKI, I PRESUME 15

I never actually went into the Little Thai Kitchen.

I reached Darien hours early, so I spent some time driving aimlessly around. I went back to the restaurant and there was a parking spot directly in front of it (no parking meters; I love small towns), so I pulled up there. I got out and walked around. Nothing I saw exactly registered, though I have a vague memory that the term "picturesque" was in my mind. I can also tell you nothing about who I saw on the street; for all I know, I could have walked right past Whittier without being aware of it. When I had that thought, I realized that it was possible he was around, and might recognize me, and that would wreck everything, so I went back to the car. I was still hours early. I stood in front of the Little Thai Kitchen, and was just deciding to go inside and get something to drink when I noticed an exceptionally tall woman was approaching on the street. Her hair was done up closely, and the silver choker had quite a remarkable effect against her skin. She walked right up to me. Behind her were the two—well, shit, I have to say *thugs*. They were both more than 6'5" and I wouldn't care to guess their weight, but they weren't small. The white one had a buzz cut and a tiny gold hoop in his nose, the black one was bald and also had a gold hoop, but his was in an ear, and they were wearing fatigues, for god's sake. They had jackets on, and I couldn't tell you about guns, but I at least saw one big fucking knife in a belt.

"Shveta?" I said.

She nodded. "Nicholas?"

"Nick."

"A pleasure, Nick. You're early."

She spoke flawless American English. I had to wonder how many other languages she spoke flawlessly, but I didn't ask. "So are you. Uh—" I looked at the bruisers.

"Yes," she nodded. "Evan and Dwayne, meet Nick. Nick, Evan and Dwayne."

We exchanged nods. They didn't offer to shake hands and neither did I; those guys scared the shit out of me. I was trying to figure out a way to ask what they were doing here when Shveta said, "I heard from Charlie. He thinks we might face more opposition than he'd first thought, and suggested I take precautions."

The "precautions" had their arms folded, and I couldn't help but wonder if they were deliberately playing up the tough-guy act. But there was no chance I was going to ask; the failure condition for that move didn't bear thinking about.

I managed to say, "All right. Should we go?"

She nodded. I unlocked the car with a click of the key fob, and started to get in. "No," she said. "Let me drive."

I looked at her and waited.

"I've done this before, Nick. It might be that you're a little nervous."

I should have been offended, or at least irritated, but I wasn't.

I said, "Yeah, maybe," and tossed her the keys. She caught them, and I walked around to the passenger door. The scary guys got in the back.

"Nice car," she said as she pulled away from the curb.

"Yeah. So, what's the plan?"

"Go in. Kill or disable everyone we see. Kill Whittier. Leave."

"Okay. I like this plan. When I met him before, he was protected. Do you know what sort of protections he has now?"

"He shouldn't have any; his protections should have vanished with what Charles euphemistically called your previous mission. In case we're wrong, or we're surprised by a sorcerer, I know that one of the artifacts Charlie gave you will strip magical defenses from anyone in the room. And the other, of course, will kill someone in an especially gruesome way. And if all else fails, I can also strip his defenses, if I'm not busy."

"All right."

"Scared?"

"A little. Not too much, I think."

She nodded.

"We're early," I said.

"I know. But I swung past his place an hour ago and he was out. We'll be able to see if his car is in the driveway."

"All right."

It was a very short drive. At some point, I heard an odd click behind me, and it took me longer than it should have to identify it as the sound a semi-auto makes when you jack a round into the chamber.

"That's his car," she said as she drove by. "He's home." My mouth was suddenly very dry. She pulled ahead a little and parked the car.

||||||||||||||||

Traffic sucked even more than usual, so it took us almost an hour and a half to reach Darien. The conversation on the way was about Shveta Tyaga. Marci explained that she wasn't scared of her, exactly. It's just that she had a reputation, that was all. "She's not superhuman," Marci said. "She's very good. Better than me, in a fair fight. But her reputation comes as much from how hard it's been to find her as how good she is."

"Well," said Donovan. "All those in favor of having a fair fight, say 'aye.' . . . Okay, good. Seems like we agree about that. If there is any trouble, Marci, you see if you can get rid of any static spells like blocks, all right? Then Susan puts her down. Seem like a plan, everyone?"

"It's a good plan," said Susan, "as long as the other side co-operates with it."

"Just what I was thinking," said Marci. "I'm not saying no; I'm saying we can't be sure we'll be able to pull that off."

"Okay."

"What about you?" said Marci.

"Hell, I don't know. I'm going to, ah, try to stay alive?"

It was late afternoon, and the shadows of the trees seemed to stretch to the horizon, or would have if Donovan could have seen the horizon for the trees. They pulled up to the house in their rental Toyota Highlander and stopped on the 5 Mile River Road just short of the driveway.

"I expected a guard of some sort," said Donovan.

Susan, in the passenger seat, shrugged.

"What now?" said Marci.

"I suggest we walk up to the front door and ring the bell. Any objections?" There were none.

They got out and started walking toward the house.

"Security for the rich," said Donovan, "is the result of a really weird combination of how rich they are and how rich they see themselves as, which often have nothing in common. Except, of course, that they all have a hell of a lot more money than the rest of us."

No replies came to this profundity; Donovan shrugged and walked up to the front door.

"The Senator's house was bigger," said Marci.

"Don't be judgmental," said Susan. "Whittier mostly lives in the condo; this is just a sort of a retreat."

Marci snickered a little.

The guy who answered the doorbell could have been a butler, if butlers generally stood around 6'3", weighed somewhat north of 240 pounds, worked with weights, and carried a semi-auto concealed under a flannel shirt and a backup piece in an ankle holster.

"How do you do," said Donovan. "We're here to see Mr. Paul Whittier. My name is Donovan Longfellow, and I'm with the Spanish Foundation. Would you mind asking Mr. Whittier if he'd like to see us? Oh, and tell him we're here to save his life. We'll wait here."

Donovan gave him his best smile. The man nodded to him and closed the door.

He opened it again about five minutes later and said, "My name is Mark. Paul will see you now."

Paul, Donovan thought. *He calls his employer by his first name. That means something. I wish I knew what, and if it mattered right now.*

They came in past an entryway with a closet where Mark offered to take their coats and they declined. The ceilings were twelve feet high. The next room had a projection screen. The seating was a sectional sofa with reclining pieces and glass side tables. There was a bar in the corner, and a credenza in back. The carpet was heavy wool shag and Donovan would have bet his next paycheck it was Persian. He'd have bet the one after that that Whittier didn't know the difference, but had just bought the most expensive one on principle. There was a bit of abstract art on the wall that looked like originals done by people who got paid a lot of money to paint things to look like they're worth a lot of money. Donovan felt like if he looked up "nouveau riche" in a dictionary he'd see this guy's picture.

Whittier stood next to the bar. He was a sandy-haired man who wore clothes that cost more than Donovan had ever seen in his life, and who wore a ring on his right pinky finger that was worth even more. "How do you do," he said. "I'm Paul Whittier. I am somewhat familiar with your Foundation." He felt around his pocket like he was looking for a pack of cigarettes; maybe he'd just quit or something.

"Good," said Donovan. "That saves time. I'm Donovan Long-fellow." He introduced the others. "We think you're about to be attacked again."

"Then, you know of the first one?"

"Yes."

"Very well," he said. "What should I do?"

Well now, thought Donovan. *That certainly is the question, isn't it?*

IIIIIIIIIIIIII

As we approached, a black guy and two white women got out of an SUV and walked up to the door.

"Wait," said Shveta.

"You know them?"

"No. But the small woman's a sorcerer. I can smell it."

They rang the bell, and someone answered, and the guy talked to him for a while. The big dark-haired woman started to turn and Shveta pulled me back behind a tree. She watched through the trees for about fifteen minutes, then said, "Okay, they've gone in. Come on."

I was fingering the stone in my pocket. Then I fingered the other. *First the left, then the right. First the left, then the right.* I followed her.

"When I say 'now,'" she said, "use the first one. The glass bead. That will take down the defenses of everyone in the room, including you. You know that, right?"

"Yes. The glass bead. Left pocket. Not the stone. If I need to. Whittier's defenses are already gone."

"I know. But we don't know if the others have their own protections. Assume they do, at least the sorcerer. I need you to back my play."

"Yeah, I get it. When do I use the stone?"

"Depends on how things go down. If everything works, I'll just tell you. If not, you'll have to pick the moment as best you can."

"All right."

"But you need line of sight with him."

"I know."

"Good luck."

"Thanks."

We reached the front door. She gestured with her hand and the door blew inward.

||||||||||||||||

Donovan was still searching for an answer when there was a muffled thump from behind him.

Donovan's first clue that it might be important was when Susan reacted by turning and facing it, and she had that every-nerve-alert-ready-to-kill look that she'd had back in '13 just before the newsstand guy pulled a gun. Then the "butler" came back into the room, running, a pistol in his hand. He stepped between Whittier and the door and started to speak. Maybe he was going to tell Whittier to get to a safe spot, or ask for orders or something.

Whatever he was going to say, he didn't. Whatever he was going to do, he didn't. He flew against the wall next to Donovan, and the sick, awful, sucking thump of his body hitting the wall made its way into Donovan's ears and took up residence in his head in a way that Donovan knew would never go away. He pulled the bag of marbles with his left hand and the blackjack with his right

Well, all right, he thought. *This is going to suck.*

Four people came charging into the room like an out-of-control subway train.

IIIIIIIIIIIIIII

She walked so calmly, so smoothly, like there was nothing going on, nothing to worry about.

Yeah, I'd done some shit. I'd stood there in a crowded restaurant and blown a guy apart with a shotgun. I'd watched a woman drown. But those were matters of just deciding to do something and doing it; this was everything happening at once, from every direction, and I know you want me to tell you what happened, but I can't. I *can't.*

I remember Shveta moving, her hair blowing back as if she were walking into a windstorm, with one hand pointing forward, flanked by her toughs, me behind them. I remember the sound of glass breaking. I remember pictures falling from the wall, and one of them flinging itself across the room as if to attack someone.

And there were gunshots that echoed so much I have no idea how many there were, and there was the smell I remembered from the restaurant, from the shotgun.

There was a loud crack, very loud, and my memory tells me it was deafening, and I know there was ringing in my ears, but somehow I heard—or maybe saw?—Shveta say "now" and I used the bead, holding it over my head, squeezing it, and saying the word Charlie had taught me. I don't know how I remembered to do all of that; it's crazy. But I did it, and the dark-haired woman was flying across the room at Shveta, and the girl was on her knees shouting something that seemed an invocation to the gods, and everything spun and the room dipped and, God help me, I don't know what happened next.

|||||||||||||||||

Donovan was still standing, and so was Whittier, stock still and shaking, and so was the guy who held something clutched in his fist. The woman next to him was also standing, but her right arm was at an odd angle, there was blood coming from the corner of her mouth, and her eyes didn't seem to be focusing very well.

Donovan found his voice. "Let me guess. Nick Nagorski, am I right?" He nodded to the woman. "And you would be Shveta?"

Nagorski's voice was raw, like he'd been shouting, and maybe he had been. "Stand aside, please. I need to kill that guy."

"That's not going to happen," said Donovan.

"Why?"

Donovan glanced around the room. Marci's legs were twisted up oddly underneath her, and Susan was pressing a hand against her own chest trying to stop the bleeding. There were two large men he didn't recognize. One was gasping and holding his stomach and seemed to have a broken leg; the other's head was at an odd angle.

Donovan turned back. "You're going to get existential with me, motherfucker? That thing in your hand. You drop it right now, then lie down on the floor with your hands behind your head."

"Naw," said Nagorski, and raised his fist. The woman, Shveta, blinked, shook her head, and looked up.

The top of the doeskin bag was already open. Donovan threw all the marbles at them.

||||||||||||||||

The ceiling was textured, a sort of pink that, no doubt, appealed to someone, somewhere. Donovan didn't care for it much. A sudden panic gripped him as he realized he had no idea who had done what to whom, or what state anyone was in, and he heaved himself to a sitting position.

Nagorski was on his face, whimpering and clawing the carpet. Shveta was on her back, eyes open and staring, her body rigid.

Donovan pulled himself to his knees, then his feet; then he stumbled toward the two bruisers who'd shown up with Nagorski. They both had guns near them, one a Beretta .340 semi-auto, the other a Ruger .357 revolver. Donovan kicked both guns aside. It was only then he noticed the guy—*what was his name? Mark. Yeah, Mark.* Mark was on his back, his eyes wide and staring and glassy, and he was dead dead dead. Whittier was shrunk against a wall, but had no sign of injury. So, a win for the good guys. *Yay.*

Donovan knelt next to Susan. "Hey, Hippie. How you doing?"

"Hey, Laughing Boy. How are the others?"

Donovan looked around. "You're hurt the worst, Marci's banged up, but she'll be fine. Bad guys are down; target is safe."

"A win, then."

"Yeah. Can you hold on for me, Hippie?"

"I think so," she said. "I'd feel terrible about giving you a guilt complex or something."

She was pale. Scarily pale. There was a lot of blood—Donovan was kneeling in it.

Donovan looked up and caught Whittier's eye. He was about to ask him to call 911 when Whittier said, "It's part of the service to clean up this mess, isn't it? I need this cleaned up."

Donovan stared at him for a minute; then he nodded. "Yeah," he said. "It is. I'm all about cleaning up messes."

He picked up the Ruger, raised it, and put four shots into Paul Whittier's chest. Four red spots blossomed on his chest, spreading and growing, and Whittier fell back and started twitching.

Donovan used his shirt to wipe down the gun, then dropped it and turned his attention back to Susan.

"Damn, Laughing Boy," she said. "I don't think you were supposed to do that."

"Shit," he said. "Must have got my orders confused."

"Yeah," she said. "That'll happen from time to time."

His hand found hers. She gripped it tight; then her grip relaxed, and her eyes rolled up, and she stopped breathing.

He heard sirens.

IIIIIIIIIIIIII

You—Donovan, right? I didn't know your name then, even though I guess we'd been playing cat and mouse for a couple of weeks. I can tell you what happened from my perspective, if you want, though, I mean, you were right there. I watched you put the dead woman's head on the floor, close her eyes, and stand up. The effects of whatever you'd done to me were just wearing off, leaving nothing but a memory of vertigo and synesthesia. I looked for Shveta, but she was gone. I wasn't able to stand yet—there was still some dizziness—but I could speak.

You remember what I said? I don't, exactly. I think it was, "You motherfucking son of a bitch," or words to that effect.

You looked up and made eye contact with me.

If I had to put words to your expression, they would be, *I can't decide if you're worth the trouble of squashing like a bug.* Then you twisted your head in a circle like your neck was stiff and said, "What, that I killed him instead of you getting to, or that he died too easy?"

"Both."

I saw you look at Whittier. "He's still alive. Even . . . yeah, I think he's still conscious. So there's that." You shrugged. Your face was expressionless, but there were tears running down your cheek. I guess that hit me, because all of a sudden my anger drained away, leaving me feeling empty—I mean, completely empty, scoured out, like the idea I might ever feel something again was absurd.

You went over to the girl—I call her that because I swear she barely looked eighteen—and said, "You okay?"

"Yeah. Susan?"

"She didn't make it."

The girl started sobbing. It was around then that I realized the ringing in my ears was actually the sound of sirens and they were getting close—probably right outside the house.

You said, "Marci, I need you to focus. Just for a minute, then we can both collapse. The extraction team is coming to transport us out of here ahead of the cops, and they'll get this asshole"— you gestured toward me with your head—"and I don't trust Becker with him."

She said, "What—"

"Can you get this guy back to my apartment?"

"I guess—"

You walked over to me and knelt.

"Hurry up," you said, and I saw something dark in your hand.

I don't remember what happened after that, but I'm pretty sure you hit me with it.

||||||||||||||||

"I was pleased," said Donovan carefully, "that you were able to extract us before the PO-lice arrived."

He was in Madrid, on a hard chair in Becker's cubicle at the Foundation headquarters. The fluorescent light overhead was nearly the only one on in the office area—empty offices, thought Donovan, had their own, special kind of spooky. Becker, in his desk chair, looked at him steadily for a long moment, then said, "Mr. Longfellow, I am truly sorry for the loss of Ms.—of Susan."

Wow. Genuine emotion from Becker. Must be a sign of the Apocalypse. "Thank you, Mr. Becker. How is Marci?"

"She'll be fine, Mr. Longfellow. She has two broken legs, which we are endeavoring to help knit."

"Where is she?"

"In the infirmary."

"Do you know if she's awake? I'd like to visit her."

"I don't know; you can certainly go down there and check."

"Okay."

"I wish you could have saved Mr. Whittier."

"Yeah."

"And held on to Ms. Tyaga."

"I'll get her. We'll get her. Marci and me."

Becker nodded, then shifted in his chair. The chair squeaked. *Wow. The man actually looks uncomfortable. Definitely a sign of the Apocalypse.*

"Mr. Longfellow, what I can't help but wonder about is who wasn't there."

"Mr. Becker?"

"It was clear that this—" He stopped and glanced at a paper on his desk. "That this Mr. Nagorski was there, and that it was he who wanted to, and apparently did, kill Mr. Whittier. And yet, when the sorcerer arrived to extract you, there was no sign of him."

Longfellow looked him in the eye. "Things were pretty confused there, Mr. Becker. He must have escaped."

"I see."

Looking someone in the eye is a sure sign of lying. Donovan knew that, and he knew that Becker knew it as well.

"If that is all, Mr. Becker. I believe I'll head to the infirmary and see Marci."

"Of course, Mr. Longfellow. I'm going to email you a JPEG of a Mr. Charles Leong, who may be involved in this in some capacity."

"Some capacity, Mr. Becker."

"It is possible." Becker looked him in the eye.

"I'll see you later, Mr. Becker."

The infirmary was in the basement, on the opposite side from the holding cells. Donovan took the elevator down and followed signs. Marci was next to what looked like the nurses' station at any hospital, though on a smaller scale and with less equipment sitting in the hallways. She was in a wheelchair, both of her legs in casts.

Donovan walked over to her and knelt. He took her face in his hands. "I'm sorry," he said.

She nodded. "Not your fault."

"It is, though. I should have said no to the operation."

"We all agreed."

"It's not a democracy."

"Yeah, it is. Because we could all refuse to go."

"Shit. Why are you consoling me? Fuck."

"Because it makes me feel better. Shut up and take it." She smiled.

He pressed his forehead against hers. "Yes, ma'am."

"Your hair is scratchy."

"Fuck you."

"What now?" she said.

Donovan straightened up. "I need to get back home and open the package you had delivered."

"Wish I could be there."

"I'll give you all the details."

"You know this isn't over, right?"

"Oh yeah. I know that."

"Are we going to end it?"

"Oh yes. We surely are."

"Good," she said.

||||||||||||||||

My head hurt like a sonofabitch, and it was pitch-black. At least, I hoped it was pitch- black, because if it wasn't I was blind. I brought my hands up to see if there was anything covering my eyes, and there wasn't.

I felt my head, and found a lump high on the temple. Touching it hurt a lot, so naturally I kept doing it, trying to figure out how big it was. I couldn't tell—lumps on your head are really deceptive. Then I brought my fingers away to see if there was blood, but obviously I couldn't see. Was that liquid on my fingers? Hard to say. Maybe sweat.

I felt a little sick to my stomach. Concussion. All right, then. Not too bad, though, or the nausea would be worse. I wondered if my vision would be fuzzy if I had any vision.

My pants were wet, and the smell told me I'd pissed myself. *Goddammit.* I wanted to take my pants off, but I didn't dare until I had some idea of where I was, or what was going on.

I tried to remember what had happened, how I'd ended up here. I kept almost remembering being hit, but then the memory would slide away. I tried to get there. I remembered the last meeting with Charlie, the drive to Darien, meeting Shveta and the thugs. Sounds like a band name. Shveta and the Thugs. Not bad. I thought I remembered that the term "thug" originally came from—

Stop it.

I shook my head.

I resolved not to shake my head again.

We'd gotten into the car, and then—nothing after that would come into focus.

I was on a cement floor, with walls close by. A little exploring with my hands told me that I was at the bottom of a stairway. Had I fallen down the stairs? Was that it? The way my head felt, I might not even notice other bumps and bruises. When did I turn into a guy who ended up blind and bleeding in a tiny room, smelling his own urine? I knew the answer to that; I decided not to go there.

I got to my feet and steadied myself against the wall. I felt around. It was a small area, and I found no indications of a door. So, I was at the bottom of a stairway that went nowhere. That would have struck me as more impossible if I hadn't spent the last months hanging around magic.

Whittier.

Whittier was dead.

I hadn't killed him; some other guy had. I almost remembered who. Just picked up a gun and shot him, like it was nothing. I hadn't gotten to kill him, and he hadn't suffered enough, and now I was at the bottom of a stairway to nowhere, blind, my pants wet with piss, and my head hurting.

Stairway to nowhere. That could be the name of my memoir.

But things started to fill in—from Whittier's death to the blood and the bodies around the room—and I finally remembered you slugging me. Some things still aren't clear, like, I don't know exactly what happened between when we blew the door of the house down and when I came back from whatever it was that made the world spin and all my senses fuck up—or, for that matter, what caused that to happen.

I thought about climbing up the stairs to see if maybe there was a door up there. But if the place was magical, maybe I'd be getting into more trouble. *Shit.* I wished I could see. *Hell with it.*

I went up the stairs slowly, on my hands and knees, carefully touching each step ahead of me, feeling it, before I moved onto it. I should have counted the stairs; it felt like there were a thousand of them.

I reached the top and felt around the walls. My hand reached a doorknob, and I almost cried with relief. I turned it. It was locked.

I put my back against one of the side walls, closed my eyes, and let the tears come.

16

NOODLES DONOVAN

He appeared after the slipwalk, and clapped his hands to turn the light on. At first, he thought Nagorski wasn't there and he started to panic, but no, there he was, huddled up at the top of the stairs. Awake, too: When the lights came on he covered his eyes and used language Grandma would have rapped Donovan's knuckles for.

Donovan took his time going up the stairs. He smelled urine.

"Sorry," he said. "I didn't mean to keep you here so long. Let's go get you cleaned up. You can use my shower, and I have a spare bathrobe."

Donovan took his arm—Nagorski didn't seem inclined to resist. The door had unlocked when Donovan had turned on the lights. He checked the peephole to make sure the laundry room was empty, then turned the handle, opening up the door and the wall behind it.

He guided Nagorski carefully around the folding table—his eyes had obviously not adjusted yet. Donovan led him to the elevator. They did not, fortunately, run into anyone on the way to Donovan's apartment.

By the time they got there, Nagorski was obviously seeing

better. Donovan pointed him toward the bathroom. "Towel and bathrobe hanging on the door. Take your time; the one nice thing about this place is that there's plenty of hot water, though the water pressure kinda sucks. I'm going to cook us something. Do you eat meat?"

Nagorski nodded and stumbled into the bathroom, shut the door.

Donovan had some hamburger defrosted, so he cooked it up along with some tomato sauce and a few spices, then turned the heat down and boiled some macaroni.

Nagorski came out of the bathroom and stood there while Donovan drained the pasta, put it on some plates, poured the hamburger over it, and added some Parmesan cheese. "There," he said. "Noodles Donovan. Want a beer?"

He nodded and Donovan got them each one.

"Donovan," he said. "That's your name?"

"Yeah, and if you call me Mellow Yellow I'll hit you again."

They sat at the kitchen table. The day before, it had been him and Marci and Susan.

Susan.

Shit.

Nagorski was pretty hungry, so Donovan just let him eat, and then realized that he was, too. He got them each seconds, and another beer. He had three bottles left from the case. *Always keep track of how much beer you have.*

When they'd both gotten some food down, Donovan went off and grabbed a pair of old coveralls. "Not what you'd call stylin'," he said, "but you should be able to fit into them, and they don't smell like piss."

Nagorski nodded, then went off to change. When he came back, Donovan didn't make any remarks about what Nagorski looked like in them. Instead he said, "So, tell me something—"

"Is this the interrogation?"

"Yeah. If you don't answer, I might torture you by making you get the next beer. I just want to know, for my own curiosity, how it started."

"How it started? Jesus. I got a job, and I got married. What the fuck. How it started. I don't know."

He was tired, Donovan could see that. No, not tired, *weary*. A bone-deep kind of weariness, where you feel like you'll never be truly rested again.

"Nick—can I call you Nick?"

"Yeah."

"Nick, I'm not about torture, or putting pressure on you, or whatever. But my friend is dead, and I'm sort of a little ripped up about it. So if you don't want to talk about shit, then okay, don't. But if you start getting sarcastic with me, I'm going lose it all over your face. Feel me?"

Nick nodded.

"So, yeah. I'm curious about what happened. Like I said, you don't have to tell me. But you seem like a nice guy. Like someone who wouldn't do that stuff I know you did. I just wonder why."

"I don't want to talk about it," he said.

"All right. That's cool. I'm pretty sure I know most of it anyway."

They continued eating.

After about five minutes, Donovan said, "Except there's this one piece I just can't figure out."

"What's that?"

"The time-stop."

"What about it?"

"That was your heavy artillery, man. That was the one you could have been saving for an emergency. Why blow it so early?"

"Charlie's idea. He—you know about Charlie?"

"Your supplier? Yeah."

"He needed me to be convinced. I mean, in magic. We couldn't do anything more if I didn't know, all the way into my bones, that it was real. And, man, when I clicked that thing, and walked through that restaurant full of, like, statues. It was weird. It was creepy. I mean, if you ever want someone to know for sure that this shit is real, have him cast that."

"I get it," said Donovan. "Makes sense."

They went back to eating.

A little later, Nagorski said, "I had a list, you know."

Donovan kept eating.

"It was—I had to—it was supposed to work out different."

Donovan nodded.

"It was in order of how fucked up they were. Charlie gave me the details about them. He said he had his own thing going, but he wouldn't tell me what it was, just that he'd help me with Whittier, if I'd help him with the others. There was a whole plan."

"I know," said Donovan. Under the table, he started his cell phone recording.

"The first one on the list," said Nagorski, "was Georgio Byrne Lawton-Smythe."

||||||||||||||||

Marci wheeled herself back to her room, took a long, slow breath, then made a call. It was answered at once. "Sweetie! Where are you?"

"I'm all right, love. I got banged up a little, but nothing serious."

"Jesus, honey! What does 'banged up' mean?"

"My legs hurt, but that's all."

"What happened?"

"An accident."

There was a long pause from the other end. Then, "I hate this."

"I know."

There was another long pause. "All right. What do you need me to do?"

Marci felt herself smiling, and felt tears at the same time. "Feed the goldfish?" she said.

"We don't have a goldfish."

"Oh, right." She sniffed. "Okay, never mind that then."

"Are you okay? You sound like—"

"I'm fine. You're just making me fall in love with you all over again, and it isn't fair."

"Ha," he said. "My fiendish plan works." He sounded like he was crying, too.

"I'll be home in a couple of days. I may need crutches for a while, to be safe—"

"Crutches!"

"I promise, it's nothing serious."

"All right."

"Should we get a goldfish?"

"Maybe. It'll give me something to do when you get banged up."

"We'll talk about it. I'll see you soon."

"I love you."

"I love you, too."

||||||||||||||||

Nick had gotten Donovan up to the point where he was about to use magic to murder a California State Senator when the buzzer rang. Nick stopped talking and looked at him. Donovan shrugged. "I'm not expecting anyone."

He got up and pushed the intercom button. "Hello?"

"Hey, Donovan. Can I come up?"

Matt. Well, son of a bitch.

"I can't think of anyone in the world I'd rather see. Uh, are you armed?"

"Yes."

Well, fuck. Donovan thought about it, then said, "Do you have beer?"

"No."

"Go get some, then come back."

"Sam Adams all right?"

"In that case, hurry back."

"All right."

Donovan sat down again.

"Who's that?" said Nick.

"Someone who wants to be a good guy."

"Yeah, don't we all."

Nick went back to his story as if there'd never been an interruption. Half an hour later the buzzer sounded again. Donovan buzzed Matt in, and opened the door when he knocked. He stood there, wearing a coat that was a bit too big for him—something of an accomplishment. Donovan took the case of Sam Adams and went into the kitchen, sticking all of it in the refrigerator. He brought Matt one.

"Well," said Donovan. "I assume you're here to get your cell phone back? Bad news about that. It's kind of in pieces."

"Oh, you found it?"

"Well, you know, it wasn't like you hid it all that well."

"Yeah."

"This is Nick. Nick, meet Matt. Nick worked for the guy who hired you to kill us."

"I didn't work for him," snapped Nick.

"Right. Sorry. He was working *with* the guy who hired you to kill us."

They sat down, Matt on the other side of the couch from Nick.

"I'm checking those cushions this time when you leave," said Donovan.

"How are things?"

"Susan is dead."

Matt stared at him. "How—"

"We ran an operation. Things went bad."

"I'm sorry. Shit. Was that in Connecticut?"

"How the fuck—"

"I got a call from a guy named Becker, who wanted me to show up there. I missed my flight and by the time I got there it was all over except the flashing lights."

"Mother fuck," said Donovan.

"I'm sorry."

Donovan nodded, and focused on his kitchen window for a while. Then he said, "Nick was just telling the story of his life. Want to listen?"

"Sure."

"Carry on, Nick. He'll get to hear about all the excitement he missed."

Nick nodded and continued his story.

⁣IIIIIIIIIIIIIII

Manuel Becker sat down at his computer. He typed in the password: a random set of numbers, letters, and symbols that he memorized anew every week when he changed it. He opened the file called "Personnel" and let his mouse hover over "Kouris, Susan Dionisia." He clicked it. He checked the box marked "Deceased." When another screen opened up, he checked the box marked "Line of duty." He meticulously filled out the other fields that would see to it that death benefits and funeral costs would be released, then clicked "Close."

With her file still open, he clicked on "Next of kin."

It read: "Father: Andras Lyric: South Barrington, Illinois, USA. Mother: Dionisia Kasia: South Barrington, Illinois, USA." It gave a single phone number for both of them.

Becker picked up the phone and started to punch in the number, stopped, and stared at the hand holding the phone. He tried to think of the last time his hands had trembled. He couldn't remember.

He punched in the number.

IIIIIIIIIIIIIIIII

Nick spoke about waking up in the narrow stairwell, reciting it almost in a monotone up to the point where he fell asleep. Then he stopped and looked down at the remains of his food.

Donovan got up and cleared the plates, put them in the sink.

"Well," said Donovan. "Okay. That gives me some stuff to play with."

Nick nodded. "Now what?"

"Now what? What do you mean?"

"What happens to me now?"

"Oh. Now you finish your beer."

"Then what?"

"Then I make a call to a guy named Becker, and he comes and picks you up."

"What's he going to do?"

"Talk to you."

"Is that all?"

Donovan shrugged. "I don't know exactly. And, you know, I don't care all that much."

"I—"

"Shut up. I got some sympathy for you. Some. You went through bad shit. I get that. But you know, you're a fucking psychopath. How many people have you killed in two weeks? A lot of people had their lives fucked up, they didn't go on a magic murder spree. So shut your hole, and finish your beer."

Nick finished his beer. Donovan felt Matt looking at him, but didn't look back.

Donovan turned to his computer and brought up Skype. "Mr. Becker," he said when the pale bald guy came on. "I have Nicholas Nagorski here for you. You want to come fetch him?"

Becker gave no indication that there was anything surprising in the call. "Can you deliver him to your slipwalk room? We'll pick him up from there."

"Sure. Five minutes." Then he looked at Nick. "Let's go. You can keep the coveralls."

Ten minutes later, Donovan let himself back into his apartment. He got himself a beer, drank some, nodded to Matt. "That's done," he said.

"Now it's my turn," said Matt. "What's next?"

"You want to help?"

"Yeah."

"Okay."

He picked up his phone, and punched in a number.

"Hey, Marci. How you feeling?"

"I'm okay. I still can't walk."

"Still in the infirmary?"

"Yeah."

"Okay. Hang tight. We're going to get this taken care of."

"I know."

"You remember Matt."

"Sure."

"He's working with us now."

"You trust him?"

"Yeah."

"Okay."

"When can you be here, Marci?"

"The casts come off tomorrow, but I'll be on crutches. If you don't mind, I don't."

"I don't. I need you here. We got to deal with this."

"Yes," said Marci. "We do. And we will. I'll be there tomorrow."

"What about your boyfriend?"

"I'll talk to him. It's all right. I'll be there tomorrow."

"See you then."

He disconnected and said, "Matt, do me a favor and take a walk, all right? I need to make a couple of calls, and I'd rather do it alone. Give me an hour."

"See you in an hour," said Matt.

When he was gone, Donovan brought up Skype and punched in a number.

"Mr. Longfellow."

"Mr. Becker. I need contact information for Susan's next of kin."

"I've made that call already, Mr. Longfellow, so you don't need to."

"I don't give a fl—" Donovan closed his eyes, opened them again. "If it's all the same to you, Mr. Becker, I would like to call as well."

Becker hesitated. "I need to tell you the cover story."

"No, you don't."

"Mr. Longfellow, this is not a negotiable matter."

"Mr. Becker, I have no intention of telling them how she died, or anything related to her death beyond hearing that it happened. Yeah, I'm going to lie to them. I'll leave it to your imagination how much I like doing that. But I'm going to. I knew her; I worked with her; I cared about her. I would like to call and express my sympathies to her family even if I have to lie to do it. But I'm not going to play your game. Please provide me with the contact information."

There was a short pause, then, "One moment, Mr. Long-fellow. There. It should arrive in your email shortly."

"Thank you, Mr. Becker."

While he was waiting to make the unpleasant phone call, he made an unpleasant Skype call.

"Well, this is a surprise, Chumpy. You forget about me for almost a year, and now two calls within a week."

"It's not good, Grampa."

"Oh. What happened?"

Donovan's mouth felt dry. He was suddenly afraid that if he didn't say it Croshack would guess, and that would be worse, so he blurted it: "Susan is dead."

He watched on the screen as the old man's head drooped. The silence went on for a long time, until finally Grampa looked up and said, "Oh, Chumpy. I'm so sorry. Was it the thing you called me about?"

"Yeah. A rogue sorcerer backed by a couple of foot soldiers and a guy with an artifact that strips magical defenses. It was a mess."

"And you're blaming yourself, aren't you?"

Donovan laughed in spite of himself. "Sure. And Marci is blaming herself. A guy you've never met who isn't even part of this is blaming himself. Even Becker is blaming himself. We got a whole thing going down here. Gonna get T-shirts."

"Well, don't leave me out of it."

"Huh. I think you're the one person who's got no reason to beat himself up over this."

"More reason than the rest of you, Chumpy. I'm sorry."

"That's bullshit."

"Shut up and let me talk. It's the least I can do."

"I . . . all right, I'm listening."

"Years ago I was ordered to keep a secret. I kept it. I shouldn't have. Hang on a minute. I need a glass of water. No. I need a whiskey. Be right back."

Donovan got up and poured himself a horseradish-infused vodka on the rocks. When he returned to the screen, Crosheck was already there. He gestured toward the drink in Donovan's hand and said, "Good choice," then had a drink himself. He didn't sip it; Donovan watched as the old man tossed it down, then poured himself another, which he set somewhere out of sight of the camera.

"The secret," he said. "I was on the team that caught Becker and stripped him of his sorcerous ability."

"Fuck," said Donovan. Then, "That's a lot to take in, old man. For one thing, it means Becker's been lying a lot. Or misleading. He keeps claiming not to know how sorcery works."

"Yeah, he knows. He has many faults, has our Mr. Becker, but excessive trust has never been among them."

"Fuck. Okay, you'd better tell me about it."

"He—Becker—used to be with the Mystici. He was a sorcerer in their R and D division, which is considerably bigger and better funded than ours. And mostly, their R and D department works on good things, or at worst harmless. It's all the other stuff the Mystici do that got to him."

"I know about some of that. There's probably a lot I don't know."

"Yeah, me too. So Becker and another guy got pissed off at all the bad things the Mystici were doing, or allowing to happen, and just started going after the worst of them. Near as we could tell, one or the other of them had a brother or sister or mother or father or wife who was killed by a sorcerer. The sorcerer was protected by the Mystici, so they weren't allowed to take any action."

"You never learned the details?"

"Neither of them would talk about it. And to tell the truth, once we caught them, we didn't need it. It was a hell of a hunt, Chumpy. Three continents, four teams. They killed nine people before we got to them, and did a lot of other damage. And those were nine tough sons of bitches, too."

"Them," said Donovan. "Who was the other guy?"

"His name is Charles Leong."

"Charlie," said Donovan. "Motherfucking son of a bitch."

"I'm sorry, Chumpy. If I'd told you this before, maybe things would have been different."

"I don't see how. I knew about Leong, I just didn't know Becker was involved. I don't see how it plays out if any different if I knew that."

"Maybe."

"And if it was anyone's job to tell me, it was Becker's."

After a moment, the old man said, "Maybe so. Or maybe it was his boss's. I don't know. Following orders, keeping secrets, doing the right thing. All sorts of decisions, and they're never easy, Chumpy."

"Sometimes they are."

"Yeah."

"Okay, Grampa. Thanks for the information. I'll put it to good use."

"I know you will, son."

Donovan clicked off, then checked the time. Then he placed the call to Susan's family.

When Matt returned, Donovan was so engrossed in staring at the mountains of British Columbia that he wasn't sure how long Matt had been buzzing. He got up, let him in, and returned to the computer. Matt got himself a beer and came over to the kitchen table, sat down.

Donovan looked up.

"All right. Enough fucking around. We need to find Charlie," he said.

|||||||||||||||

Marci showed up around 9:00 AM Eastern. Donovan gave her time to set her crutches against the wall before wrapping her in a hug. It went on a long time. Then she took her crutches again and made her way to the couch.

"Already walking," said Donovan. "They do good work."

"They tell me I'll be done with the crutches in a week."

Marci and Matt exchanged nods.

Donovan plugged in his speakers. "All right," he said. "Matt's heard a little of this already, but you should both hear the whole thing. Sorry about the sound quality. I recorded it on my cell holding it under the table."

He started the recording. When it was done, he said, "That was a little harder to listen to again than I'd expected. I don't mean the sound quality."

Marci nodded. "I'm all cried out for now," she said.

"Me too," said Donovan.

He got up and paced a little, then sat down again.

"Anything else?" said Marci. "I need to—I want to dive into this."

"Yeah, I know. There's something else. I talked to your predecessor. He had some info. I've been holding off on telling Matt until you were both here."

"Okay."

He summarized what Grampa had told him, using as few words as possible.

Then he said, "Any questions?"

Marci said, "How do we find Charlie?"

"You should have put a tracker on Nagorski and let him go," said Matt.

"First of all, I don't have a tracker. Second, it's pointless. Charlie isn't going to come anywhere near him. Third, the last thing I'm gonna do is let that psycho fuck loose on the world. So, here's the thing: Charlie's the one who's had all the artifacts, controlled them all."

"Sure," said Marci. "That's been clear all along."

"There has to be a way to—hang on," he finished as his computer informed him of a Skype call. It was Becker. He clicked answer.

"Good afternoon, Mr. Longfellow. This concerns the 'script' placed to detect an email from the individual who created the dummy email account."

"Who we're assuming is your old friend, Charles Leong; is that correct, Mr. Becker?"

Either Becker didn't react, or Skype concealed his reaction to Donovan's *your old friend*. "That is correct. Half an hour ago, we received what our computer expert called a 'hit.'"

"And?"

"We have just now confirmed the location."

"Excellent. Where is he?"

"A city called Atlanta."

"In a state called Georgia?"

"Yes. Your country, of course."

"It's not *my* country, Mr. Becker. Can we get any more specific than Atlanta? It's a big place."

"The neighborhood is called Mechanicsville. That is as close as we could get."

"Good. That ought to do it. Thank you, Mr. Becker."

"Good hunting, Mr. Longfellow."

He disconnected, and turned around.

"Well then," he said.

"What now?" said Marci.

"Now we head to Georgia. Probably fly instead of slipwalk, but I'll ask Upstairs. Matt? You look like you got something on your mind."

Matt nodded. "Yeah, there may be a thing."

They both looked at him and waited.

"I was in Madrid a few days ago," he said. "And I might have learned something. If I'm right, I may have an idea on how to get the guy who's behind it all. Let me run it by you."

"Is it anything that will make it a bad idea to go to Atlanta?"

"No."

"Then tell us on the plane. I'll grab my lighter."

"Lighter?"

"Never mind. Let me call in about travel arrangements; may as well save Fenwood from apoplexy."

"I didn't think people got that anymore," said Matt.

"Let's go," said Marci.

Marci and Matt stood up. Donovan went to the closet, unlocked it, and took his blackjack, a lighter, a knotnot, and the car keys. He closed the closet and started whistling "Marching Through Georgia," even though he was pretty sure neither of the others would get it.

||||||||||||||||

Eight hours later, they were in the Atlanta airport, Oversight preferring to pay for three short-notice tickets as opposed to three slipwalks. Donovan wondered if some poor clerk had had to laboriously calculate the costs and come up with a comparison. Probably.

They waited while Matt picked up his suitcase—a suitcase purchased at the airport, because Matt had firearms, and going back and forth through security to get the bag, bring it back, check it, and return had put Matt in such a foul mood that he hadn't spoken the entire trip until Donovan pointed out that he had information to share. He told them about his visit to Madrid, and they talked over plans. They had things fairly well figured out when they landed in Atlanta. After collecting Matt's suitcase, they took a shuttle to a Ramada near Mechanicsville that had a vacancy. The desk clerk looked like she still belonged in school, but she gave the three of them a double-double without comment, though she did purse her lips in disapproval. *They must learn that early around here*, thought Donovan.

Once they got to the room, Marci announced that she would use all of the sorcerous power at her disposal to destroy anyone who tried to beat her to the shower. Donovan tossed his suitcase into the corner and collapsed on one of the beds. Matt shrugged, tossed his suitcase next to Donovan's, and collapsed on the other.

How they worked it out Donovan didn't know, because he was asleep before the bathroom door closed.

He felt better the next morning. He stumbled out of bed while Marci and Matt were still asleep in the other. They were still asleep when he was finished in the bathroom. He looked at them, and tried to decide from how they were sleeping if they'd had sex. He couldn't tell, but it wasn't any of his business anyway, except in the vague, general sense that Matt was now sort of on his team and protocol had things to say about it. But Donovan wasn't about to start paying attention to protocol now of all times.

He went downstairs to the restaurant and had a long, slow

breakfast. They joined him about halfway through and he still couldn't tell. He gave himself a firm talking-to for paying so much attention to it.

"So," said Matt. "Is there a plan?"

"Yes," said Donovan. "Unfortunately, it's too complicated to actually work. In general, we find him, we take him, we have a big party."

"Complicated is bad," said Matt. "Complicated means everything goes south."

Donovan nodded. "I've been trying to figure out ways to simplify it. I prepare an email, but don't send it. Marci prepares a spell, but doesn't cast it. That's the tricky part, really: If everything goes down the way I think it will, we'll need Marci to do two things at once, and neither one is easy."

"I know what the obvious one is," said Marci. "What's the other?"

Donovan pulled out the car keys. "This thing needs to penetrate. It needs to get past any protections or defenses, just for a second."

Marci twirled a finger in her hair, then stopped and put her hands in her lap as if it required an act of will. "Breaking down a shield is a test of strength, whether it's a protection against magic or physical attacks."

"And?"

"I'm not confident."

"Fuck."

She bit her lower lip. "Unless."

"Okay," said Donovan. "I like unless. Let's go with unless. Unless what?"

"Unless we can prep the room. I mean, if I can set it up ahead of time, like a thing that just happens, I can spend some time putting extra power into it, like an artifact."

Donovan studied her face; there was something she wasn't saying. "Is there a downside to that?"

"Well, I'll need to stuff a lot of power into it. You know what happens when your ability to stuff power into an artifact exceeds your ability to prepare the artifact to contain it?"

"Let me guess—something not good?"

"Right."

"Well, okay. Um, do the spell thing, but not the too much power thing."

"Great plan," said Marci dryly.

They fiddled around with the details as Matt and Marci ate. Or, well, Matt ate; Marci sort of picked at her food.

"So," said Matt. "Now we're in the area, and we have a whole plan except how do we find him? We can rent a car and go driving through every neighborhood until we spot him, but that doesn't sound like such a good idea."

"We have his picture," said Donovan. "There are such places as grocery stores, convenience stores, and gas stations."

"Cover story? I mean, just walking up to people and showing his picture will make them suspicious, right?"

"We won't need a cover story," said Marci.

"Oh, right. Yeah."

"Finish your breakfasts," said Donovan.

He charged it to the room, which put it in the hands of the Black Hole to deal with, and much joy may it bring Fenwood.

Donovan secured a rental, which took a couple of hours to arrange and acquire. They settled on a blue Ford Fiesta, because Marci said she hated SUVs, though she hadn't objected in San Diego or Connecticut. She sat in back as punishment and because she was the smallest. They followed the GPS to the Mechanicsville neighborhood and began checking convenience stores. The clerks acted like it was no big deal seeing Donovan walk in with Matt and Marci, and he realized that it didn't make him nearly as nervous as he'd been with Marci and Susan, and then immediately felt guilty. Fortunately, it didn't take long. The fourth one they tried, they walked in, Marci did her Jedi mind trick, and they showed the picture.

"Oh yeah," said a fat clerk who looked like he owned the place. "Yeah. That's Charlie. Lives down the street. I don't know which house."

"Well, damn," said Matt. "Is it all going to be that easy?"

"I hope so," said Donovan. "Now, may I suggest that we all take this opportunity to use this nice man's restroom? And then maybe buy something, on account of he's such a great guy?"

Matt bought a pack of Camel 99's, Donovan's old brand, which Matt promised not to smoke in the car, and Marci got a Snickers bar.

They got back into the car, drove it to the middle of the block, parked, got out, and stood around as if they were having a conversation, all of them scanning the street. Marci did her thing to make them less conspicuous, and they waited.

"There's a part of this plan we didn't talk about."

"Well, shit," said Donovan. "What is it?"

"When we find him, Marci does something so the guy starts acting drunk, right?"

"Right."

"And we bring him into his own house, right?"

"Right."

"What if someone's there?"

"That's why we have you, big guy."

They sat in the car, and Donovan composed the email, just waiting to press send.

At 6:47 in the evening, Charles Leong came out of his house, almost square in front of them, and set off down the street toward the convenience store.

"All right," said Donovan, trying to sound as if his heart weren't suddenly hammering. "Let's take him."

17

It was a small house, two-bedroom, one-bath, built in the fifties. There was no one else there, so that was good. Charles Leong was on a plain wooden chair at his kitchen table, with Donovan and Matt. The back door opened to the kitchen. Marci was working. She muttered under her breath as she ran her finger across the casting above the door, back and forth. At first Donovan thought she was muttering a spell, but eventually he realized it was something on the order of, "Goddammit, don't fuck this up. How did that go? Shit, forgot that part," and so on. Matt and Donovan sat at the kitchen table with their guest, who wasn't so much conscious just then.

"All right," said Marci. "I think I got it. Time to do the other one."

She wasn't terribly good with her crutches, but she managed not to fall over. A few minutes later she was back. "All done," she said. "I hope." She looked exhausted.

"You got this?" said Donovan.

"I got it," said Marci.

"Okay. Then we ready to start the show?"

"Yes," said Marci. Matt nodded.

"Okay," said Donovan. "Snap him out of it."

Marci touched his forehead, then sat down. Charles Leong woke up, shook his head, tried to move, failed. Donovan opened up his cell phone and sent the email. He nodded to Marci and Matt. "Done," he said, and put his phone away.

Then he turned to Leong. "S.R.P. Sensitivity Removal Protocol. God, these people love their acronyms, don't they? It's like their dream is to be as corporate as they can manage. I mean, seriously. Sensitivity Removal Protocol. What the fuck."

Leong focused on him and said, "I hope you aren't planning to threaten me with that, because it's too late."

"I know. Usually, when people do the sorts of things you did, and that happens, we're done with them. But you managed to continue to be a nuisance. So, good job on that, anyway."

"Thanks?"

"My friend Susan was killed in all of this."

"I didn't know her. But I'm sorry."

"Yeah, I'll bet."

"What do you want?"

"Marci, let him loose. It looks uncomfortable sitting like that." She gestured at him, and he relaxed. "Thank you."

"Charlie, how do you live like this?"

"I own a chain of Laundromats. That part of what I told Becker was true."

"That's why you live on frozen pizza, Hot Pockets, and Diet Coke?"

"It's a small chain."

"A good computer, though. Impressive. We'll be taking that with us, I'm afraid."

"Yeah, I figured."

"We going to find anything on it?"

"No."

"We'll see. My uncle—he used to be a fed—taught me that torture is one of the worst ways to get information, 'Reliable intel,' I think he called it."

"I'm relieved to hear that."

"But, God, Charlie. You have no idea how bad I want to test that."

Leong didn't reply.

"What are the chances that you'll make it easy for me, and just tell me who you're working with inside the Foundation?"

"Not very good, I'm afraid," said Leong.

Matt cracked his knuckles.

"Want a Coke?" said Donovan.

"Sure."

Matt opened the refrigerator and pulled one out, then looked around, opening cabinets. "Doritos," he said. "Want some?"

"Not just now. Is this how you work? You're going to be nice to me until I decide to tell you what you want to know?"

"It works sometimes. Usually when the person doesn't have any good reason not to talk. Or when I can come up with some clever way of tricking it out of him. I don't think either of those are going to happen here."

"What is, do you think?"

"Well, we're going to chill a bit, then we're going to put a spell on you that will make you realize everything you've done is wrong and fill you with the desire to be a good person, and then, of course, you'll be happy to talk."

"Think that'll work?"

"Yeah."

"We'll see. I thought the Foundation didn't approve of that sort of thing."

"It's kind of hard to know where to place the line," said Marci.

"Some things are one hundred percent *verboten*. Others, like making someone trust you long enough to get past him into a building, are fine, as long as he isn't going to get in trouble for it. Other things are in between. It usually has to do with long-term consequences to the person you do it to, and how desperate you are."

"You guys desperate?"

"Yeah, kinda," said Donovan.

"Whatever the spell is, if it's mental it's going to be a test of wills. I don't think it'll work."

"As you said, we'll see. But look, tell me one thing. Why did you do it?"

"Does it matter?"

"Fuck yes, it matters. My friend is dead. Her name was Susan Kouris; she had a mother, a father, and a little sister. She was funny. She was smart. She called me Laughing Boy and I never got around to asking her why. I kept meaning to. She did her job, and she saved my ass at least three times. She's dead because of you. I want to know why."

Leong popped the lid on his Diet Coke and drank some. He put the can down, wiped his mouth, and said, "I'm not fond of evil. I don't care for it. But it's part of life. There are greedy people in the world. But magic—those few who can feel the grid lines. The things they—used to be 'we'—could do for the world. Do you have any idea what those things are? So how can you just watch people use these skills to line their pockets and ruin lives? How can you?"

"It gets easier with practice," said Donovan.

"Maybe for you. I put up with it as long as I could. When I couldn't, I acted."

"You and Becker."

"Yes."

"So my friend is dead because you want to fight evil."

"Not all evil. I'm pretty specific. I heard my friend managed to kill Whittier."

Donovan saw no reason to enlighten him. "Nick? Yeah, well. Good work on that."

"He ruined Nick's life."

I know all about it. "I figured it was something like that."

"The world is better with Whittier out of it. Not to mention all the others."

"And you don't think you're taking a lot on yourself, making decisions like that?"

"I suppose." He shrugged and took another drink from his can. He frowned and looked at it. "Did you put something in this?"

"No," said Donovan. "No need to. Marci."

Leong nodded. "Well, you asked why I did it; I answered. You want to argue about it, or do we move on?"

"I dunno," said Donovan. "I got nothing going. How about you?"

"No, I'm good."

"You sure? Because you seem to be in a hurry. Expecting company?"

"Alas, no."

"Then let's talk philosophy."

"You think I haven't gone over this in my head? You think, the first time, with Becker, that he and I didn't go around and around on it before we decided to act?"

"Jesus Christ, you fucking psycho. How am I supposed to know what you were thinking?"

"You're calling me a psycho? What about those—what was that?"

"What?" said Donovan. "That little chiming sound? I didn't hear it."

As he spoke, Matt and Marci stood up. Marci picked up her crutches, and went to the back door, Matt to the front.

"This way," said Marci. "Just one."

"Two coming this way," said Matt. "You're sure there's no invisibility out there?"

"I'm sure."

"What if there's a time-stop?"

"Then we're fucked."

"You guys got this?" said Donovan.

"Yeah."

"Yes."

Donovan pulled a pistol from his coat pocket—a Colt Python .357, four-inch barrel. He cocked it, pointed it at Leong, aiming for center mass, elbows braced on the table, supporting hand firm but relaxed, finger off the trigger, just as Uncle Gary had taught him. "If you want to live through the next five minutes," he said. "Don't move."

"What's going on?"

"That's him," said Matt. "We've got him."

"Not yet we don't," said Marci. "Switch."

"Right."

They exchanged doors, Marci moving noticeably better on her crutches.

It was only then that Donovan noticed out of the corner of his eye that Matt had drawn his other pistol, and was holding it two-handed down and to the side.

"What the fuck?" said Leong.

"The chime," said Donovan, "was to let us know someone had violated the perimeter of the house."

"Who is it?"

"Who do you think?"

"I swear to Christ, I have no idea."

"Then I hope you like surprises."

Marci said, "That's Shveta."

"Okay," said Donovan. He kept the gun pointed at Leong while he dug the car keys out of his left-hand pocket. "We knew she might be here."

"I know."

"You got this?"

"Yeah."

Someone kicked open the front door.

||||||||||||||

Matt thought of combat operations as the working of a machine full of parts with unknown failure modes and unpredictable breaking points. The big advantages were, first, a reliable team, second, a flexible plan, and third, communications—whether by radio, hand signal, or even significant looks—that were dependable enough to keep everyone together as events developed.

He stood facing the doorway, carefully out of Donovan's line of fire. Behind him were two people he'd never trained with and didn't know, counting on magic—literally magic—to make things work. The possibility of the whole thing going south was so high that his only option was to fall back on the most basic, fundamental lesson: Do your job and trust your team in spite of everything.

The dark-skinned woman and the skinny man came through the doorway. Matt had been told he wouldn't see or hear anything when—if—the spell worked, so he had to take it on faith. His problem was the armed man, and nothing else.

All right then.

This, at least, was something Matt understood. The guy was

holding a semi-auto, a SIG, with both hands, pointed down and away: his pose a mirror image of Matt's own. The man's training was, if not the same as Matt's, at least similar. The man raised his pistol at the same time Matt did. A certain distant, disconnected, unacknowledged part of Matt's brain idly wondered which of them was better.

The report was very loud in the tiny room.

IIIIIIIIIIIIIII

Stay focused.

Donovan had no way of knowing if Marci's spell had worked, so he just had to assume it did. He kept the gun on Leong, but turned his attention away, hoping the man wouldn't take the opportunity to jump him.

He just had time to recognize the woman Shveta—it was only later he registered how she looked when she came in, her confidence, her air of command. Everything about her ought to have screamed, *Do not mess with this one!* and he might have frozen, if he'd had time to think.

Afterward, he also remembered—or thought he did—her eyes widening as the spell above her went off.

There was gunfire—he always forgot how loud gunfire is indoors.

He pointed the keys to the 1955 Dodge at her, and said, "Why can't we all just get along?"

Then he hoped for the best. They *said* it would work—that there was incredible power packed into those keys, power that could insinuate itself into the mind, the heart, the spirit— that soul-crushing guilt, self-hatred, acute and instant depression would cocoon and envelop the unprotected target.

Unprotected, that was the issue—was Marci's spell sufficient to remove, or at least significantly reduce, Tyaga's protections?

If not, a spell would be coming back at Donovan, and whatever the spell was, he was very unlikely to survive it.

Either it had worked or it hadn't, and, in the meantime, there was Charles, a couple of scant feet from Donovan, with a pistol between them. Donovan had steeled himself for this moment, rehearsing it in his head, but it was still the most difficult thing he had ever done in his life: Still not knowing the result, he looked away from Tyaga. He turned his attention back to Leong and said, astonished at how steady his voice sounded, "Oh, right. That spell I mentioned. It wasn't actually for you."

IIIIIIIIIIIIIIII

Roughly three-fourths of the way through her training, Marci's interests had changed from research to fieldwork. She was never entirely certain why, but from the time she mentioned it to William her instruction had changed. One of the differences she gradually noticed was an increased emphasis on formal precision—on doing everything exactly right, not taking any shortcuts to get an effect. She asked about it one day, and William said, "When you're casting a spell in the field, and your life depends on it, speed is more important than perfection. It doesn't help to get a perfect, one hundred percent conversion water-breathing spell up just after you drown, right?"

"Well, yeah."

"The more precise your technique, the more effective your spell will be on those occasions when you just have to make do with whatever you can cast right now. So we work on ingraining perfect. Speed will take care of itself."

"Oh. I think I see," she'd said.

If Susan had still been alive, and the subject had come up, Susan would have told her she'd been given exactly the same instruction by every one of her teachers.

William had given her one more tip: "If you know in advance what spell you're going to cast, of course, it helps a great deal."

When the door opened, he stepped inside, hand raised. Marci hadn't fully believed it would be him. But she'd already found the grid line, two hundred feet north, and had let it flow into and out of her until she had nearly vanished into it, so

Picture them as gray wavy spiky lines with a sour salty taste and make them thin, thinner, thinnest passing beyond the body deeper than the heart where there is space between the pieces, empty, like a lonely foghorn on a thick moonless night so nothing else exists but sound within mist holding sound the way a painting holds colors, and like draws to like so the very essence of her casting finds the essence of his and they commune and touch and tangle and gray wavy spiky thicker now thicker until it is all there—that's how you can find the grid, just like me, I'm wrapping my hands around it as if around my own, and then—pullpullpull and it is horrible that it is so easy and sad that it is done.

Marci fell to her knees and a sob burst out of her as she looked up; there he was, shock and horror only starting to register on his face, because she had understood first, because she'd been ready, because he told her to be.

"I'm sorry, William," she said, or maybe she only thought it; she couldn't tell.

‖‖‖‖‖‖‖‖‖

Becker answered his cell phone on the first ring. "Becker," he said.

"Longfellow. We got them."

"Leong?"

"And his boss."

"His boss? Who—"

"William Fauchaux, from Recruitment. He was the one

behind it. He—look, there's no time right now. I have a body, a wounded guy, and two prisoners. Get us home."

"On it," said Becker. He clicked a button on the computer, sending the necessary message.

"On the way. What happened?"

"They got a bit rowdy. Matt had to put one down, and we have Shveta Tyaga for you."

"And you?"

"We're all fine."

"I'll see you here."

"Yeah."

IIIIIIIIIIIIIIII

The receptionist behind his desk in front of the elevator managed to look like everything was normal, which impressed Donovan a great deal. They were grouped in front of the desk.

"Hello, Mr. Faucheux."

"Hello, Mr. Becker."

"I confess, I'm surprised to see you like this."

"You mean, with my hands tied behind me and a gun at my head?"

"Excuse me," said Donovan, "but would it be all right if we put this guy somewhere? Guns are heavy."

"I got it," said Matt.

"You got Faucheux. I got Leong, and my arm is getting tired, and if someone wants to see to Shveta, I think she's going to recover soon, and this could get ugly if you don't get her somewhere safe."

"Maybe we should all get comfortable," said Becker.

"If your idea of being comfortable involves me still holding this thing, we'll have to talk about comfortable."

"I have it," said the receptionist, and a shimmering field grew up around Leong, who shrugged; then another occurred around Shveta, who didn't react.

Donovan lowered his weapon.

No one spoke for a moment, and Donovan realized that Becker was staring at Faucheux's face, and put together that Becker was recognizing on it what his own face must have looked like, back when it happened to him. It was an intuitive leap, but not for a very long distance.

Becker seemed to catch himself, and turned to Donovan. "When did you begin carrying a firearm, Mr. Longfellow?"

"Today." He handed the weapon back to Matt. "Also stopped today."

"As a rule," said Becker, "we do not issue them."

"Yeah," said Matt. "I took these off a drug dealer in New Jersey."

"I see. Well, if you'll come this way, Ms. Morgan wishes to speak to you."

"If it's all the same to you," said Faucheux, "I'd as soon not."

"And I," said Leong.

"We will have you escorted to cells," said Becker. "The rest of you, this way," and led them toward the elevator.

IIIIIIIIIIIIIII

"So, you had this prepared?" said Morgan. They sat in her office, Donovan on one side, Marci in the middle, then Matt. Becker was behind them, standing.

"Yes," said Donovan. "I sent an email to William Faucheux, asking him for an interrogation specialist, as we had captured the dangerous Mr. Leong. I may have implied that we felt confident we'd break him eventually anyway, but that it would be faster with a specialist. I gave him the address, then waited." Donovan shrugged.

"How," said Morgan, "did you know Faucheux was the one behind it?"

Donovan nodded to Matt, who said, "He didn't want to hire me."

"That was it? Because he didn't want to hire Mr. Castellani you decided he was behind it?"

"Well, that's what made us look at him," said Donovan. "Once we started looking, it was kind of obvious. He was perfectly placed to recruit for his own purposes. He could hire accounting and computer people from outside, and as a department head he had access. And Marci gave me a few details about some conversations she'd had with him that, in retrospect, were efforts to discover if she was suitable for recruitment. And the fact that Leong knew about Vasilyev, and Faucheux was well placed to find that out. It seemed to add up."

"I didn't know," said Becker.

"No," said Donovan. "You wouldn't have. He wouldn't have trusted you, after you joined the Foundation, and especially since you worked for the Ranch. And of course, you, Camellia, passed on the information about Young, which proved to be the key to figuring out what the endgame was, which in turn helped us find Faucheux."

"Endgame?" said Becker.

"Sure. Destroying the board of directors of the Mystici. He wanted them wiped out and replaced with people willing to take some degree of moral responsibility for what their group did."

Morgan frowned. "That makes too much sense. But what about Whittier?"

"He was the price Leong paid Nagorski for being his dancing monkey—doing the killings Leong couldn't do himself. He convinced Nagorski that they were all evil—which I guess they were, to one degree or another—and showed him how they connected to Whittier so he had a reason to kill them. The last one—Leong's actual target—I suppose Leong killed himself, probably with a bullet; I don't know."

"Actual target? Who was that?"

"I don't know. But I'm sure if you check police records somewhere there will be a mundane murder, or maybe an accident, of whatever Mystici board member was responsible for North America. Whoever that is, it'll turn out, was protected by Young. That death is what alerted what's-her-name, the head of the Mystici. Elsa Merriweather."

"Can you verify that?" said Becker.

"I could. I won't."

"Why?"

"Because I don't give a shit. It didn't work, right? We cut the proverbial head off the proverbial snake. Done deal. They got one in North America, and then we stopped them before the next one went off. End of problem."

"So, then," said Morgan, "Faucheux had people lined up to replace the board members as they were killed?"

"Yeah, something like that. I'm pretty sure of it."

"We should question Faucheux, find out who they were."

"Yeah, you do that. I'll be counting up all the fucks I don't give."

Becker said, "Mr. Lo—"

"Oh, just leave it, Mr. Becker. They're a bunch of pricks. If you want to help them clean their house, do it. But leave me out of it."

"Your work," said Morgan after a moment, "is not unimpressive."

"I speak for my team," said Donovan, "when I say that we're just tickled as shit that you're impressed."

"Actually," said Marci, "I'm pretty happy about it."

"There's loyalty for you," said Donovan. "So, what will happen to the prisoners? I assume Faucheux's dealt with, what with Marci's sorcelectomy. What about Leong and Tyaga?"

"You are correct, William Faucheux would have faced S.R.P. if it hadn't been done already. We may decide to question him; I must consider the matter. Tyaga will certainly be given that treatment—a rogue sorcerer with that much skill is like mercury fulminate. Mr. Leong, as you suggest, is a more difficult problem."

"Removing his abilities didn't seem to help much," said Becker.

"No," said Morgan. "I'm afraid we'll have to execute him."

"I'd like to volunteer for that job," said Donovan.

"Truly, Donovan?"

"Yeah. Truly. And I'd like to talk to him first."

"Talk to him?"

"We were arguing philosophy when things got hairy. I want to continue the conversation."

"I must review the decision with the board. I can let you talk to him, but you must promise not to kill him. Wait for our decision."

"I promise."

"Then I'll arrange it."

"And afterward, you're serious about wishing to be the executioner?"

"Yes."

"Then I'll get back to you after the board meets."

"Thanks."

"It will take a few days to assemble the board. We like to meet in person for big things, and we take steps to ensure security."

"Yeah," said Donovan. "There's a lot of that. I mean, steps to ensure security."

"Do you have something to say?"

"Nope. Not a thing. Not a goddamned motherfucking thing."

IIIIIIIIIIIIIIII

Elsa came on the line with unaccustomed speed, but Camellia had expected that.

"Hello, Camellia. You're on speaker."

"So are you. Is anyone there?"

"No. You?"

"Yes. Elsa Merriweather, meet Donovan Longfellow. He is the lead investigator in North America."

"How do you do, Ms. Merriweather."

"I prefer 'Mrs.' How do you do? Do you have news, Camellia, or are you expecting your investigator to get information from me you couldn't?"

"I have news, Elsa. The matter is resolved. You and your board are safe."

There was a pause. "Well. Then, you believe we were in danger?"

Camellia leaned close to the phone. "You know bloody well you were in danger, Elsa. As soon as Alex Young died, you knew what the endgame was. You knew someone, somewhere, was planning to kill your entire board of directors, to cripple the Mystici. And, Elsa, I have two people dead because you refused to tell me what you knew. Two people. Decent people, good people, with families. People who are worth ten of you, with your secrecy, your greed, your utter unconcern with who gets hurt."

"Camellia—"

"Shut it, Elsa. Shut up and listen. We've found two of those responsible so far, and we are on the trail of the remaining four, although without the mastermind or their chief assassin I doubt they can do much. But this started, Elsa, because the Mystici refuse to accept any responsibility for the harm their members do, and it got out of hand because you wouldn't tell us what you knew."

"How—"

"How did I find out what the endgame was? Because of the fear in your voice when you called me, that's how."

"And you think that was an accident, Camellia? You think I didn't deliberately—?"

"Fuck. You," said Camellia, and disconnected.

She turned to Donovan. "Satisfied?"

He shrugged. "Best we can do, I guess."

Camellia nodded. "Yes," she said. "Best we can do."

ıııııııııııııı

Donovan, Matt, and Marci took the elevator down to the basement.

"You sure about this?" said Matt.

"Yeah."

"Just, you know," said Matt. "If you go through with it, it'll change you."

"Oh yes," said Donovan. "It will indeed."

They reached the detention area. A man sat on an uncomfortable-looking chair. As they approached he looked up from his cell phone game, and said, "Can I help you?"

"No," said Donovan. "I'm afraid we are all beyond help, by this time."

The guard waved them through. Donovan reached into his jacket and took hold of the knotnot.

ıııııııııııııı

"To summarize," said Camellia, "we have limited the damage, and the threat—the immediate threat, at any rate—is over, and we are out one head of recruiting who will need to be replaced as soon as possible. Anna Koerning is filling in as interim head. Therefore, I have asked Florencia to place on the agenda two additional items: a bonus for our field agent and his team, and a motion to set up a committee to review security policies as per Ms. Ursine's motion at our last meeting."

They all looked at one another, taking a good long moment to return their attention to Camellia. "Unless Ms. Ursine has changed her mind?"

"Hardly," said Betty.

Camellia nodded. "Good then. Are there any questions?"

Hodari cleared his throat. "Um, well, there is the matter of the prisoner escape."

"Charles Leong? Yes. Unfortunate. An administrative error. I take full responsibility."

"Do you indeed?" said Hodari.

Camellia caught his eye. "Yes," she said.

"Administrative error."

"Yes."

"Very well," said Hodari. "Then let's move on."

||||||||||||||||

When Marci got home that night, Lawrence had prepared calamari with shallots, garlic, and lemon over squid ink pasta. In a bowl in the living room there was also a goldfish, which she named Susan.

ACKNOWLEDGMENTS

My thanks to James Taylor (no, not that James Taylor), Vicka Cory, Skyler White, Will Shetterly, Pamela Dean, and Emma Bull for helpful comments. As always, I appreciate the production work of Irene Gallo and her all-girl detective orchestra. Thanks also to copy editor Barbara Wild, and to James D. Macdonald for help with research. Additional copyediting and proofreading by sQuirrelco Textbenders, Inc.